THE PATIENT

COLE BAXTER

INKUBATOR
BOOKS

Published by Inkubator Books
www.inkubatorbooks.com

ISBN (eBook): 978-1-83756-241-1
ISBN (Paperback): 978-1-83756-201-5
ISBN (Hardback): 978-1-83756-243-5

1

I paced up and down the sidewalk outside the hospital as I waited for my ride. I was sure it was either a mistake or a cruel joke, me being released like this. Some people would say the hospital was like a prison. I would say it was more like a sanctuary, a place to go to escape the overwhelming feeling that everyday life brought, and for me, it had been home for the last ten years. And now I was being thrown back into the world with no idea what to do or what to expect.

The hospital claimed to have prepared me for this. Sure, they'd sat and chatted with me at great length about the real world and its expectations of me, but talking about something and actually living it were two very different things. I could already feel the beads of sweat running down my back and pooling on the waistband of my jeans. My heart was beating a little too fast, and I was panting for air as though I had been running when, in actuality, the opposite was true. I couldn't remember the last time I had run anywhere.

A silver car pulled up, and I knew it was my ride. I was

tempted to run straight back into the safety of the hospital, but something stopped me when I saw my probation officer getting out of the car. I had been expecting someone mean-looking. Yes, I was expecting someone who would bully me, boss me around, and demean me.

What I wasn't expecting was Brianna Caldwell.

She was tall, but not in an imposing way, and she had a nice figure, curvy and womanly. She made her way around to the trunk of the car and popped it open. She smiled at me, and her dark brown eyes seemed to light up from within. A gust of wind blew her curly black hair into her face. She rubbed one hand up her forehead and held her hair back, still smiling at me.

"James Owens?" she asked.

I nodded, mute.

"Come on then; let's get you home. Pop your bag in the trunk."

Her tone was friendly, but no-nonsense. She seemed like the sort of woman who got stuff done, but who got it done by smiling at you instead of yelling at you.

I stepped closer to her and put my bag in the trunk. I knew then that there was no going back. I was on my own now, and I had to find a way to integrate into a society that didn't want me any more than I wanted it.

I returned my probation officer's smile with one of my own, one that I hoped looked normal. Her smile didn't falter, and she didn't run off screaming, so maybe I had managed to pull it off.

She slammed the trunk closed and headed back toward the driver's door of her car.

I made my way to the passenger side.

"I'm sorry. You must think I'm so rude. I'm Brianna Caldwell, your probation officer."

We both got into the car, and I slipped on my seatbelt. I was aware that Brianna was waiting for me to say something. "Thank you so much for agreeing to pick me up, Ms. Caldwell."

"It's Brianna." She turned the engine on and revved it up. "And it's no problem at all."

She pulled away from the curb and drove through the hospital grounds to the exit. She paused and looked both ways, and then she joined the flow of traffic on the main road.

"So, how much have you been told about me and what my role is in this?" Brianna asked, glancing at me.

"Not much," I admitted. "Just that you're my probation officer and that I'm to report to you, whatever that means."

"Your release is a 'conditional discharge,'" Brianna explained. "It basically means that, officially, you are free, but that there are certain rules you need to follow, and if you don't follow them, you will be incarcerated again. This time, because the hospital is confident that your schizophrenia is under control, if you were to reoffend, you would be taken to a real prison."

I shuddered.

"It's okay. Just follow the rules, don't break the law, and that won't happen to you."

"What are the rules?" I dared to ask.

"Well, obviously, like I said, you're expected to follow the law. As well as that, you aren't allowed to leave the country or even the state without written permission from a judge. You must check in with me once weekly, wear the ankle monitor at all times, and that's pretty much it. Easy, huh?"

I nodded, although I wasn't so sure.

Brianna glanced at me and frowned. "What is it, James? You don't think you can follow those rules?"

"No, I *do* think I can follow them. And I really want to. But the fact that I committed a crime means that I didn't follow the rules."

"That was a long time ago. Things were very different then," Brianna pointed out.

"I know," I said. "But what worries me is that I can't remember doing anything wrong. So how can I make sure I don't get myself into that kind of situation again?"

"You weren't on the right medication, and you didn't have any support in place," Brianna said in a calming tone. "Your meds are sorted now, and you have me and your counselor. If you feel like you're slipping at any point, just call one of us. Okay?"

I nodded, grateful that I had a way out if the bad side of me emerged again. Maybe I really had changed. I couldn't remember exactly what I used to be like, so perhaps it made sense for me to trust Brianna and my doctors, and to accept that I wasn't that person anymore.

"Where are we going?" I asked in a breathy whisper as Brianna pulled off the main road and into an outdoor shopping center.

She pointed across the street to a large McDonald's. The parking lot and the outside seating area were full, and I could see lines almost back to the door as we got closer.

"I thought we could grab a burger for lunch," Brianna said. "It's on our way, and I'm not going to get a chance to eat later on."

I felt bad for Brianna. She should be able to have a lunch break. But I also knew I couldn't go in there and that no amount of guilt was going to make me do it. My heart started to race, my chest tightening. I shook my head frantically and looked for a way out.

Brianna frowned. "What is it?"

I could hear the genuine concern in her voice, and it calmed me down enough to be able to get my words out. "Too busy ... I can't go in there," I managed.

"Oh," Brianna said. "I'm sorry. I didn't think."

"It's okay," I mumbled.

Brianna was still heading toward McDonald's. Was she just like the others, taunting me and pretending to be on my side, only to make matters worse for me every chance they got?

"We'll go through the drive-through. Is that okay?" Brianna asked.

I nodded as relief flooded me, replacing the adrenaline that had thrummed through me only seconds ago, leaving a taste like pennies in my mouth.

Brianna smiled at me, and I calmed the rest of the way down almost instantly. It was strange for me to settle down so quickly, but I thought it had a lot to do with Brianna. She seemed able to calm me in a way that no one else could.

She pulled through the drive-through and stopped at the first window. She leaned out her window to get closer to the speaker. "A Big Mac, please. And ..." She trailed off and turned to me, an eyebrow raised.

"Oh, no, not for me, thanks. I don't have my wallet."

She turned back to the speaker. "Make that two Big Macs, please."

A voice came down the ordering speaker and told her to pull to the next window.

"You didn't have to do that," I said, looking down into my lap, shocked that she even wanted to help me.

"I know I didn't have to, but I wanted to," she said.

I could hear the smile in her voice, even though I still didn't dare to look at her.

"I'm hoping we can be friends, and that's the kind of thing friends do for each other."

A flash in my mind and Nick's face hovered there for a moment, his soft green eyes holding mine. I knew that Nick wasn't real, and he certainly wasn't a hologram projected by my mind. He was just my one and only friend, so I figured if anyone should know about friendship, it would be him. His nod confirmed that it was okay, normal even, for me to accept the burger from Brianna. I smiled at her. Nick saluted me, and then his face slowly faded away from my vision.

"Thank you." I smiled.

Brianna returned my smile, and then her attention was taken by the server who spoke to her from the window.

It didn't take long before we were in the parking lot, munching on our burgers.

"So, how much do you know about your financial situation?" Brianna asked me between bites.

I thought about it for a moment and then shook my head when I realized no one had really told me much of anything. I knew my father had died and that I would be getting an inheritance, and that was pretty much it.

"Nothing," I admitted.

"I see. So as your father's sole male heir, you were left everything," Brianna started.

"Wait," I interrupted her. "What about Janet? Doesn't she get anything?"

"Janet?" Brianna asked.

"My twin sister," I explained.

"Of course. No, your father didn't leave her anything. His belief was that he should leave everything to his son. Your father was ... how can I put this ... traditional," Brianna said.

"That's a nice way of saying 'chauvinistic pig.'" I smiled.

Brianna giggled softly.

I felt a warm glow inside. I liked us sharing a joke, and I liked being able to make her laugh. For that tiny moment, I was more than just a mental health patient. I was a real person. Brianna saw me.

She turned serious again as she told me more about my finances. "So, you have obviously been left the house, which will be your permanent address, at least for the duration of your probation. After that, it's entirely up to you whether you remain on the property, rent it out, or sell it. I'm not sure of the exact amount, but you have also inherited a significant sum of money. Enough that your day-to-day living expenses will be more than taken care of. Out of that money, you will have to cover your medical bills and inheritance taxes. You might want to consider hiring a lawyer to manage that kind of thing on your behalf."

I thought for a moment and then nodded. "That's a good idea. I'll do it."

Brianna swallowed the last bite of her burger. "Okay, let's get you home."

I wasn't sure how to go about hiring a lawyer, but I would work it out. I didn't want Brianna to think I was totally useless. Besides, if I had as much money as she said I had, I wouldn't have to shop around and try to find the best deal. It would be a simple case of finding a firm with lots of good reviews.

I was still thinking about starting the search when the

car pulled up to the curb, and I glanced out the window and saw it. The house. My father's house. *My* house now. I felt my stomach turn at the mere sight of it, but I swallowed down the feeling. The house had never been the issue. It was my father.

"Thank you," I said to Brianna as we both got out of the car and made our way to the trunk to retrieve my things.

"No problem. I'll give you a call later on to check that you're settling in okay. And then we'll make arrangements from there."

"Okay," I said. "Thanks again. Goodbye, Brianna."

"Bye," Brianna said as she got back into her car.

I stood on the sidewalk and watched her drive away, and it was all I could do not to scream after her and beg her not to leave me here.

2

I stood watching the road for a long time after Brianna drove away. Finally, I forced myself to face the house. *My* house. Why couldn't my father have done us both a favor and left it to Janet? She was always at home here in a way that I never was. I would have given it to her if I had anywhere else to go, but I didn't, so I vowed to make the most of this.

I turned and forced myself to open the wooden gate. The hinges squeaked just like I remembered, and I made a mental note to fix that. My father always said it was a good thing; it alerted us to anyone coming up the path. I just found it annoying, and it wasn't like I was going to have a line of people wanting to visit me.

I reached the front door and took out the key I had been given before leaving the hospital. I had thanked the nurse who gave it to me, although I had secretly believed she was a hallucination at that point; I wasn't aware that I was coming back here. I was glad now that I had been polite to her all the same. I let myself into the house and stood in the foyer for a moment.

The familiar smell hit me first. The smell of home. It wasn't any one specific smell; it was just the smell of my house, the way every house had its own smell. Memories surged through me on a whiff of that smell, but I managed to push them to one side, ignoring the desire to look at them, to allow myself to be pulled back down to their dark depths.

I swallowed hard and looked up the stairs, but I wasn't quite ready to tackle the memories of the bedrooms just yet. I put my bag on the bottom stair, ready to take upstairs when I got up the courage. For the moment, I was content to take on the ground floor.

I moved toward the living room door. It almost didn't feel real being back here. I had to keep reminding myself that it was real, but it was also different than the old days. My father wasn't going to appear from somewhere, his face like thunder, rage simmering off him in waves.

I pushed open the living room door and stepped in. It had been over ten years since I had last set foot in this room, and nothing had changed. Everything was exactly like back then, and this time I couldn't stop the memories from over-whelming me.

My legs felt like jelly, and I pitched forward, landing on my hands and knees on the floor. I stayed that way, my head down, retching and gasping as panic overtook me.

I saw it as clearly as I had every time it really happened. My father coming toward me, his nostrils flared, his cheeks flushed, and the vein at the center of his forehead bulging. In his hands would be his belt, and he would snap it together menacingly, the sound echoing through the room.

"No," I whimpered. "No. Please no!"

"Take it like a man," my father bellowed, and the belt came down, swishing through the air.

I felt the sting of the leather as it connected with my back, but that was nothing compared to the sharp pain where the buckle connected with my lower spine.

I cried out in pain, tears springing up, and my father hit me again, screaming at me to be a man, but the more he screamed, the harder he hit me, and the harder he hit me, the harder it was to control my cries of pain. The onslaught went on until my father tired himself out, and then he would stand over me, his chest heaving, beads of sweat on his red face.

"I'm just trying to help you, James. When will you learn that you have to be tough to make it in this world?" he would snarl down at me before he stalked out of the room and left me there crying, my back smarting, blood running down my sides.

I slowly became aware of my surroundings once more. I was lying on my side, my knees drawn up, tears streaming down my face. I winced slightly in advance before I moved, knowing how much it was going to hurt, but also knowing that if my father caught me lying here feeling sorry for myself, I would really suffer.

I forced myself to roll onto my front, ready to push myself up, and I was surprised that my body didn't hurt at all. Was I finally becoming a man, learning to cope with the pain? Would I finally be able to make my father feel proud of me?

I got to my feet, and I slowly pushed my hand beneath my shirt at the back. The skin there was dry, unmarked. I frowned, more confused than ever. Even if I stopped feeling the pain, surely my body would still react to the leather, the metal. Surely I would still bleed.

"Hello?" I managed to say, noting that my voice was no longer a whimper. "Dad? Janet?"

I moved forward and caught a glimpse of myself in the mirror. I stopped and stared at the man looking back at me. His pale skin, his shaggy hair, his beard. He could be me in twenty years' time, but why was I seeing him now? Was I finally broken?

"The reflection is real. It's the rest that's not," a voice whispered in my head.

I panicked for a moment, but then I realized that I wasn't going mad—the voice was my voice—and I listened to it more closely.

"The beating wasn't real. It was a memory, brought back by being here again. Think about it. There are no marks on you. Your father isn't here. You are a thirty-year-old man, and this is your house now," the voice said.

It was true. I was free of my father. Free of the abuse. Free of my incarceration. But I didn't feel free. I felt trapped by the memories, but more than that, I felt trapped by the holes in the memories, the things they said I had done that I couldn't remember doing. Terrible things that I had buried deep in my subconscious.

I sat down on the couch and tried to think of something else, but it was too late. The shock of being thrown back into my childhood was too much for me, and I could feel the all-too-familiar fluttering in my chest, the dizziness in my head, which meant I was on the verge of a panic attack. For a moment, I didn't know what to do, but then I felt my cell phone in my pocket. I would call my therapist.

It was only when I had my cell phone in my hand that I realized I didn't have the therapist's number—as an in-patient at the hospital, I had never needed to have it before

—but surely I could find it on the internet. Searching for the number kept my mind occupied, and although I knew I was far from clear of the panic attack, I managed to hold it at bay.

I found the number, and I called it.

It rang a few times, and a woman's voice came down the line. "Dr. Jenkins's office, Margo speaking, how can I help?" it trilled.

"I need to speak to Dr. Jenkins," I blurted out, barely able to keep myself together now that I had nothing to do to distract me from my emotions. Only the promise of speaking to my therapist was stopping me from going into a full-on attack. "It's urgent."

"Is he expecting your call?" Margo asked.

"No," I said. "But I'm his patient, and I need to speak to him."

"Where are you calling from?" Margo asked. "If you're on one of the wards, the registrar should be the one calling. And if you're not on one of the wards—"

I knew it was rude to cut her off mid-sentence, but I couldn't bear to wait another second. I was losing control of myself fast. "Just put me through to my therapist. This is a personal matter that I don't wish to discuss with you."

"Very well," Margo said.

It was clear from her tone that I had offended her. Well, tough. She started it by asking me three million questions instead of doing what I asked her to do when it was so obvious that I needed Dr. Jenkins's help.

"Anthony Jenkins," a voice said a couple of seconds later.

"Oh, Dr. Jenkins, thank goodness," I said, relief covering my panic for a second. "I'm sorry to bother you, but I'm having a panic attack, and I didn't know who else to call."

"Okay, deep breaths; remind yourself that there is absolutely no reason to panic. Now, what's your name?" Dr. Jenkins said.

"James Owens," I said.

I could hear the sound of typing.

"I'm just looking up your records, so I can see where we are with your treatment. Ah yes, here we are. Mr. Owens, it says here you have been discharged from the hospital. Is that correct?"

"Yes," I replied. "But I was told I would still need therapy."

"Yes, but it won't be from me," Dr. Jenkins said. "You have been referred to a therapist who deals with people outside of hospitals and facilities. Were you not told this?"

"No," I said. "At least I don't think I was. To be honest, Doctor, I was given so much information all at once that it's all become a bit of a blur."

"I understand," Dr. Jenkins said. "Do you have a pen handy? I can give you the details of your new doctor."

I stood up on shaky legs and went to the ottoman that stood beneath the large bay window. I opened it and almost smiled when I saw that it, too, hadn't changed. The notebook and pen, which my mom had always refused to leave out in sight because she said it spoiled the look of the room, were still nestled away in the ottoman, a habit my father kept long after my mom died.

I grabbed them both and went back to the couch. "Okay, go ahead."

"Your new doctor's name is Dr. Andrew Sellers." Dr. Jenkins rattled off a number.

I scrawled it down and read it back to him.

"That's it," he said.

"Thank you," I said. The calming effect of having something practical to focus on was starting to wear off now that I had the pen and the paper and the new number, and I could feel the adrenaline flooding my system again. My heart began racing once more, my breath speeding up. Lights flashed in front of my eyes, and I felt as though my throat were closing. I was only one step from losing control of myself completely. "Can you help me now?"

"I'm sorry, I'm afraid I can't. You are no longer my patient. I do wish you well, though. Call Dr. Sellers. He'll be able to help you," Dr. Jenkins said, and then I heard the line go dead.

I tried to focus on my breathing, but my airways were so tight that I could barely breathe. I started wheezing. My heart was pounding, and I knew I was going to die. My brain would be starved of oxygen, or my heart would just give out from being overworked.

I managed to jab my finger at my cell phone and get it back to the screen to make a call. I typed in the number Dr. Jenkins had given me, but the line was dead. Panic's icy fingernails ran down my neck and my back, and sweat ran freely down my back and sides.

I squinted slightly, willing my eyes to work properly, and I saw I had mistyped the last two digits of the phone number. I deleted them, re-entered them, and tried again. This time, the call connected.

"Dr. Sellers's office," another receptionist trilled, her voice echoing through my head.

Why do they all have to sound so damned cheery all of the time? I thought.

I sucked in air through my nose, trying to calm myself down enough to speak. "I n-need to talk to D-D-Dr. Sellers," I managed.

She must have realized that I was on the edge of having a complete meltdown because she didn't mess about asking if I had an appointment. She didn't even ask my name; she just put me through.

"Dr. Sellers speaking."

His voice was warm and kind, and I felt a tiny bit better hearing it, although I was still in a full-on panic attack at that point. I tried to respond to the doctor, but I couldn't get my words out. I could feel tears threatening. He was going to hang up on me, and I was going to die.

"It sounds like you're having a few problems," Dr. Sellers said, "so here's what we're going to do. I want you to take slow, deep breaths, as deep as you can, okay? Don't worry about trying to talk. Just listen to the sound of my voice and count as you breathe in for five and breathe out for seven. You are safe, and I am right here with you."

His voice was soft and calming, and somehow, when he said I was safe, I kind of believed him. I did as he said, breathing in for a count of five and then breathing out for a count of seven. The whole time, Dr. Sellers was talking to me, reassuring me, and after a few moments, I felt like I would be able to speak. My heart rate was slowing, and my chest no longer felt as though it were being squeezed in a vise. My vision had returned to normal, and I no longer felt like I was about to lose control of myself.

"Thank you, Doctor," I breathed.

"That's okay," Dr. Sellers said. "Now please, don't think me rude, but I don't recognize your voice. Are you a patient currently?"

"I'm not entirely sure," I admitted. "I have just been released from the hospital, and Dr. Jenkins, my therapist there, said you are my new therapist. I'm sorry to call like this, but I didn't know what else to do."

"Don't ever apologize for calling me. That's what I'm here for. Now, let me see if I have any information about a new patient joining my register," Dr. Sellers replied.

I waited, and I heard him typing on a computer.

After a moment, he spoke up again. "Ah. There you are. James Owens?"

"Yes," I said. "That's me."

"Okay, James, I won't go through everything right now if it's all the same to you because I do have a patient scheduled for a session quite soon," Dr. Sellers said.

Was that it? Was that all I was going to get out of my new therapist?

"So how about we schedule some phone calls first, and then we'll see about some face-to-face therapy once you get comfortable enough with me. Let's say every other day for the telephone sessions?" Dr. Sellers said.

"Yes. Thank you, that's great," I said.

Maybe he had been telling the truth about having someone already booked in and he wasn't just trying to fob me off. I would bet that he liked that other patient better than he liked me, though.

"I can see here you've been prescribed a mild sedative for when you feel a panic attack coming on," Dr. Sellers went on.

"Yes," I said.

"Is there any reason why you didn't take one when this particular attack came over you?" he asked.

I felt the heat flood my cheeks as embarrassment made me cringe mentally. At first, I wondered how he knew, but before my paranoia could go nuts, the obvious answer presented itself —if I had taken the medication like I was supposed to, my panic attack wouldn't have reached the point it had on this phone call.

"Well, I don't really like taking them. They make me tired, and I can't just lie around sleeping all day," I said.

"Why not?" Dr. Sellers asked. He didn't wait for me to answer, and I was glad he didn't because, really, what reason was there? It wasn't like I had anywhere to go, anyone to see. "Of course, you don't want to be like that forever, but I'm confident that my therapy sessions are going to help you to control your panic and anxiety. In the meantime, cut yourself a break and take those pills when you need to, alright? You are healing, and your body and your mind alike heal better when you are sleeping."

"Okay," I said.

I'd never really thought of it that way, but Dr. Sellers seemed to know what he was talking about. He had managed to stop my panic attack in minutes using only his words, something Dr. Jenkins had only ever been able to do using a sedative. If he said it was a good thing to take the pills and sleep, then I had to believe that was indeed the case.

"Good," he said. "I want you to take one of those pills now and lie down and enjoy a little nap. Okay?"

"I will," I said.

"Good," he said again. "Let's schedule your first real session for tomorrow, then, shall we? How does half past one sound?"

"Great," I told him.

"In the meantime, remember what I said about your meds, okay?" he said.

I told him that I would, and we said our goodbyes, and I ended the call.

I went through to the kitchen, half expecting another flood of memories to overwhelm my senses. My mind was already overstimulated, though, and there was no room for anything else, so no more memories or hallucinations came. I grabbed a glass of water and went back to my bag at the bottom of the stairs. I found the sedatives I had been prescribed and took one; then I went back into the living room.

I lay down on the couch and closed my eyes, already aware of the sedative working its magic, making me feel like I was floating on air. I smiled to myself as I floated along, the horrors momentarily banished from my mind.

Despite the fact that I had already had a panic attack, I was feeling quite good and positive about my release from the hospital and my future. Brianna and Dr. Sellers were nice, and they seemed to care about me.

I knew it wouldn't last. They would eventually shun me like everyone else did.

But the sedative stopped me from thinking too far down the line, and right now, in this moment, things were pretty damned good, and they stayed that way as the sedative pulled me down, down, and I fell into a deep and dreamless sleep.

3

I woke up still feeling reasonably good. I was looking forward to speaking to my new therapist, and I was relieved to know that I would soon be able to control my anxiety without sedatives. It made me feel like I was free to take them as needed in the meantime, and somehow, that thought was liberating enough that I figured I probably wouldn't need them all that much.

I was feeling a little peckish, and when I checked the clock, I saw it was definitely time for dinner. I walked to the kitchen with no idea what I might find. I looked in the fridge and then the cupboards. There was nothing, which, in hindsight, didn't surprise me. Any food that might have been left here after my father's death would have been thrown away by whoever attended to sorting out his affairs, or it all would have been green and moldy by now.

I went back to the living room and found my cell phone. I googled takeout places in my area, and within ten minutes, I had placed an order for a large pizza.

Not long after I'd placed the order, my cell phone rang. I

picked it up and looked at the screen. It was a number I didn't recognize, but it was local, and I figured it was probably the pizza place wanting to double-check something.

"Hello?" I said.

"Hi, James, I just wanted to check that you're settling in alright," a woman said.

I was confused. It certainly wasn't anything to do with my pizza. I vaguely recognized the voice, but I had no real idea who it was.

"I'm sorry," the woman said, and her inflection made me think she was smiling. "It's Brianna Caldwell."

"Oh, of course," I said. "I couldn't place you for a moment there."

I decided against telling Brianna that I had already had a panic attack since being back at the house, and then had spent the rest of the day asleep. As my probation officer, she might be able to use that information against me. I was definitely best off letting her think everything was perfectly fine.

"I'm settling in well, thank you," I said. "It's almost like I've never been away."

That much was true. The first thing I had seen in the house pretty much had been a hallucination of my father, and within seconds, it was like I had never been out from under his brutal rule.

"That's good news," Brianna said.

Again, I heard the smile in her voice. It made me want to smile, too.

When she spoke again, the smile seemed to be gone. She sounded a little bit worried. "It didn't occur to me until after I dropped you off that you would have no electricity or gas, no running water, and likely no food."

"It didn't occur to me either until about twenty minutes ago," I said with a laugh.

And that was just the no-food thing. The part about the electric and the water and the likes hadn't occurred to me until Brianna pointed it out. I wasn't about to admit that, though.

"Oh no," Brianna said.

"It's fine," I hurried on. "I do have water since it's on a well. It's plenty warm enough, and I've ordered a pizza for dinner. I'll get everything switched back on tomorrow morning."

"Are you sure?" Brianna asked. "I might be able to get you a hotel room for the night."

A hotel room sounded nice—it would get me away from this place that seemed to be haunted by my father's ghost and, worse, by my own ghost, the sad little boy I once was. But I knew I couldn't take Brianna up on her offer. If I did, I was afraid I would never get the courage to come back here again. I had to face this place, and I felt like if I got through the first night, it would start to get easier.

"No, honestly, I'm fine," I said.

"Well, if you're sure …" Brianna said, giving me another chance to take her up on her offer.

"I am," I said firmly before I could let myself say otherwise.

"I'll let you get back to waiting for your pizza," Brianna said. The smile was back in her voice. "Have a lovely evening."

"Thank you. You too."

It occurred to me after I ended the call that checking in like that was probably outside of Brianna's job description. Did that mean she actually did care about me? Maybe it did.

And maybe, instead of worrying about her going away when she learned the full truth about me, I should just enjoy her being in my life.

Speaking to Brianna reminded me that I had promised to call Nick once I was out of the hospital. If it was anyone but Nick, I would have left it until tomorrow. I was emotionally drained from earlier, and I really didn't fancy a big, deep chat. But Nick was my best friend. Hell, he was my only friend.

We had spent a lot of years together in the hospital, and Nick had gotten me through some of the tougher times. He would say I had done the same for him, but I genuinely thought he was just being polite. I could barely help myself, let alone anyone else.

Despite that, Nick and I had grown close, and when he was released from the hospital three years ago, he told me that he had befriended his demons and could move on with his life now. He had told me that, one day, I would do the same thing. I had taken that as a goodbye, assuming Nick wouldn't want anything more to do with me now that he was free of his demons. I had been wrong. I had massively underestimated Nick.

He came to visit me in the hospital once a week, sometimes more when he had time to spare around his writing. When he won a publishing contract for his first thriller, I was the first person he told, and when he gifted me a copy of his book once it was printed, I read it cover to cover that very day. I have read it so many times since then that I feel like I could recite most of it word for word.

So Nick is not someone I am willing to let down completely, but he is also someone who would understand my emotional fatigue, and he would likely be the first person to tell me our catch-up could have waited until tomorrow. I decided to go for the middle ground and text Nick rather than call.

I picked up my cell phone, opened my messages, and then thought for a moment before beginning to type.

> Hey there, Nick, how's things? So, I'm officially free. I'm taking today to just kind of settle in, and then tomorrow, I'll be starting my life over.

I read back over the message before I sent it, and I asked myself if it was a little bit too intense, but I quickly decided that it wasn't. That was how I felt, and Nick and I had never really held back on our feelings with each other—we both knew too well the consequences of doing that. I hit send.

I didn't have long to wait before my cell phone pinged. I opened the message and smiled.

> Yes! So glad to hear that you're out of that place and looking to the future. You've got this, and I'll be with you all the way.

I felt better. It was good to know that I had someone on my side so completely.

> Thank you, that means a lot. I'd love for us to chat properly either on the phone or to meet up sometime soon. I would have called tonight, but I am emotionally drained. It's in a good way (I think), but you know how it gets when you just don't have a spoken conversation left in you at the moment.

I didn't have long to wait before the answer pinged in,

and I relaxed a bit. For as sure as I was that Nick would get it without me having to try to explain it further, there was still a small part of me that was worried he would be offended that I hadn't wanted to talk in person.

> I completely understand. I was the same way when I first got out. Lasted a few days, and then I started to settle down properly. Just give me a buzz whenever you're ready. Don't wait too long, though. My new book is being released next week, and I'm assuming you'll want the copy I kept for you?

I didn't hesitate in replying.

> Yes! Congratulations on the book. I can't wait to read it.

A knock on the door startled me, and I felt the first roots of panic sneaking in, before I remembered. I laughed shakily to myself. It was just the pizza I had ordered. I stood up, ready to go and answer the door, when I had another moment's panic. Did I have any money? It was okay, Brianna telling me all about my inheritance, but did I have any physical cash here and now to pay for the pizza?

I had a twenty-dollar bill in my pocket, I remembered. A gift from Uncle Sam that was meant to get me home. But Brianna had brought me home, so I had the money. I shrugged. Let Uncle Sam buy me dinner instead of a ride home. I made a mental note to repay Brianna for the Big Mac. I felt awful knowing she had bought my lunch when I'd had money the whole time. I had been so jittery, I had completely forgotten about it.

I hurried to the door and got my pizza. I took it into the

living room and went to the kitchen to grab my cell phone and a napkin. I returned to the living room and put YouTube on my phone, then flicked aimlessly through the videos as I ate. Then I stopped flicking and left one running that appeared to be some sort of sitcom about nothing in particular. I ate and watched, although I wasn't really taking a whole lot of notice of the video; it was more for background noise.

While I finished the last slice of my pizza, I picked up my cell phone and looked through my call list. I found Brianna's number and saved it to my contacts. I smiled as I looked at her name sitting there on my cell phone, and I told myself not to go getting any silly ideas. It didn't matter that Brianna was the prettiest woman I had ever laid eyes on. It didn't matter even that she was nice to me. As if she was going to want anything to do with me, the local nutjob. No, I definitely needed to let go of any notion of anything like that.

To distract myself from stupid thoughts, I found Dr. Sellers's number and added that to my contacts list as well.

I put my cell phone back down on the couch, and I took the empty pizza box out into the kitchen and set it down on the side of the trash can. I looked out the kitchen window, noting that the grass in the backyard needed to be mowed. It was a long way from fully dark, but the night was slowly rolling in, and I was conscious of the fact that, once it became fully dark, I would have no light source. I might have thought that everything in the house was familiar, but walking through it in the pitch black would most likely result in me tripping and falling over something.

I knew that at the very least, I should take my bag up to my room and unpack the things I would need for tonight, such as my toothbrush and the half-full tube of toothpaste I had been assigned back at the hospital.

I told myself that now was as good a time as any, and I'd started toward the stairs when the sound of my cell phone ringing in the living room caught my attention. I sighed. I still didn't feel up to talking to anyone, but I knew that I couldn't just ignore the sound. It would drive me crazy if I did, and I already had more than enough crazy to go around. I turned back and went to my cell phone. I picked it up, looked at the screen, and saw Janet's name.

I went to take the call, but at the last second, I pulled my hand back. I wasn't sure why exactly; I just knew that I didn't have it in me to talk to Janet right now. I knew she wouldn't give up without hearing from me, though, so I let the call ring out, and then I sent her a text, hoping it would work the same way with her as it had with Nick.

> Hey. Sorry I didn't take your call. I'm okay, I'm just tired and emotionally drained. I'll give you a call in a few days when I've had a chance to adjust a bit.

I didn't have to wait long before the ping sound caught my attention, and I opened the text message from Janet.

> Oh, don't be silly. I'm not waiting a few days to talk to you. Don't worry about being emotionally drained or whatever. I want to talk to you, not have you confess your undying love for me. Now answer!

I had barely had a chance to read the message when my cell phone started ringing again. I could ignore it, but she wouldn't take the hint. She would keep calling until I

answered. I could turn it off, but then I might miss a call
from Brianna or Dr. Sellers. I sighed and swiped up, taking
her call.

"Janet," I said.

"Hello, James," she said. "I can't believe you weren't going
to take my call. After everything I've done for you. So rude.
What would Jesus say to you ignoring your own sister?"

With an effort, I bit back the sigh that was trying desper-
ately to escape. Couldn't she see that this was part of the
reason why I didn't want to take her call in the first place?
She was always so dramatic. I supposed that was why she'd
become an actress. She was good at being theatrical. And as
for what she'd done for me, I wasn't sure what that might be.
I decided against asking. She would have some answer, and
she would never let me forget it again.

"I thought it was rude taking your call when I don't have
the energy to chat. I thought you deserved me when I was
more with it," I said.

It wasn't a total lie.

"Oh, never mind all that," Janet said.

I could picture her waving her hand through the air,
waving away my concerns like they didn't matter, like she
always had.

"I won't keep you. I just wanted to tell you this in person
so I could hear your reaction."

"Go on," I said, already dreading what was coming.

"I'm leaving New York and coming home. I'm going to
look after you for a week or so, because you clearly can't look
after yourself," she informed me.

"Excuse me?" I said, my anger overtaking the dread for a
moment.

"Oh, don't go getting all huffy. You know what I mean.

You've become so used to people taking care of you all the time, I bet you don't even know how to cook a basic meal," she said.

"I'll manage."

"Sure you will. But you don't need to just manage if I'm there, do you? You can learn to be independent, to have your own life," Janet said. "I'll teach you everything you need to know, but until you've learned it, I will look after you. I'm sure that's what God wants me to do, as your sister."

"Okay," I managed to say.

The last thing I wanted was Janet here, but I knew that once she had set her mind on something, there was no talking her out of it. It would be easier to let her come, endure the visit for a week, and then be done with it.

"See, I knew you wanted me to come. The Lord told me so. You were just thinking of me, weren't you? Aww, you always were a sweetheart. But I've got you, James. I'm in your corner. Just like always. Love you. See you soon," she said and ended the call.

I moved the cell phone away from my face. I supposed it was fair to say that Janet had always had my back. Or so she kept on telling me, and she wouldn't lie to me, surely. And seeing her wouldn't be so bad, right?

I tried my best to convince myself that this was true, but the feeling of dread that had lodged itself in my stomach just wouldn't go away this time, no matter how much I willed it to.

4

fter my call with Janet, I sat in place, staring at the wall. I knew she loved me and wanted what was best for me. Yet somehow, talking to her always left me feeling strangely unsettled. It took me a good few hours to shake off that feeling, and then I realized that Janet's unsettling call was nothing compared to what was coming next.

I had to get my things upstairs and get them put away before night fell and the darkness would mean I couldn't see anything in front of me. I dreaded going up there, but the longer I put it off, the more I would build it up in my mind, and the last thing I needed right now was to make this thing bigger than it already was.

I stood up before I could change my mind and pushed my cell phone into my pocket. I figured I might as well have it with me just in case. Besides, when night fell, it would serve as a flashlight, so I could get around without breaking a bone.

I moved to the bottom of the stairs where I had dumped

my bag earlier. I picked it up and began to slowly climb. As each step took me closer to the top, I felt the dread in the pit of my stomach grow a little bit denser. It was a bizarre feeling, one I couldn't really put my finger on. I supposed it was just being back here after so long. Surely the strange mix of familiar and alien would be enough to leave anyone feeling a little disconcerted.

I tried my best to shake off the feeling as I reached the top of the stairs and looked both ways. The left-hand side of the upper floor had always been out of bounds for me. For everyone except my father, really, and I guess my mom when she was alive. I suddenly felt a streak of rebellion, and instead of turning right into the familiar, I went left and made my way into my father's private quarters.

There were two doors leading off the hallway. I pushed open the first one, my stomach swirling with excitement and dread in equal measures. I held my breath as the door swung inward. I let it out in a sigh that was half disappointment, half relief. I wasn't sure what I had expected to find behind that door, but it was definitely something a bit less mundane than a bathroom.

It was a large bathroom, and the fixtures and fittings seemed to be high-end, something I expected from my father, but it wasn't what I was looking for. That had to be behind the other door.

I closed the door, then walked to the other one and put my hand on the knob. For a moment, I was frozen to the spot. I was so conditioned from my childhood and my father telling me that this room was out of bounds that even now that he was dead and buried, I still believed it.

I told myself I was being silly—this whole house was mine now—and I pushed open the bedroom door. A giant four-poster bed sat in the center of the room, still made up with dark purple silk sheets and pillowcases and a white duvet cover. The furniture was all matching oak, and I knew it was real wood, not just particleboard with a bit of sticky-back plastic on it. A chandelier-style light hung above the bed, and a plush red carpet adorned the floor. In short, the room looked fit for a king, which was apt as, in some ways, my father had believed himself to be a king, at least of our household.

As his heir, that likely made me king of the house now. But I didn't want that. I didn't want any of it. I just wanted to be me.

I walked into the room and put my bag down on the bed. No sooner had the bag left my hand than I spun around, sure there was someone behind me. There wasn't, of course. There was no one in the house but me, but I could still feel my father's presence. That was what it was. That was why I felt like I was being watched. Even now with my father not just gone, but actually dead, I knew I wasn't going to be able to take his room.

Even after hearing the story of my father's death from several people, I still felt almost as though it were all just a delusion, a part of my illness. I kept picturing my father walking through the door. If he caught me in his room, I wouldn't live to see tomorrow, and despite knowing that I was being paranoid, I decided against taking the master bedroom.

I felt better as I picked my bag back up off the bed and left the room, closing the door behind me. I walked past the top of the stairs, then went down the other side of the hall-way. The doors of the guest rooms stood open, and I peered into them. They were out of use: their furniture covered with plastic sheets, all the beds stripped bare.

Finally, I came to the end of the hallway, the last three doors. The door opposite me was the bathroom I had shared with Janet. The room on the left-hand side had been my bedroom, and the one opposite it on the right had been Janet's. I instinctively moved toward my old room, but at the last minute, I turned away, and instead, I opened the door to Janet's room.

Her room had also always been forbidden territory to me when we were growing up, although she seemed to think that my room was fair game and just marched in whenever she felt like it. I went into her room now, feeling brave and rebellious and really quite good about the whole thing.

I could instantly see why Janet had been so protective of her space as a child. Her room was two or three times the size of mine. She wouldn't have been afraid that I would take it from her—she wouldn't have allowed it, and my father would have taken her side like always—but she probably didn't want to hear me moaning about it not being fair that her room was so much bigger and grander than mine.

I debated taking the room for myself. What would Janet be able to do about it when she got here? Nothing, that was what. The whole house was mine now. But even as I thought about it, I knew I wouldn't take the room. I didn't have the energy to put up with Janet complaining about it. And besides, it wasn't like I needed a huge bedroom. I was only going to be sleeping in there, not hosting a party.

I backed out of Janet's room and closed the door, and then I crossed the hallway to my room. I had genuinely believed that this room would be the least problematic, but it seemed I had been wrong. For starters, there was a lock on the outside of the door, one my father had had no qualms about using when I was a child and he decided I needed punishing for some imagined wrongdoing. Even though I was alone in the house, the thought of someone coming along and locking me in the room did nothing for my nerves.

I decided to go in and sort my things out and then go find a screwdriver to remove the lock. I could worry about repairing the damage done to the paint tomorrow. For now, I just wanted to get settled.

I pushed the door open and stepped in. Instantly, a shiver passed through me. I felt a deep-rooted sense of dread in my stomach, the cause of which I couldn't put my finger on, but I knew it had to do with this room, and no doubt it also had a lot to do with my father and his treatment of me.

I forced myself to remain in the room long enough to unpack my bag. It wasn't like I had a lot of choice about where to keep my things, and of the three rooms that I wouldn't have to mess around taking dust covers off every-thing in, this one was the lesser of the evils. It didn't take me long to unpack the few bits of clothes I had, and then I moved through to the bathroom to sort out my meager toiletries. That was something else I would have to sort out —new clothes, shoes, toiletries. Everything, really. But that was another job for tomorrow. For now, all I had to do was work out which of the rooms I was going to sleep in.

I felt my head swim and my vision swoop in and out for a second. My breathing sped up, and my heart slammed in my chest. The start of a panic attack. I knew by that feeling that I wouldn't be sleeping in any of those rooms, not unless I wanted to have a full-blown panic attack again.

The decision made for me, I left my bedroom and headed back for the stairs. As I did so, my breathing began to return to normal, and my heart rate slowed. My vision stopped swimming in and out, and my head stopped spinning. As far as my anxiety was concerned, I had made the right decision to walk away from the bedrooms. I wasn't sure my pride would agree, but in that moment, I really didn't care.

I descended the stairs and wandered into the living room. I shrugged as I looked at the couch. I hadn't left myself with a ton of options, so I walked over to it and lay down. This was my bed, at least for tonight.

I thought it would take me a long time to fall asleep—experience had taught me that much about myself—but on this occasion, I fell asleep almost as soon as I lay down.

I WALK THROUGH THE HOUSE, *trying to get away from the shadow, but it follows my every move. It's not my shadow. My shadow cowers from it in fear. It's bigger than my shadow— taller, wider. It's my father's shadow. He is following me around the house, letting me lead the way until he is ready to pounce on me and teach me a lesson.*

I duck into the bathroom and close the door, but where the lock should be, there is just an empty space. Even as I tell myself not to leave the room, I reach out, open the door, and leave.

The shadow still follows me. It seems that the laws of physics don't apply to the shadow, because it was in the bathroom with me without my father being in there. Despite knowing that, I am more certain than ever that the shadow is my father's shadow. I can hear him breathing. I can smell his scent—a woodsy after- shave he always wears, and a slight hint of sweat; the latter is only present when he is about to beat me, the smell of his excitement.

I take a chance and start to run. I make it to the top of the stairs, down each one. The shadow stays with me, never getting any closer or farther away. I reach the bottom of the stairs and keep running. I make it into the living room, and I see that the shadow hasn't followed me in here.

I have done it. I am free of my father. Free of the beatings and the abuse. I sit down on the couch, and a laugh bubbles up in my throat. I try to keep it in, but I can't. It bursts out of me, a sound so pure, so full of joy. I keep laughing, and it feels good. In that moment, I am truly happy.

But it doesn't last long. I hear loud, pounding footsteps. My father's footsteps. They are on the stairs once more, but this time, they are not coming for me. They are heading up instead of down. I feel a pang of guilt stab at me like a needle worrying my skin. Has he gone after Janet? Is he going to hurt her because I escaped him?

No, he won't hurt Janet. Janet never bears his bruises, never gets yelled at by him. Janet is his favorite by far, but I'm not sure if that's a good thing or a bad thing for her. My father has his balance all wrong. He doesn't love me enough, but he loves Janet too much.

I screw my eyes tightly closed, not wanting to hear her bedroom door opening, not wanting to hear her quiet whimpers and pleas for him to stop. I put my fingers into my ears, but I realize I can still hear him. And he's not with Janet. He's behind me again.

I open my eyes and wail in despair as I realize I am back at the start. I start to run, the shadow looming over me ...

I WOKE UP WITH A JUMP, cold beads of sweat coating my skin. I felt the icy fingers of panic inside me, swirling everything around in my stomach. I didn't know where I was. I only knew that I was being watched. By my father.

I took a couple of deep breaths, forcing myself to breathe deeply, focusing only on breathing in for a count of five and out for a count of seven. I slowly became aware of my surroundings, and I knew why I'd had that particular dream again. It was being back here. I could call it my house all I wanted to, but deep down I was worried that it would always be his lair.

I sat up and ran my hands over my face. I had accepted that my father chasing me through the house had been nothing but a horrible dream, but even now, fully awake and calm again, I still felt as though someone were watching me. It made the hairs on the back of my neck stand up. I wanted to spin around and see who was behind me, but at the same time, I didn't dare look.

I stood up and grabbed my cell phone. There was no way I would get any more sleep unless I searched the house, and without any real light, I would need to use my cell phone as a flashlight. I would just have to hope that the battery held out.

5

My Journal—Day Five After Release

I really thought things were going well. Since my release, I've managed to contact the gas and electric companies, and I now have light, heat, hot water, everything. I bought groceries and clothing and toiletries. Of course, I have to be back home before six or my ankle monitor sounds an alarm. I don't mind the curfew—I hardly want to walk the streets at night anyways.

I have cooked meals and tidied up after myself. I have spoken to my new therapist and Brianna again. I have found a lawyer and employed his services to help me with probate and accessing the money I have been left. I explained that I don't have a bank account, and he told me to leave everything to him, so that is what I am going to do.

Between all of the busyness, I have made sure to take care of myself, too, because if there's one thing I learned in the hospital, it's that if you stop taking care of your body, you might as well give up on taking care of your mind.

I have showered at least once a day, brushed my teeth morning, noon, and night, and gotten in at least thirty minutes of exercise and thirty minutes of meditation per day. I have kept on top of my medication and made sure not to miss any doses. I found a small safe, more of a lockbox, really, and I keep it in there so that I know where it is at all times. The only medication not in the box is my sedatives. I like to have them on me so if I do have an attack, I don't have to get to my lockbox.

Taking everything into account, I think it's fair to say I have been functioning like any normal adult.

That all changed today. I arranged to have some groceries delivered. They arrived on time, and I went to the door feeling happy and, I think, acting perfectly normal. Until I opened the door.

Call me sexist, but I was expecting the delivery driver to be a man, so the fact it was a woman threw me slightly. I got over the initial shock and looked a bit closer at her. She was young, and she had pretty blonde hair. But what caught my attention were the freckles scattered across her nose and cheekbones. I don't know why, but the sight of them triggered a panic reaction.

It got so bad so quickly that, before the girl could speak, I was on my knees, clawing at my throat, gasping for breath. The girl wanted to call 911, but I managed to croak out enough to tell her it was a panic attack. She stayed there with me until it had mostly passed, and I got myself back under control. I thanked her without looking at her face, and when she left, I took one of my sedatives.

I am so angry with myself. I was doing so well, and then that happens. And I don't even know why those freckles set me off. But I feel as though if I tried really hard to remember, I would. I can see the tail-end of the memory of the girl with the freckles on her nose and cheekbones dancing away in my peripheral vision.

I feel that I could grab it if I wanted to. But something stopped me. There's a voice inside me that tells me that if I see that memory, I might just go all of the way mad, and that this time, there will be no meds, no coming back from it.

I can't risk that. I make a mental note not to order any more grocery deliveries. It feels like I have just slapped a Band-Aid on the bleeding stump of a severed leg, but it will have to do.

6

I picked my cell phone up as it started to ring. I checked the screen, and as expected, it was Dr. Sellers calling for my therapy session. He was right on time, and I smiled.

"Hello," I said.

"Hi, James, it's Dr. Sellers," he said. "How are you feeling today?"

It was a good question. I wasn't particularly happy, but I wasn't particularly sad. I just ... was. I'd had another bad dream the night before, as I had done every night since coming back to the house, and I decided to focus on that.

"I'm okay, Doc, just a little bit tired because I keep having night terrors so bad that they wake me, and then once I'm awake like that, I can't get back to sleep."

"Tell me a bit about the night terrors," Dr. Sellers said. "Can you remember them when you wake up?"

"Mostly," I said. "Or at least I think I can. Who knows how much I may have forgotten, though."

"Fair point," Dr. Sellers said, with a smile in his voice. When he went on, he was serious again. "Tell me about the worst one."

"My father is following me around the house. He isn't yelling or anything, but I can see his shadow no matter which direction we are moving in. I end up in different rooms each time I have the nightmare, but that's the only thing that changes. Other than that, there is always him following me and then us ending up in one room or another, and from that room, he leaves me alone."

I paused for breath, and then I went on. "When he goes away, I am worried he is going after Janet, my twin sister. I close my eyes and block my ears. When I open my eyes again, I am back at the start of the dream, and it begins again. It plays on a loop until it wakes me up. And when I do wake up, I always feel unsettled, like I'm being watched."

"So part of the dream invades your reality?" Dr. Sellers said.

"Yes," I agreed. "I guess it does."

"And Janet? How does she fit into all of this?" Dr. Sellers asked. "Are the two of you close?"

"She's in my corner," I replied, automatically repeating her words.

"What does that mean?" Dr. Sellers asked.

"It's just something she says. Like she has my back, you know," I said.

"And do you feel like that's true?" Dr. Sellers asked.

I thought for a moment, and then I sighed. "I don't know. Sometimes I believe that she has my best interests at heart, but then I wonder if I just think like that because it's easier than questioning everything. But other times, I feel like she's far from on my side. I remember her and my father ganging up on me when I was a child. But the truth is, I don't know if it's a real memory or a hallucination, and I can't be mad at someone for something they only did in my head, can I?"

"No, you can't," Dr. Sellers confirmed. "Do you find that happens a lot? Not knowing whether something from your childhood is real or imagined? Or is it an issue that stems solely around your sister?"

"It happens a lot," I admitted. "Sometimes I can work out if it's true or not, but other times I have no idea."

"How does this affect you now?" Dr. Sellers asked.

"It makes me paranoid sometimes, like I feel that what I'm seeing and experiencing now can't be real. I also hate the fact that when I look back at my childhood, I'm not sure what is real, what is imagined, and what is not real, but I was led to believe was real by my father."

"Okay," Dr. Sellers said after a few moments. "I think the first thing we need to do, and perhaps the most important thing, is to find a way for you to distinguish between the real and the not real."

I didn't know if he was asking me or telling me, but he paused, so I felt like I should answer him. "Yes. If you can tell me how to do that, I would be grateful."

"We're going to use two different approaches. Firstly, I'm going to schedule a face-to-face session with you if that's okay? I really think you could benefit from some hypnotherapy. I hope to be able to regress you, and we can work out what's real that way. Would that be alright?"

I didn't really know a lot about hypnotherapy, but I was desperate enough to try anything. My mind had become my own worst enemy, and I hated it. And for this to have a chance at working, I knew I had to trust my therapist. I already liked Dr. Sellers a damned sight more than I had liked Dr. Jenkins, so I figured I might as well go all in and trust that he knew what might work for me.

"Yes, if you think it will help," I replied.

"I do," Dr. Sellers said. "I have a waiting list for that kind of appointment, so we'll likely have a few more phone sessions before that. I'll have my secretary add you to the list and let you know when you can expect me. Now, in the meantime, the other thing I would like you to do is search out things from your childhood that might help you determine if your memories of certain things are real or not. Can you do that for me?"

"I don't know what you mean," I replied. "Like try to hypnotize myself?"

"Oh goodness me, no," Dr. Sellers said.

He laughed softly, but I felt as though I was in on the joke, like he was laughing with me rather than at me, and I laughed myself. It was bizarre that I had thought for even a moment that my therapist might recommend I do his job for him.

"I mean try to find actual physical things. School reports, journals, anything like that. See if there is any evidence of you being violent or antisocial. Seeing the events written down might help you to know what was real and what wasn't."

"Yes, I can do that," I said.

I felt happy, hopeful even, for the first time in a long time. It wasn't just that Dr. Sellers had set me a task I could actually do; he had set me a task I felt like I *wanted* to do. It would be interesting to find things from my childhood, and those things might contain some of the answers I so badly needed.

By the time my therapy session finished, I was still feeling positive. I could hardly wait to start my search for memories from my childhood.

7

I jumped up, eager to start searching the house for the sort of things Dr. Sellers wanted me to find. I was ready and raring to go. There was just one problem—I had no idea where anything like that might be kept.

I thought for a moment. It certainly wasn't in any of the guest rooms. It wasn't in my room, and I doubted it would be in Janet's room. It wouldn't be in my father's room. He wasn't sentimental enough to keep things like that. No, if there was anything to be found, it would be things my mom had kept. So where might she have stashed them?

I was pretty sure she would have put them in the attic. It would have been a good place to make sure my father never found those things and threw them away.

I climbed the stairs quickly, my enthusiasm for the task carrying me. It wasn't until I reached the top that I realized that the hatch was on the side of the hallway that belonged to my father. I shook my head. The house was mine now. All of it was mine. None of it belonged to my father.

I marched purposefully down the hallway to the hatch to

the attic. The hatch was a couple of inches in front of my father's bedroom door, and I wondered, not for the first time, why it wasn't in the center of the hallway. I had once asked my mom, and she told me that if the hatch were in the middle, it would prevent us from storing anything large, whereas with it at one end, it left the majority of the floor space clear. I didn't know if this was a real memory or a hallucination, but I thought it was probably real—it felt real, but all my hallucinations felt real. The difference was that this one felt a little bit too mundane to be a hallucination. Like seriously, even crazy people have their limits. And surely, I wasn't boring enough that the best thing my broken mind could conjure up was a conversation about an attic hatch.

The pole wasn't anywhere in sight, and I swallowed hard, knowing I needed to go back into the master bedroom. I told myself that nothing was in there, nothing was going to hurt me. My little mantra didn't calm me down completely, but it did seem to stop me from having a full-blown panic attack, so I opened the master bedroom door quickly while I felt able to do it.

I stepped into the room and instantly looked down at the floor, not wanting to look at any of my father's things again. But I knew I wasn't going to find the pole that way. I took another deep breath and forced myself to lift my head, then glanced around the room.

Relief flooded me when I spotted the pole resting against the side of a wooden closet. I grabbed the pole, then turned and practically ran from the room. I slammed the door shut behind me and leaned against it. As I concentrated on getting my breath back, I tilted my head back and closed my eyes.

I was on the verge of another panic attack, and I had to ask myself whether this was really worth it. I told myself that I knew it was. If I could find out the truth of who I had been, then I would be more confident. And if I could find a way to establish the difference between my real memories and fake ones, then I would feel much more stable.

Knowing that what I was doing was a good thing didn't really affect my panic level. It was like my brain knew something, but my body refused to accept it as the truth. I knew I had to take one of my sedatives. I didn't particularly want to —they left me feeling exhausted, and I didn't want to sleep. Not yet. First, I wanted to find anything I could about my childhood.

I realized, though, that I wasn't in the right frame of mind to look at much of anything, so I made my decision. I would take my medication like I was supposed to, and then I would go up into the attic and have a look around. If I found anything, I wouldn't look at it until after I had crashed for an hour or two from the sedative.

I took the bottle from my pocket and opened it. I shook a pill out into my palm, recapped the bottle, and put it back. I looked at the pill for a second, all white and innocent. But it wasn't innocent. It was a thief that stole parts of my life, and I couldn't wait for the time when I was no longer dependent on them to get me through the day.

With a sigh, I brought my hand up to my mouth and dry swallowed the pill like I had done a hundred times. As usual, I imagined the pill sticking in my throat. I swallowed hard, once, twice. I bit down on the inside of my cheek, causing my mouth to flood with saliva, and I swallowed again. The blockage in my throat didn't move.

I was going to die. The irony of being killed by the very

pills that were meant to stop me from doing something stupid to myself wasn't lost on me, even in that moment. I swallowed again, again. Nothing was working, and I was starting to feel like I couldn't breathe. I reached up with both hands and massaged my throat, but it was no use.

I needed a drink of water. But I was too far away from the kitchen or my bathroom. I would die before I reached either of them. My father's bathroom was right there, the door in touching distance, but the last thing I wanted to do was go into any part of my father's lair again.

I would just let myself die. My legs were turning to jelly, and my vision danced with black spots. With a growling sound born of determination, I reached for the bedroom door and stumbled into the room. I wasn't going to let him win. Not now. I wasn't going to let him keep torturing me from beyond the grave.

I staggered to the sink in his bathroom, turned on the cold faucet, and bent down. I pushed my face into the flow, holding my breath and swallowing water. After a few big gulps, I stood up and swallowed cautiously. The blockage was gone. I could swallow, and I could breathe again.

I walked back through the bathroom door to the bedroom door and, as I shut it behind me, I peered back into the room for one last second and smiled.

"Fuck you, Dad," I whispered. "I'm not afraid of you anymore."

It was a lie, but it felt good to say it, and I hoped that, one day in the not-too-distant future, it would become the truth.

I got the pole and used it to open the hatch and pull down the ladder to the attic. I leaned the pole back up against the wall and climbed the ladder. In the attic I stepped off the ladder and pulled the string that turned the light on. I blinked against the sudden brightness as the neon bulb burst into life.

I stood still for a moment, looking around. Most of the things up here were covered with dust sheets, large bits of furniture, and paintings that could be worth a fortune now, but probably weren't. My father had always fancied himself an art connoisseur, but in reality he had never discovered the next big thing.

I turned my attention to the piles of cardboard boxes at the other end of the attic. I made my way toward them, pleased to see that they were labeled, which would save me a lot of time going through each box.

I looked down the first stack at the labels. Christmas. Halloween. Kitchen stuff. Outdoor lights. Tax returns. More Christmas. More Halloween. Photos. I moved on to the next stack and found much the same sort of thing. The third stack contained old bills and receipts, a box for every year going back at least two decades.

I was beginning to give up hope when I spotted a box tucked away behind the stacks. It looked much the same as the rest, but it wasn't labeled, and something told me that was a good sign. I started to move the stacks of boxes so I could get to the lone box. It wasn't easy—my sedative was kicking in now, leaving me exhausted and drained. I just wanted to curl up in a ball on the floor and sleep. Normally I would have, but I really wanted to see what was in that box.

I finally made enough of a gap that I could reach through and grab the box. I lifted it into the air and placed it on top of one of the other stacks. I took a deep breath, butterflies fluttering in my stomach as I took the lid off the box.

Inside were piles of papers, handwritten, not printed. I knew I had hit the jackpot with this box, and I decided to take it downstairs before I started going through it. That way, if I passed out, I would at least be comfortable.

I put the lid back on the box and crossed the attic back to the hatch. I stepped onto the ladder, sure for a second that I was going to fall and break my neck. I kept my balance despite my hands being full, and I made my way carefully down the ladder. When I reached the bottom, I set the box on the floor and pushed the ladder back up into place. I debated putting the pole away but decided against it. I might want to go back up there and see if there were any more boxes like this one.

I picked the box back up, then made my way down the stairs and returned to the living room. I sat down on the couch and took the lid off the box again. I could smell the mustiness of old paper, and I smiled to myself. These had to be my old journals.

I had stopped journaling not long after my mom had died because, like everything I did, my father said it was pointless. It had never felt pointless to me. Writing down my thoughts and feelings had often helped me to clear my mind, and, later on, if I referred back to the entries, they helped me to clarify things. I started journaling again in the hospital, and I intended to keep going with it, but these journals here would all be from before my mom died.

I reached in and pulled out an envelope, the address of this house scrawled on it in blue ink. The envelope was torn open, and protruding from it was a sheet of lined paper. I pulled the sheet out and found the same blue scrawl on the paper. I sat back and began to read.

By the second line of the letter, I had established that it was from Great-Aunt Muriel updating my parents on how she was doing. I had never met her, and now that I thought about it, I didn't even know if she was my mom's aunt or my father's. By the third line, the monotone in which the letter was written and the strength of my sedatives worked together, forcing my eyes to close.

I dragged them open and tried my best to keep reading, but the writing all blurred into one big, blue smudge as I fought to stay awake. I thought about the nights I'd had since coming here, my sleep broken and plagued with night terrors. No wonder I was so tired. Even without the sedative, I would have been exhausted by now.

Still, I fought on, blinking and running my hand over my eyes. I managed to focus long enough to get to the end of the letter, although twice I didn't realize that I had fallen asleep until I jumped awake and found my chin resting on my chest.

Once I confirmed that the letter contained nothing helpful, I slid it back into its envelope and put it on the coffee table, and then I leaned back against the couch and folded my hands in my lap. I allowed my eyes to close, and this time I didn't fight the exhaustion as it pulled me down to sleep. I would be able to concentrate on everything else in the box so much better once I felt more awake.

8

I woke up the next morning feeling rested for the first time in ages. I was a little bit surprised that I had slept right through, and if I'd had a bad dream, then I didn't remember it, and it hadn't disturbed my sleep. I couldn't help but think it was because of the box of papers I had found yesterday.

I kept thinking back to how Dr. Sellers had told me that things like this could help me learn about what was real and what was imagined. The memory of those words soothed my soul. All I had ever wanted was to know the truth about my own life. And maybe to fill in some of the gaps of the times I didn't remember.

I went into the kitchen and made two slices of toast and some coffee. I ate the toast with butter and jam, and I drank two mugs of coffee. I poured a third one and took it into the living room. I was ready to start my journey of discovery.

I put the box on the couch beside me and took off the lid. I was once more greeted with the mustiness of old papers. I smiled to myself, enjoying the smell. I reached into the box and began to pull things out one by one. The top ones were more letters between various family members and one or the other of my parents. I glanced through these, but there was nothing of any real interest in them, and I thought it was likely that my mom had only kept them out of sentimentality. Maybe one day I would read through them, but not now. I had a mission to complete, and they would only slow me down.

After all of the letters were out of the box, I found a sketchpad. I didn't recognize it at first, but once I opened it, I realized it was mine. I flicked through the pages, looking at the various doodles and cartoons. If I was honest, I supposed it would have been fair to say that I was looking for something dark. Drawings of graves, weapons, massacres. I didn't know exactly what, but certainly something more disturbing than the superheroes I had drawn. Despite being pretty run-of-the-mill, the drawings did bring back a memory—one I could now confidently say was real—I had enjoyed reading comic books when I was little. Spider-Man, Superman, Iron Man, I loved them all.

I wondered briefly what Dr. Sellers would make of it. I figured he would say something along the lines of, "You and every other kid in America," and make me realize that not everything had to have some deeper meaning. Dr. Jenkins, on the other hand, would have made something out of it. He would have said something pompous like I was looking for a male role model, a hero, a father figure. He would have been wrong. If anything, I would have been looking to those heroes to rescue me from my father, not to become him. But overall, my sketchbook felt as irrelevant as the letters, and I closed it and put it on the pile on the coffee table.

Next was a large folder, which I lifted from the box with

both hands. I wiped my palm over the front of it, wiping off the dust, and opened it. It was a folder containing all of my school reports until my mom died. After that, there was nothing. That wasn't something I would have expected, knowing my father like I did.

I flicked through the reports, but nothing jumped out at me suggesting I was a problem child or anything, or at least not at school. I'd go back to the reports later as well, as I was interested to read them, but they weren't my priority right now. My priority was finding something that told the true story of my life in the house. I closed the folder and put it down with the other things, and then I peered back into the box.

There was only one thing left. A leather-bound notebook that looked awfully like a journal. I felt excitement spread through me, goosebumps chasing each other around my skin. This was it. One of my journals. I reached into the box and lifted the notebook out and ran my hand over the smooth, black cover. I loved the feel of it. I brought it to my nose and sniffed it, savoring the scent of the real leather.

Finally, I opened the journal and instantly realized it wasn't my handwriting that filled the pages. My excitement didn't dampen, though. The handwriting belonged to my mom. It was her journal. I lifted it to my face and sniffed, hoping for a whiff of her floral perfume or her strawberry shampoo, both scents I could recall as though it were only yesterday that I had last hugged her.

All I could smell was the paper, but still, holding her journal in my hands made me feel close to her. A lump formed in my throat. I really missed my mom, and I still didn't really know what had happened to her, only that she had died.

Plenty of times over the years, my father had screamed at me, telling me that I was just like my mom. He thought it was an insult. He had no idea that the thought of being like my mom warmed my heart. It was the one time I felt like I was managing to get one over on him.

I started to read the journal, absorbing its words, and turning the pages as if in a trance.

Before I knew it, three hours had passed, and I was still glued to the spot on the couch, with the journal open on my lap.

The main thing that stood out, and made me sad and angry in equal measure, was that my father had abused my mom in much the same way as he had abused me. She made several references to him hiding her medication when she voiced her opinion or disagreed with him. And if she tried to stop him from taking it, he would deny what he was doing, and then he would get angry and hit her. It also sounded like my mom and I shared the same mental health issues.

Nowhere in my mom's journal did she mention that I was a problem child. There was nothing to insinuate I was violent or even that I misbehaved. She did refer a couple of times to me having attacks. I wasn't entirely sure what she meant by that, whether I had had some sort of seizure or whether it was her way of referring to things that my mind blocked out. It definitely didn't sound like a word a parent would use to describe a misbehaving child.

There was one entry in particular that had caught my eye, and I went back to reread it:

Oh, what a day. Cain was in a bad mood from the get-go, yelling at James from the moment he opened his eyes. Not Janet of course. Never Janet.

God help me, I hate how bitter I seem when I say that. I make it sound like I don't love my girl. I do. I swear I do. But I don't think she loves me. She claims to, but it's true that actions speak louder than words, and the things she does tell a different story.

Of course, it could be that she's even more terrified of Cain than James and I are, and so she does whatever she thinks he wants her to do so she can stay on his good side and be daddy's little girl.

So, Cain began the day by yelling at James over some imagined misdemeanor. I'd hoped that was it, that he had gotten it out of his system, but of course that was just wishful thinking on my part. By lunchtime, my nerves were shot, and I was sick of hearing Cain yelling. I had told James several times that it was okay, to just ignore his father, he was just in a bad mood, but I could see it was taking its toll on James, and I was getting angrier by the moment.

As soon as James and Janet finished eating their sandwiches, I sent them off upstairs to read. Janet began to protest, but I must have looked as mad as I felt because one glance at me and she scurried off behind James without another word—something that was quite unusual for her.

I waited until I heard their feet leave the stairs and run across the hallway, and then I turned to Cain and asked him to lay off James.

He bit my head off, shouting about how James could do anything he wanted, and I would take his side. I tried to explain that that wasn't true, but that the truth was, James hadn't done anything to deserve the way he was being treated, by his own father no less.
Cain laughed at me, a bitter laugh, and told me that one day, James would kill me, and with my dying breath, I would apologize to my husband for not seeing the truth earlier.

Honestly, the man is on another planet. How he can believe for even a second that James is violent or nasty is beyond me. I might be the one with schizophrenia, but make no mistake—Cain is the only one who is crazy around here.

I don't have a plan yet—Cain controls everything in the house, including all of the money—but I am going to get out of here. I am going to take James away somewhere safe. I am going to ask Janet to come, too, but I know in my heart she will refuse. But at least I can save James.

I have more to say, dear diary, so much more, but Cain has hidden my meds again, and my thoughts are fuzzy and frayed, and I can't think for much longer. I just wanted to get this down before I forget.

At face value, my mom's words told me everything I needed to know. My mom was meant to be my savior before she died. We weren't the problem. My father was. And maybe even Janet. I wasn't sure about her, just like my mom hadn't been. But I also knew from the entry that she hadn't taken her meds, at least that day.

What if the whole thing was a paranoid delusion? What if I was actually a bad kid, and my mom chose not to see it, and my father just wanted to straighten me out so that I didn't end up in prison or something?

I still didn't know what to believe, and trying to guess the answers was giving me a headache. I decided on a whim that I was going to put everything back in its box for now and go and look up in the attic again to see if I could find anything else.

Maybe then I would get some answers. And if I didn't, maybe Dr. Sellers's hypnotherapy sessions could help me to figure out what was real and what wasn't. He certainly sounded like he believed it could work, and that was good enough for me.

9

It was almost 4 p.m. when the doorbell rang. I felt a moment of panic. I knew I hadn't ordered anything, and I wasn't really up for a social call from someone trying to be neighborly.

The letterbox rattled. "James? James?" a voice called in through the flap.

I relaxed, though not all of the way. The voice belonged to my twin sister, Janet. She had said she was coming, but I had forgotten all about it.

"Coming," I called as I headed for the door.

"Quickly now," Janet responded, and then the letterbox slammed closed.

I rolled my eyes. Considering Janet was the same age as me—technically, she was a minute and a half older—sometimes she sounded like an old lady trying to get a grandchild to behave when she spoke to me. I told myself to give her a break. She didn't have to come all this way to look after me. And, after all, she was the one person I could truly rely on. The one person who was in my corner.

I opened the front door, and Janet pulled me into a rather awkward hug. I tolerated it for as long as I could before I wriggled free of her hold. She didn't seem to notice my discomfort; she just walked past me and headed for the living room. I picked up her suitcase, closed the front door, and, with a sigh, I followed her back into the house, leaving the suitcase at the bottom of the stairs.

Janet was already in the living room, sitting on the sofa, and I took the other end. As she looked me up and down, her mouth was a tight O of disapproval.

"What?" I said when I couldn't stand her scrutiny anymore.

"You look so skinny. Are you eating properly?"

"Yes," I said. "I'm not that skinny. I—"

She cut me off. "Breakfast, lunch, dinner?"

I nodded, not even bothering to try to speak.

"Give me an idea of what you're having for each of your meals. Like on an average day."

"For breakfast, I have either toast and jam or oatmeal. Lunch is generally a sandwich or a wrap, and dinner is something like steak or chicken with potatoes and vegetables."

She pursed her lips. "Maybe it's your meds that are making you lose weight. Are you taking them how you're supposed to?"

"Yes," I said.

"I might take over dispensing them to you while I'm here, just so it's one less thing for me to worry about," she said.

While I would normally give in to whatever she wanted for a quiet life, my medication was the one area I wouldn't do that for. It was a crutch for me knowing that I was handling my meds on my own, and to be honest, I wasn't sure I could give up that control.

"That won't be necessary," I said firmly. "I've told you I'm taking them properly, and you don't need to worry about that side of things."

"Well, there's no need for that attitude. I'm only trying to help you," Janet huffed. "It's my duty."

I tried my best to bite my tongue, but old habits were hard to break, and I soon found myself apologizing to her. She gave me a smug smile, and I was glad because that smile stopped me right before I changed my mind and gave her permission to dole out my meds. Instead, I just smiled back and then looked down into my lap.

"Tell me about your daily schedule," Janet said when it became clear that I wasn't going to say any more.

I shrugged. "I don't have a schedule per se. I just go about my life like anyone else. Of course, I have appointments to keep track of, but that's it. The rest of the time, I do what I want. I eat when I'm hungry, and sleep when I'm tired. That kind of thing."

"Okay, that makes sense," she said.

I felt myself smiling, happy under her praise despite myself.

"And your appointments. I take it you have a therapist?"

"Yes. I like him much more than the one I was assigned to while I was in the hospital," I said.

"Good," Janet said. "Maybe you'll respond better to him if you like him. Do you have a probation officer or a cop you have to report to?"

I nodded, unable to stop myself from smiling when I thought of Brianna. I was pretty sure that reporting to your probation officer was meant to be a nuisance, a punishment to an extent. For me, it was the opposite. I looked forward to seeing Brianna each time I had to prove I was still here. I loved being in her company, and I loved the way she talked to me like I was normal.

Janet frowned. "You're not supposed to look pleased with yourself. Do you have any idea how embarrassing it is for me to have to tell people my twin brother is on probation?"

I resisted the urge to tell her not to tell anyone about it if she felt that way, and, instead, I just shook my head.

She reached out and squeezed my forearm. "I'm sorry. I know it's not your fault you're ill. Just don't be breaking your probation. Okay? Now that you have your meds sorted and everything, doing so would be a choice rather than a symptom. Do you understand what I'm saying here, James?"

I nodded. I had no intention of breaking my probation conditions. I didn't want to go back to being locked away, and honestly, I figured if I broke the rules, I wouldn't get to see Brianna anymore. That thought was guaranteed to keep me motivated.

"Can I see your ankle monitor?" Janet asked.

I rolled up my jeans slightly and lifted my leg.

She glanced at the monitor, then grinned. "I could have that off in minutes, if you have a screwdriver or a chisel and a hammer."

I instinctively pulled my leg away from her, and she laughed.

"What?" she said.

"You've just made a big deal about me following the rules and then suggested I have you break my monitor off. It's alarmed, you know," I said.

"Jeez, will you chill out a bit? I was joking." Janet laughed and shook her head.

I tried to laugh, but I couldn't quite bring myself to do it. Something told me she hadn't been joking at all. The best I could manage was a smile. It must have been enough to appease her because she didn't say anything else about my lack of a sense of humor.

"So, are you managing with your bills and everything?" Janet asked.

I nodded.

"Are you sure? Because if you're struggling, I can help you set up direct debits and everything," she went on. "Yes, I think that's the best idea. Let me have your bank details, and I'll sort it out for you."

"It's sorted already," I told her. "My solicitor took care of it."

"You let him have access to your bank account?" Janet said.

"Of course not," I replied. "He has set up payment arrangements with the utility companies and an account for online groceries. I don't have a bank account yet. He's sorting it all for me."

"You don't have a bank account? So where are you keeping our father's money?" she asked.

I noticed that she didn't refer to it as my money, but *our father's* money. She was obviously bitter about the inheritance, and to be honest, I didn't blame her. She had always been my father's favorite, and it wouldn't have surprised me in the least to learn that our fates had been the other way around upon his death.

It must have come as a nasty surprise to Janet to not be in his will. I wished I could give her the lot and walk away from it, because I didn't want anything of my father's, but the truth was, I wasn't in that position, so we would both have to suck it up. The final disservice from my father.

"My solicitor is dealing with it," I repeated. "Look, Janet, I'm sorry about the way it turned out. That he left me the money and not you, and—"

"Please." Janet cut me off with a wave of her hand. "As if I need his money. I'm successful. I have my own money. You think our father didn't know who would need to be babied and who would make it? He left you everything because he knew you would never amount to anything on your own."

I didn't bother to argue with her. We both knew that wasn't why he had left me the inheritance. It was because he was a misogynistic pig, but if that was what Janet needed to believe to make her peace with the situation, then I wasn't about to argue.

"I'm sorry," she said after a second, mistaking my silence for upset. "I'm just saying what he thought. I'm not saying I feel like that toward you."

"I know," I said. "It's fine, really."

"Right," Janet said. She clapped her hands and stood up. "Let's get some groceries ordered, shall we?"

"I've got groceries."

"I know, but I want to make sure you have plenty to eat and it's not all junk food," she said.

"Go ahead." I sighed. "The laptop is in the dining room."

She disappeared and reappeared a second later with my laptop. I could have argued the toss or refused to give her the password for the groceries account, but what would have been the point? I needed to pick my battles with Janet, and it wasn't like she was going to order things I didn't like.

I sat beside her as she made the order. She spoke aloud,

letting me know each time she put something in the basket. When she eventually checked out, I had spent $183 on things I didn't really need, but it wasn't like I couldn't afford it, and it would save me from grocery shopping for the next week or two.

She finished up and put the laptop down on the coffee table. She turned to me and gave me a sad smile. "You know I only want what's best for you, don't you?"

"Sure," I replied.

I did know that. Didn't I?

"Well then, I think it's best if I deal with your medication," she said. "I know you said you're handling it, but if you give me whatever you keep it in, then I can give you the right pills at the right times. It'll be one less thing for you to worry about. You can just concentrate on getting better, then, without any stress."

"No," I said. "I know you're trying to help me, but right now, I'm okay. I feel like you're kind of smothering me with talk about my meds and ordering groceries when I told you I already had the shopping done."

Janet looked down into her lap for a moment, and then she looked up at me, her eyes meeting mine. "I didn't want to have to tell you this, but you're making me out to be the bad guy here and leaving me with no real choice. I'm worried about you not taking your meds because you said you had your groceries under control, but I checked in the fridge earlier, and so much of that stuff is out of date. Honestly, I don't know how you haven't made yourself ill," she said quietly.

I opened my mouth to tell her that wasn't true, but it must be true if she'd looked. Why would she lie? And why would she order me a load of groceries if mine were all okay?

Yes, she had to be right. I obviously wasn't doing as well as I thought.

"Don't look so sad," Janet said with a flicker of another smile. "You'll get there; I know you will. Look, why don't we compromise? You can take your own meds, but whenever it's time to take them, I'll remind you. If you forget, then we'll make sure I'm present until you physically take them."

I nodded. That sounded like a good compromise. I was worried now. If I could eat out-of-date food, what else could I fuck up without even noticing? I ignored the little voice at the back of my mind, the one that insisted Janet hadn't even been in the kitchen to know this stuff. That was just my mind trying to trick me, to make me crazy again. This time, I wasn't going to fall for it.

"Thank you," I said. "I'd appreciate that."

Janet smiled at me.

I was suddenly choked full of emotion. I wasn't ready to show her that level of vulnerability, so I jumped up. "Nature calls."

I hurried away to the downstairs bathroom. I locked the door and leaned back against it while I fought to get myself under control.

Was I still crazy? Would I ever not be crazy? I didn't feel crazy, but do crazy people know that they're crazy? Do they feel crazy? I shook my head, shaking away the thoughts, and gulped hard, trying to swallow down the lump in my throat.

Even if some of my food had been out of date, I hadn't been ill, so it couldn't have been that old. I had never had to worry about checking expiration dates when I was in the hospital, so surely it was normal that it might have slipped my mind. I wasn't crazy. I was just a little bit forgetful.

Once I realized that, I saw that I might have been a bit

too hard on myself. I had probably been a bit too hasty to agree to Janet supervising me taking my meds, too, but it was harmless enough, and it would put her mind at rest. It might even make her see that I was more capable than she gave me credit for.

When I was confident that my emotions were under control, I stepped forward and flushed the toilet. I washed my hands absent-mindedly, and then I went back to the living room.

My jaw dropped when I saw that Janet had dug into the box of papers from the attic. I thought it was pretty damned rude that she should come into my house and snoop like that, but I also knew if I appeared angry about it, it would make it seem as though there was something of value in the box, and Janet wouldn't rest until she had it.

I wasn't ready to share Mom's journal. I wanted to scrutinize every word before I even considered showing it to Janet. She had one of the letters in her hand, and I was relieved. She could read those. I really didn't care about them.

I sat down beside her. "So, tell me, how's work and everything?" I asked, hiding my annoyance, and forcing her to put down the letter and reply.

I was only half-listening to her answer, already wondering where to hide the box once she wandered away. I pretended to listen until she stopped talking, and then I asked her if she wanted a drink.

"I'd love a cup of tea," she said.

I stood up and headed toward the door. "Tea. That's the one with the little bag, right?"

Janet rolled her eyes and got up, just as I had known she would.

"Sit down. I'll make it," she said in a long-suffering voice.

I waited for her to reach the kitchen, and then I picked up the box and hurried upstairs to my bedroom. I put the box in a corner of the room, but not before I had removed Mom's journal and locked it away in my lockbox.

10

"Where did the box go?"

It was almost midnight, and I was almost asleep. I had no idea what Janet was talking about.

"Huh?" I said, sitting up straight and running my hands over my face.

"The box of letters and stuff. Where did it go?" she said.

Her tone was casual, but I knew there was nothing casual about the question. She had planned to finish snooping through the things in that box. I didn't want to tell her I had locked it away from her, because she might ask why, and I would have to tell her the truth—that I didn't want her anywhere near Mom's journal—or else I would have to lie, and I couldn't think of any lie that would convince.

"I put it back up in the attic," I lied. "Why?"

"No particular reason," Janet said with a shrug. "I was reading through some of the letters, that's all. Never mind. It's not like I recognize any of the names on them."

"Same here," I said. "Hence why I put them back upstairs."

Janet nodded, and I thought she actually believed me. It helped that she, too, had started with the letters from the very top of the box, and it wasn't a lie that they were from people we didn't know, and none of them seemed to be about anything of any great importance.

"I guess I'll start the paperback I brought with me instead," Janet said with a yawn. "I think it's past my bedtime. And you look tired yourself."

"Yeah, I am. I reckon it's sleep time for me, too," I said.

I shuffled slightly on the couch as Janet stood up, and I put my feet up where she had been sitting.

"Night," I said.

She turned back from the door with a frown. "What are you doing? Why aren't you going to bed?"

"I've been sleeping down here," I admitted.

"Why?"

"I don't know, really," I said. "It sounds stupid now, but upstairs felt ... I don't know. Wrong."

Janet came back into the living room and sat on the edge of the armchair opposite me. "Please try to sleep in your room. It'll be a good sign that you're moving on from your paranoid issues. There's nothing to be afraid of, James. The Lord is with us always; you shouldn't be afraid."

"I'm not afraid—" I started.

"Good," Janet interrupted. "Then it won't be a problem to be back in your old room, will it?"

I wasn't entirely sure how I had gotten to this point, but it looked like I was spending the night in my old room. There was one thing I was going to do first, though. I didn't care if Janet thought I was paranoid because of it. I got up off the couch and went into the kitchen. Janet followed me as I opened the drawer beneath the sink that contained a mixture of things, including some basic tools.

"What are you doing?" Janet asked.

"I'm looking for a screwdriver," I told her. I pushed things aside in the drawer and finally found one. I held it up with a triumphant smile. "Got it."

Janet was looking at me with a worried frown. "James, it's the middle of the night," she said softly. "It's not the time to start a DIY project."

"No shit," I replied, rolling my eyes. "I want that lock off the outside of my room. You can scoff all you want to, but I will never settle with it still on there."

"I hope you're not suggesting I would lock you in your room," Janet said.

"I'm not suggesting anything. I'm just saying that the lock doesn't need to be there, and I want it gone." I led the way out of the kitchen. As I climbed the stairs, I wondered about Janet's words. Did I think she would lock me in my room?

No. I didn't. Not now. But I couldn't help but wonder if she would have back then, especially if my father had prompted her to do it. Was the only reason she had never done it back then because she couldn't reach the lock? *No, that's stupid*, I told myself. Janet was always on my side. Why would she want to do something so cruel to me?

"Well, goodnight, then, don't forget to say your prayers," Janet said from behind me as I turned to the right and Janet reached the top of the stairs behind me.

I looked back, and my jaw dropped when she turned left.

"What?" She laughed. "I thought I'd take the master bedroom. You're not using it, and it seems like a shame to let such a nice room go to waste, don't you think?"

I didn't think that at all. I thought anywhere that had my father's essence lingering in it should be closed off and never used. If I told Janet that, she would think I had lost the plot, so I forced a smile.

"Good night, Janet," I said.

She gave me a half-smile, then walked down the hallway toward the master bedroom. She turned back for a second. "Don't forget to take your meds or say your evening prayers."

"I won't," I assured her.

And I wouldn't. But would I have remembered without her reminder? I didn't think I would have forgotten to take my pills, but it was hard to tell. As for saying prayers, I had never been very religious, but it seemed Janet had become somewhat since I'd been locked up. Maybe I should start?

I was suddenly glad of Janet's presence. It was nice to have someone here who would keep an eye out for me, someone who was on my side.

I AM ALONE, and yet, I am not alone. I can't see or hear anyone, but I can feel their presence. I can feel their eyes on me, and if I concentrate hard enough, I swear I can hear quiet breathing. The hairs stand up on my neck as icy-cold fear turns my stomach into a rattling mess. Cold fingers of dread drag themselves across my skin, leaving behind trails of goosebumps. I pull my knees up and wrap my arms around them where I sit on my bed. I rock back and forth, my eyes squeezed tightly shut and tears running slowly down my face as I wait for my watcher to reveal himself.

Nothing moves. Still, I can feel the eyes watching me. I force myself to lift my head and look around. Nothing is out of place. There are no shadows that could be hiding anyone. But I know someone is here. Him. He is here. I can sense him like an animal senses a predator.

I get up off the bed, my legs shaking, and I move slowly across the room to my closet. He has to be in there. My father. Watching me. Biding his time to attack. I will still be attacked this way, but at least I will have a modicum of power. I get to choose the moment that it happens to me.

I creep across the floor on my tiptoes. I reach for the closet door when I am close enough. I grab the handle, take a deep breath, and pull the door open in one quick movement. I jump back as the door slams open, but there's nothing out of place, and no one there. The only things in the closet are my clothes.

My heart racing, I push the closet door closed, and then I spin around, pressing my back against the door. I look around, frantic, knowing he is watching me still. It feels as though he is in the walls, like he is watching me from every direction at once.

I know this can't be true, but knowing it's impossible doesn't stop it from being true. I know he is there. I know it as sure as I know my own name.

The moon pops out from behind a cloud, casting a silvery glow over my room. The moonlight glints in the full-length mirror hanging on the wall opposite the window, and I know then. He's in the mirror. Somehow, my father is in the mirror watching me, taunting me, waiting for the perfect moment to jump out and get me.

I run at the mirror, and with a roar that is part fear, part anger and part animalistic rebellion, I smash my fists against the mirror. I slam them into it harder and harder until it first cracks and then shatters into a thousand tiny shards.

My fists bleed, the shards of glass sprinkle over my feet, and they bleed, too. Still, though, I don't stop beating the mirror with my ruined fists. I won't stop until every mirror is destroyed, and then he will be trapped in the world on the other side of the mirrors; the world he uses to torment me will become his prison.

Manic laughter bubbles up through my chest and throat and out of my mouth as I think of him trapped somewhere all alone with no one to watch, no one to bully. I keep pounding with my fists, but all that's left of the top half of the mirror now is the wooden backboard.

I drop to my knees, barely feeling the stinging of the glass shards that embed themselves in my knees, my shins, and the tops of my feet. I pound my fists on the bottom half of the mirror, the half that still has glass left in it.

More shards rain down on me, but I am not afraid of the glass. I am afraid of what lurks behind it. I keep punching. I am hot, sweaty, and out of breath. I gasp and pant, but I don't let myself stop to rest for even a moment. I will rest when the job is done, when his eyes can no longer follow me.

There is only a small bit of glass left in the mirror now, way down in the bottom right-hand corner. I move my fists toward it, banging on the backboard all the way down. I almost reach it. I almost beat him. But it's only almost.

As I reach the last little piece of intact glass and go to hammer on it, my father's hands burst out of the mirror shard and grab me around the throat. I try to scream, but I can't get any air in. He's squeezing my throat, cutting off my airway, choking me. This is his revenge, his punishment for me trying to trap him in the mirror world.

I reach up and try to pry his fingers loose. I am not strong enough to make them budge even a quarter of a centimeter. I scratch at the backs of his hands, and although I draw thin ribbons across his hands, ribbons along which appear small red beads of blood, he doesn't seem to feel it.

I reach down and grab one of the bigger glass shards. I bring it *up and stab toward my father's hands. As the shard arcs toward them, they are gone, dropping me like I am burning them.*

I take in a big gulp of air. It is the last real breath I will ever take.

The shard of glass finally hits its target, except its target is gone, and only my throat remains. The shard pierces through skin and flesh and veins, and a geyser of hot blood splatters what was once my mirror.

I try to breathe, but all I manage is a gurgling of bloody bubbles that makes me choke again, and it occurs to me that I am drowning in my own blood.

I woke up gasping for air. I reached up with my hands, expecting to feel warm, sticky wetness. But I felt only smooth skin. It was slightly damp, but I knew I was back in reality, and in reality, the dampness was just the layer of sweat brought on by the night terror.

I pushed off the duvet and let my hands fall to my sides. I lay panting for breath, waiting for the last remaining shreds of the dream to go away and leave me in peace.

My breathing slowly evened out, and the initial panic dissipated, but I realized that despite knowing everything that had just happened was merely a dream, I still felt as though I were being watched. I told myself I was being irrational and silly, and for all I knew, that was true on a rational level, but my subconscious was anything but rational, and it insisted that I was being watched.

I sat up with a sigh and flicked on the lamp that sat on my nightstand. I should have stayed downstairs, I told myself, although it wouldn't have made any difference. It didn't matter where I slept; if I was going to have a night terror, I was going to have a night terror.

I knew what I had to do to get rid of the feeling. I took a deep, shaky breath and stood up slowly, testing to see if my legs would hold my weight. It seemed that they would, and, feeling mildly ridiculous but not caring, I moved to my closet. I pulled it open. Nothing but my clothes and the lockbox on the floor of the closet, and of course the box of letters sitting beneath an old pillow where I had hidden it after taking my meds tonight.

I closed the closet door and turned to the mirror. It wasn't the same one from my dream, but I knew I wouldn't settle while it sat there on the wall, a window to who knew what.

I had no intention of smashing it, but I had to do something. I went to lift it down from its hook, but it was screwed into the wall. *Great*, I thought. *Now what?*

I debated going back down to the living room to sleep on the couch, but I knew I still wouldn't be able to shake the feeling of being watched, so I might as well deal with it in the bedroom. I went to my chest of drawers and grabbed the screwdriver I had used to take the lock off my bedroom door. I went back to the mirror and unscrewed one side. I supported it with my shoulder and unscrewed the other side. After I lifted it down, I carried it to the bedroom door and opened it.

It was blocked by a long black shadow creature. I made a sound that was half a scream and half a moan.

"Fucking hell, James, you scared me half to death," said a shaky voice.

Relief flooded me. "Sorry. I didn't realize it was you."

"Who exactly were you expecting? And what the hell are you doing with that mirror?" Janet asked.

"I wasn't expecting anyone; that's why I got a shock," I said.

"And the mirror?" Janet pressed.

I sighed. She wasn't going to leave it alone until I told her what I was doing with the mirror in the middle of the night like this. I was so exhausted from the spent adrenaline in my body that I couldn't make up a convincing lie. With shame flooding my cheeks, I told Janet the truth about my dream and how I knew I wouldn't sleep if I felt like someone was still watching me.

Janet took the mirror from me. She opened the door to her old room and took it inside; then she came back out and shut the door. "There. It's gone. You know this is irrational, right?"

"Yes, but I pick my battles, and this isn't one I wanted to waste my energy fighting."

"Alright," Janet said with a nod. "As long as you know that there isn't really someone living in the mirror about to attack you."

It sounded even more ridiculous the way she said it. She made no effort to hide the scorn from her tone. I looked down, embarrassed.

"It's okay," Janet said, her voice softer now, almost comforting. She reached out and gently stroked my cheek. "There's only me here, James, and I promise you I have your best interests in mind. Okay?"

"Okay," I said, finally looking up at her.

She smiled, a warm smile that made me wonder how I had ever doubted her intentions. Of course, she wasn't the enemy here. She was my sister; she had my back. She was just worried about me, that was all.

"Try to get some sleep. You look like hell," she said.

We both laughed.

Janet turned serious again. "You really do need to get some sleep, or your mind will keep playing tricks on you."

"I will, I promise," I said.

"Goodnight," she said, and then she turned and started walking down the hallway.

Something occurred to me then. "Janet?" I called after her.

She paused and looked back.

"How did you hear me taking the mirror down from the master bedroom?"

"I didn't hear you." She laughed. "My goodness, how good do you think my ears are? I just felt like something was off, that you needed me, so I came along to see if you were okay. I reckon it's a twin thing." She turned and walked away.

I'd heard of that kind of link between twins. But Janet and I had never experienced it before. Or had she always felt my pain and just never mentioned it?

It was all too much to worry about now. My mind was overloaded enough, and Janet was right. I needed to sleep. I went to my closet and got my lockbox out. As always, I had one of my sedatives in my pajama pocket, but I wasn't panicking, and I decided to keep that one there for emergencies and get a different one now.

I got the key out and unlocked the box. I pulled out the things I wanted to go through first, and then I got one of my pills out. As I started to return the journal and the other things, I remembered the deal I'd made with Janet that she could watch me take my meds if she felt like it was necessary.

It was no good keeping these things in the lockbox, especially now that I'd lied to her and said I'd put them back away in the attic. It was one thing laying it on a bit thick and acting a bit fuzzier headed than I was when it served a purpose, but it would be just as easy to move these things and not give Janet any reason to watch me more closely.

I took the things from the lockbox and then grabbed the other box from beneath the bed. I put them in the bottom drawer of my chest of drawers and pulled a few pairs of pajamas over the top so even if Janet did come snooping around, all she would see were my pajamas.

I locked my lockbox and put it back in the bottom of my closet. I went to the bed with my pill in my hand. I slid beneath the duvet, ignoring the slight dampness my panicky sweat had left behind. I swallowed the pill, and then I flicked the lamp off and lay down.

As I lay waiting for sleep to take me, I thought of Janet coming to check up on me tonight and the fact that she had essentially uprooted her own life to come here and take care of me. I vowed to try not to let my paranoia extend to her. I told myself that, from tomorrow, I was going to be a lot nicer to her.

11

After breakfast, I went to the living room and sat down.

"Have you remembered to take your medication this morning?" Janet asked as she joined me.

I felt a wave of irritation run through me. She had no reason to think I might not have taken it. I started to snap at her, but then I remembered our deal and my vow to be nicer to her, so, instead, I nodded and thanked her for her concern.

She smiled, her real smile, the one that made her face light up.

I told myself again that I had let my own paranoia take over my feelings for my sister. I decided to go a step farther and confide in her about my therapist's plan for me to delve into the past and try to remember things that I had thought were lost to me forever. I patted the couch cushion beside me, and Janet came over and sat down.

"I suppose you've been wondering why I had that box of old letters out?" I asked.

"I did think it was a bit strange," she said. "Especially with them being in the attic. If they had been somewhere in the main part of the house, I probably would have thought that you had just stumbled across them and were curious. But it was like you had purposely gone looking for them."

"I did go looking for them," I told her. "I spoke to my therapist, and I told him that a lot of my paranoia stems from not knowing which memories from my childhood are real and which aren't."

"Some things are best left in the past," Janet said.

"That's easy for you to say. You can make an informed decision about what to leave behind because you know what happened to you. It's like when people say money isn't important—the only people who say that are people who have money," I said, trying my best to make her understand.

"I know what you're saying, but you do know that some-times—most times, in fact—your mind represses things to protect you, right?" Janet said.

"So I've heard. But I barely remember my childhood. It was pretty traumatic from the bits I do remember. With father knocking the shit out of me. Mom upset. Being scared that if he left me alone, he would start on you."

"It makes sense for you to repress those memories, though, doesn't it?" Janet said.

"Of course it does. But here's the thing. It feels even more traumatic not knowing what went on."

Janet shifted uncomfortably on the couch. She looked down at her lap, refusing to meet my eyes.

I felt dread gnawing at me. "Just tell me. Please."

She finally looked up and met my eyes. "I'll tell you if that's what you really want, but I am advising against it."

"I want to know," I insisted.

"Fine." She took a deep breath. "It's like Dad and I told you for years while you were in the asylum—"

"Hospital," I interrupted her.

"I know you've changed, so please don't let this upset you, but you were a bad kid, James. Like *bad* bad. You were horrible to me and our parents. You were rude; you didn't follow any of the rules at home or school. You were physically violent with us sometimes."

I swallowed hard. Janet had been right to an extent. This truth was a bitter pill to swallow. But I still felt like I needed to know everything that had happened to me, and now, maybe I also needed to know everything I had done to other people.

"Why do you think there was that lock on your bedroom door?" Janet said gently.

"I thought it was because our father used to lock me in there as a punishment," I said.

Janet shook her head sadly. "The only time our parents locked you in your room was when your behavior was even worse than usual. It was on the days when you were completely uncontrollable, and they worried you would end up hurting someone."

I felt a dark depression wash over me as I thought about being capable of something like that, but, even in the midst of it, there was a light. The light of doubt. The light of hope. Something deep inside told me that there was more to it than what I was being told. Despite the pain that even this glimpse of the past had brought me, I decided to keep working with my therapist and do the hypnotherapy. If it turned up things I didn't want to hear, then I would deal with it. In the meantime, I just wanted the truth, no matter how horrible it might be.

"Oh, James. I'm so sorry," Janet said, tears glistening in her eyes.

I shrugged, dismissing her apology. "I asked you to tell me."

"I know, but it doesn't make it any easier to hear, right?" she said.

I shrugged again. I didn't want to admit that she was right, but if I said I wasn't finding it hard, it would make me sound like a sociopath, and I could do without that label sticking on me along with all the rest of them.

It was difficult, but I had to ask her one more question. "What did I do to get sent away?"

"Your violent tendencies reached a level the family could no longer cope with," Janet said softly. "Trust me, it's better if you don't remember what you did." Without warning, she got to her feet. "Come on." She walked away, obviously certain I would follow her.

For a moment, that certainty annoyed me so much I almost didn't move, but I knew curiosity would get the better of me, so I sighed and followed her.

"Where are we going?" I asked when we reached the top of the stairs and Janet turned and headed toward the master bedroom. There was no way I was going in there. My head was messed up enough. "Janet."

She turned and smiled when I said her name. "We're going to find that box of old letters and journals and what-not. It's done you no good delving into it. If anything, it's upset you."

I opened my mouth to protest, but I knew Janet. Once she got an idea into her head, there was no convincing her to do something different. She might just believe I had flaked and couldn't remember exactly where I had put the box when it wasn't anywhere to be seen. She wouldn't, though, if I made a fuss about not going up there first.

"Okay. If you think us going through it together will help," I said.

"I do," Janet said, looking pleasantly surprised that I was seeing things her way.

She got the rod and pulled down the hatch and began to climb the ladder. I made my way toward the bottom of the ladder and climbed up it once Janet was clear. She turned and looked at me. I knew what she wanted, but I played dumb.

"What?" I asked.

"Where did you put the box?" Janet said with an exaggerated eye roll.

"Oh. Um. Over there somewhere, I think," I said, pointing at the stack of boxes I had looked through before finding mine.

Janet moved closer to the pile, and I followed her.

She frowned. "The top ones both say Christmas decorations."

"Huh, yeah they do," I agreed.

She sighed, another exaggerated gesture. "Why wouldn't the box you just put away be on the top?"

"Oh. I knocked them down by accident. I picked them all back up, but they're not in any sort of order," I said.

"Great." Janet sighed and hefted the first box off the pile and placed it on the floor at her feet. She worked in silence, lifting each box, putting it on the pile on the floor and then checking inside it. The only time she spoke was when I asked if she would like my help, and she muttered that I had already done enough. I stayed quiet after that, dreading the moment she came to the last box and realized I had lied.

"Ah, here we go," she said when she was three-quarters of the way down the pile.

"I ... huh?"

"Don't look so shocked," Janet said. "It could have only been in one of these stacks, right?"

I nodded even as I pictured the journal and the other bits and bobs in the bottom drawer of my chest of drawers. I was suddenly mortified when the truth hit me. Janet must have stumbled across another box of things. What if there were more of Mom's journals in there and she wouldn't let me see them?

I edged closer to the box as Janet restacked the others. I relaxed a bit. The box was full of my old sketchpads. It would be nice to look through them, but if Janet kept them back from me, it wouldn't be half as bad as it would have been if they were Mom's journals.

That reminded me; I really wanted to get back and finish reading the journal I already had of Mom's. Between my medication, the panic the house seemed to bring out in me, and Janet's intrusions, I hadn't managed to read any more of it yet.

Janet finished rearranging everything and put the lid back on the box with the sketchbooks. She bent down and picked it up.

"Would you like me to carry that?" I asked her.

"No, I've got it," she said. "Just turn the light off and close the hatch behind me, please."

I did as she asked, and we went downstairs.

"There's something I need to do before we deal with this," Janet said, gesturing at the box. "Can you give me, like, half an hour?"

I nodded. I was eager to know what was in the sketchpads now, but I could wait. And besides, this way I might get to sneak a peek while Janet was busy.

As though she had read my mind, Janet turned and left me in the living room, taking the box with her. If I asked her to leave it behind, it would be too obvious that I wanted to go through it without her, so I bit my tongue.

I sat down and tried to read that day's news on my cell phone. I struggled to concentrate, but what did it matter? I was only killing time anyway.

It seemed like more than half an hour had passed when Janet came back. I noticed she didn't have the box with her, but that didn't really surprise me. She had taken it away from me. That didn't mean she was going to carry it around the house with her.

Janet beckoned to me, and I got up and followed her. She led me into the kitchen, where she paused and picked up the box. She had left it on the kitchen table. Dammit. It had been so close and yet so far away.

She kept walking and led me to the old firepit in the garden. As I got closer, I smelled the burning branches, the singeing papers. Janet had made a fire. She nodded to a deckchair facing the firepit. I sat down.

"Where's your chair?" I asked, looking around.

"I'm okay standing." She smiled.

It was an odd smile, and I was starting to feel uncomfortable.

She moved closer to the firepit and dropped the box into it. I gasped, and Janet looked at me. There was no malice on her face, and she even smiled.

"There," she said. "Now that stuff can't hurt you anymore. Would you like a cup of tea?"

I nodded mutely, unable to process the jump from Janet

destroying the old papers to the mundanity of drinking tea. I was glad that she left me alone for a moment, though, while she went to make the tea.

I thanked my lucky stars that the box she'd burned wasn't really the right box, but I didn't know what to think about her actions. On the one hand, she knew how important it was to me to look back at my childhood and try to retrieve my memories, and she had willfully destroyed something that might have helped that retrieval. And for that I should be so angry with her.

On the other hand, she had seen how upset I had become when she told me just a few things from my childhood, and she was only trying to protect me from learning more. I guessed I loved her for that. She really did have my back.

While I waited for my cup of tea, I stared into the dancing flames, wondering if Janet had done this because she was hiding something, or whether my paranoia was making me doubt her motives.

12

I was just walking out of the bathroom when I heard a noise coming from one of the closed-off rooms leading to the master bedroom. Icy cold fingers of fear caressed my neck, and I shook my head, refusing to believe that the ghost of my father had come back to haunt me when I was awake.

The noise came again, only slightly louder this time. It was a whooshing sound, like the sound a sheet makes when you shake it out before you put it on the bed.

"Hello?" I called, remembering how some of my father's valuables were protected by dust sheets. My voice came out sounding so quiet that I barely heard it, let alone anyone living or dead down the hallway. I cleared my throat, stood up straight, and put my shoulders back. "Hello?"

"James, is that you? Don't just stand there shouting hello at me like an idiot, come and help me, for goodness' sake," a voice replied.

I relaxed when I realized the voice belonged to Janet. My fear turning to curiosity, I headed into my father's wing and walked toward the room with the door that sat ajar. I raised my hand to knock, and then I brought it back down again. This was my house. Why would I knock? Even knowing I was being absurd, it still took everything I had not to knock on that damned door. Instead, I pushed it open and stepped inside.

Janet stood in the center of the room, tugging at one of the dust sheets. She glanced at me over her shoulder, and I automatically went to help her. We wrestled the dust sheet to the ground to reveal a tall glass cabinet full of various antiques.

Janet opened the cabinet and began to lift the pieces out one at a time. She turned them this way and that and either shook her head and returned the piece or nodded and slipped the piece into the duffel bag that sat on the floor beside her feet.

"What are you doing?" I finally asked after watching her bag three pieces and reject four.

"What does it look like? I'm taking some stuff that belonged to my father. Why?" she challenged suddenly. "Are you going to have me arrested for taking a share of the stuff that was left to you?"

Of course I wasn't going to have Janet arrested. I thought for a moment and realized I really didn't care about these pieces. Janet could take the lot if she wanted.

"It's just stuff," I said with a shrug. "If you want it, take it. Like I said before, for what it's worth, I believe you should have been left an equal share of the inheritance. So if you want to take a few pieces, don't think of it as stealing, think of it as getting your share."

Janet paused with a silver clock halfway to her duffel bag. She looked up at me and then she deposited the clock in the duffel bag and straightened back up. "If you meant that, you'd add me to your bank account like I asked you to do."

I thought she deserved half of my father's money, but I didn't think that she deserved to control my half of it, too. I was perfectly capable of looking after my own money, so I did the only thing I could think of that wouldn't set her off. I lied.

"My bank account still isn't sorted yet," I told her. "But once it is, I can talk to my solicitor and have half of the money transferred to you."

It felt like the least I could do. I was sure Janet would be pleased at my generous offer, which would be a nice bonus for her.

"I've told you, James, I don't want your pity money. Unlike you, I am quite capable of earning my own," she said icily.

"I ... I don't understand," I said honestly. "I thought you would be grateful."

"Grateful? To you?" Janet snorted. "If that were the case, I would really know I had hit rock bottom."

I ignored the jibe and instead focused on the part that I couldn't work out. "So if you don't want any of the inheritance, why are you so keen to have your name on my bank account?"

Janet laughed, a short, bitter laugh. "You don't get it, do you?"

"No. Please help me understand," I said.

She smiled at me in the way a person might smile at a child they were about to humor. "Oh, James, you should know by now. I have your back. I just want to be able to keep an eye on what's coming and going from your account to make sure you're not overspending and that no one is taking advantage of you, that's all."

She spoke to me like she really did have my best interests at heart. But did she? I just wasn't sure anymore.

I went from thinking that Janet was ready to rob me at any given moment, to thinking that she just wanted what was best for me, and then back again at least once a day. I had no idea which of those was the real Janet. Maybe in truth, she was as clueless as I was, and she wasn't sure whether it was more important for her to take care of me or take what she felt was rightfully hers.

I genuinely didn't mind the idea of giving Janet half of the money, but I wasn't going to be a fool for her or anyone else. Not anymore. I wasn't going to give her the chance to take it all. And if she was genuinely just looking out for me, then she really didn't need to be in my bank account or any of my other business. I was fine. My meds were working as they should, and I was perfectly capable of managing my own finances.

I didn't want to upset Janet, so I smiled meekly.

She returned my smile, and then she pointed a long bony finger at me. "Tell me when your account is set up."

I nodded, although I had no intention of doing any such thing.

Janet frowned as though sensing my deceit. "Actually, I might call this solicitor myself and see why he's dragging his feet. I won't have you being taken advantage of."

Except by you.

The thought popped into my head unbidden, as though it were someone else's. I felt my cheeks color at the accusation, even though I hadn't spoken it aloud. Janet seemed not to have noticed my discomfort. That suited me. It meant I didn't have to try to come up with an explanation for my sudden embarrassment.

"James?" Janet snapped her fingers to get my attention. "Your solicitor. I want his name."

I shook my head. She wasn't getting that, but if I wanted to keep her sweet, I would have to have a good reason why not. I thought for a second before inspiration struck.

"He's court-appointed," I said. "And the judge ruled that he's only allowed to talk to me about the estate."

"Hmm," Janet said. "Okay."

I wasn't sure if she believed me, and I couldn't ask her. If I were telling the truth, I would never ask her that.

"Just tell him to get a move on and then let me know when it's sorted." She bent down, picked up her duffel bag of goodies and left the room without saying anything else.

I stood there looking down at the discarded dust sheet and wondering what exactly had just happened. I couldn't help but think that Janet wanted all of my father's money, not simply a share of it. She must have been able to see that I was managing my meds and my life effectively now, and that I didn't need handholding with my money. Or could she not see that? Maybe she was genuinely worried that I would relapse and do something with the money that I would later regret.

Technically, that made more sense. Janet had only ever looked out for me. She was the only one who had ever had my back. Why would that change now? I had to let my paranoia stop threatening my relationship with the only member of my family I had left.

My thoughts left me feeling sluggish and tired, and I picked the dust sheet up off the floor and draped it back over the glass cabinet. I left the room and ambled off toward my bedroom. My plan was to read some more of my mom's journal, but when I stepped into the room and saw my bed, I gave a big yawn, and I knew it wasn't going to happen.

I was just so tired; I wouldn't take in anything I read right now. Instead of bothering to get the journal out, I just lay down on the top of the duvet. Within minutes, my eyes were closing, and I was asleep.

13

I woke up slowly, like I was swimming through treacle, and glanced at my bedside clock. It was just after ten, and the sunlight streaming in through the open curtains told me that it must be ten in the morning rather than at night. It seemed that my nap had lasted all night. I shrugged. It wasn't like I had any better plans, and I must have needed the extra hours of sleep.

I yawned again, and then I sat up, pushed the duvet back and got out of bed. My head felt slightly fuzzy, but I knew that would clear once I had taken my meds. I opened the closet and then my lockbox, and my eyes widened in horror.

My tablets were gone.

I took a deep breath and told myself that they couldn't possibly be gone. They wouldn't just up and leave, and no one but me had access to my lockbox. I closed my eyes and counted to three, and then I opened them again, but it made no difference. My tablets were still gone.

With mounting horror, I stood up and closed the closet door. Had I let myself run out of my medication? No, surely not. I remembered taking my pills yesterday, and there had been plenty left. I must have left them out after I had taken them. Yes, that must be it.

It wasn't a perfect realization. I was a little bit disturbed to realize I could do something so careless without even remembering doing it—but it was still better than thinking I had let myself run out of them without noticing I was even getting low.

I couldn't think where my meds might be, so that meant I had to search the entire house, even the rooms I would very much liked to have ruled out.

I was searching one of the guest rooms when Janet came in and found me peering underneath dust sheets.

"There you are. I thought you were still sleeping," she said.

"Still sleeping? It's almost two in the afternoon," I replied.

"What on earth are you doing?" Janet asked, ignoring my statement.

I debated lying to her, but I couldn't think of anything to say that didn't make me sound a bit crazy, so I settled for the truth.

"My medication wasn't in my lockbox this morning. I must have left it out somewhere yesterday," I admitted.

"Honestly, you're such a scatterbrain. Those meds are important. You've got to be more careful with them," Janet said.

"Yes, I'm aware of that. Now, are you going to help me search for them, or are you going to stand there and berate me?" I asked.

Janet didn't answer me verbally—she just rolled her eyes —but she turned to her left and started going through the drawers in a large bureau that stood there, and I supposed that, really, that was answer enough. I was irritating to her as usual, but she was still willing to help me because she had my back.

We searched the full house. My bedroom, the bathroom, the kitchen, and the living room all got searched at least three times each. And still, we didn't find any sign of my medication.

I was certain we wouldn't find it before my next dose was due. It was okay, though. I had no need to panic. I knew I had to call my therapist, and strangely, I wasn't particularly nervous about it. If it had been my old one, I would have had a knot of anxiety in my stomach just thinking about it. But Dr. Sellers didn't scare me like my hospital-appointed therapist always had; instead, he made me feel safe, something I felt was important for a good therapist. Maybe it was the one defining quality that separated a decent therapist from a good one.

"I'm going to call my therapist," I said as we sat down in the living room.

"Why? To let him know you can't be trusted alone?" Janet said.

"No," I corrected her. "To tell him that I have accidentally misplaced my meds and to ask for a small emergency supply until I find them."

"Won't he think you're terribly irresponsible?" Janet asked.

"No. Anyone can misplace something." I picked my cell phone up and went to my room, sure that Janet would appear in any other room that I made the call in, so that she could eavesdrop. I scrolled through my contacts as I sat down on the edge of my bed. I found Dr. Sellers's office and hit call. I didn't have long to wait until my call was taken.

"Dr. Sellers's office, Mandy speaking; how can I help you?" a chirpy voice trilled.

"Hi. It's James Owens," I said. "Can you put me through to Dr. Sellers, please?"

"The doctor is almost finished for the day. Would you be able to call again tomorrow, please?" Mandy said.

"I'm really sorry, but I can't," I told her. "It's urgent. If it makes it any better, I won't keep him long. I have an emergency with my medication."

"Please hold," Mandy said.

I waited as patiently as I could, anxiety turning my stomach into knots and making me rub my fingers together like I was trying and failing to tie them into knots. I relaxed a bit when I heard Dr. Sellers's voice come down the line.

"James? What can I do for you?" he asked, his voice warm and gentle.

I quickly explained the situation. I knew I was babbling a little, but I couldn't seem to reel it in.

"It's okay," Dr. Sellers said. "Calm down, James; these things happen. They could have easily ended up getting thrown away by accident or something. I don't have a single patient who hasn't lost some meds at one point or another."

"Really?" I dared to ask.

"Really, you did the right thing by calling," Dr. Sellers confirmed. "I'm going to call you in a prescription for an emergency supply of pills. They will last until your next main prescription is due to be filled again. I'll get them sent out overnight, and they'll be with you in the morning. You'll be fine missing one day, just start taking them as normal again tomorrow. Make sure you remember to take them as soon as they arrive, because if you miss two days' worth of these pills, you will start to get withdrawal symptoms, hallucinations, that kind of thing."

"I understand," I replied. "I'll take them first thing in the morning when the mailman drops them off. Thank you, Doctor."

I ended the call and went off in search of Janet. I found her sitting in the living room, where I had left her, the TV remote in her hand as she flicked through the channels. She looked up as I walked in.

"Did you get it sorted?" she asked.

I instantly felt guilty for assuming she would try to follow me and eavesdrop on my conversation. She clearly hadn't moved, and she seemed to trust that I could deal with it by myself.

"Yes," I replied. "Dr. Sellers is going to overnight me an emergency supply, so I'll have them again tomorrow. He said missing them for one day will be fine."

"As long as it's only one day though, yes?" Janet asked. "Because more than that can send you back to crazy town, right?"

"I'd prefer not to refer to my mental health issues as me going to crazy town, but yes, any more than one day can be dangerous for my mental health," I told her as I sat down beside her on the couch.

"Well, let's pray that doesn't ever happen, then, huh?" Janet said as she finally settled on a channel where an old black-and-white movie was just starting. She put the remote control down.

I was sure she had a smirk on her face as she spoke, but I must have been mistaken. It must have been a shadow from the TV dancing over her face.

I took a long drink of my coffee, leaving an inch or so in the bottom of my cup to take my pills with. Janet had gone out to the mailbox to get them for me. I heard the front door open and then shut again.

A moment later, Janet came into the kitchen and shook her head. "Sorry, James, there were no meds in there."

"Maybe the mailman is running late today," I said. I was clutching at straws, and I knew it.

"I don't think so. I saw a few of your neighbors opening their mailboxes and coming up with mail," she said.

"I'd best call Dr. Sellers and see what I should do," I said.

"Yes, good idea," Janet said. She looked at her watch as I started to get up. "Not yet. It's not even nine. He won't be in this early."

I sat back down and nodded. She was probably right. Or wrong. Dr. Sellers would be in, but he wouldn't be taking patients' calls yet. He'd be going over his paperwork and doing whatever else doctors do before, after and between patients. Would he mind me calling? He said I did the right thing calling yesterday.

That was different, though. That was a real problem. This was just me being impatient. Either that or Dr. Sellers changed his mind and decided I don't really need my meds. But he said if I missed two days in a row that I'd regress. But maybe he was wrong about that. Maybe. Maybe. Maybe.

It was like I didn't know anything anymore.

I slowly raised my hands to my temples and began to massage them in small clockwise circles, one of the gestures I used to make before I started my current meds, whenever I was beginning to get overwhelmed.

I couldn't sit here a moment longer. It was driving me mad being so still. I stood up and headed for the door.

"Where are you going?" Janet asked.

I didn't answer her. Not because I didn't want to but because I didn't know the answer. Where was I going? Anywhere. Nowhere. Maybe neither. Maybe both. All I knew was I had to be up and moving. I headed for the stairs, and I took them two at a time, my hands pressed against the sides of my face. I could feel my mouth turning down, the skin of my eyes being pulled down. I didn't care. All that mattered was that I kept moving. Why? Because my father was behind me. Yes, of course that was why.

My father was chasing me through the house. He was going to catch me, and he was going to beat my ass, because boys who lose things need to have their memory improved. With an evil grin on his face, he snapped his leather belt and told me that I would learn my lesson.

I could hear him behind me, gasping and slobbering, and I upped my pace to a jog and then to an all-out sprint. I ran like the devil himself was on my tail, and who knows, perhaps he was. Or perhaps the devil would have been an improvement on my father. At least with the devil, the need to hurt me wouldn't be personal. He liked to torture everyone.

I slammed into something hard enough to bring tears to my eyes as I bounced down onto the floor. I sat up, rubbing my nose. There was a door in front of me, and as I looked around, I saw more doors opening off a hallway. It was the hallway that ran down through my father's quarters. I had somehow wandered down here toward his room. Was that why he was so angry? Or was he so angry because I was meant to be here earlier?

I turned around and pressed my back to the door. I bent my knees, pulling them up to my chest and wrapping my arms around them. Tears dripped from my chin and soaked into the material on my knees, leaving a cool, damp patch.

"I'm sorry," I said as my father's hulking figure towered over me. "I'm sorry."

"For what?" he replied with a grin.

I had no idea. I just wanted to make him go away and leave me alone.

He snapped the belt again, and I flinched.

"I'm waiting for an answer," he said.

"For everything. I'm sorry for everything. Please don't hurt me," I blurted out.

"Wrong answer," my father said, his eyes aglow with glee. "You should be sorry for not taking your meds."

"My meds?" I repeated stupidly.

"Yes. They keep you sane. And look at you. Forget them a couple of times and you're crazy all over again."

"I'm not crazy," I blurted out without thinking of the consequences of arguing with him.

"Really? Then how come you're hallucinating?" my father asked me, looking genuinely puzzled.

"I ... I am?" I stuttered.

"Sure," he replied. "Look down at yourself, James. You're not a child. You're a grown man, although heaven help me, you don't fucking act like it."

I slowly looked down, and my eyes widened. I wasn't a child anymore. My father was right. I was a grown man.

"How did you ...?" I started to ask, but as I raised my head, he was gone before I had a chance to finish my question.

All that was left of him was an echo of his laughter hanging in the air.

I took a moment to breathe, and then I pushed myself to my feet. My legs were wobbly beneath me, but they held me solidly enough, and I began to walk down the hallway. I didn't know where I was going, but I was a grown-up now—my father had said so—and I had to be independent.

I kept walking until I reached a dead end, and then I turned around and began walking once more. I walked, and I walked, and I walked. The house seemed bigger, like I was walking down hallways I had never seen before, and it came to me with startling, sudden clarity that I was lost in my own home.

I stopped walking and looked around for something familiar, but there was nothing. The walls were the wrong color, the carpet replaced with bare stone. Where the hell was I? I was starting to panic when I heard a voice calling my name. It sounded like Janet, and I turned toward it.

She was standing in a doorway, the light behind her turning her into a silhouette.

"Janet?" I said quietly. "Are you real?"

"Of course I'm real," she said. "What happened?"

I started walking toward Janet. "I got lost," I said as I reached her. She moved to one side, and I stepped past her. "Look. That hallway. It's not ..." I stopped talking as I turned around to show her. There was no hallway there, just a packed bookcase.

Janet stood beside the bookcase, a frown of concern on her face. "What do you mean? You came to look for a book."

Was that what the ghost of my father wanted me to find? No, no. That hadn't been real. But Janet was real. She had said I was looking for a book. That made sense. Didn't it?

"I got worried about you because you were gone so long. I found you standing here staring at the bookcase."

"I ... But ... I don't know." I paused, and then I looked up and met Janet's eye. "I think I might be going crazy again."

"Nonsense," Janet said. "It's just a blip, that's all."

"No. I thought I was somewhere else. Somewhere that didn't exist. And I was hallucinating earlier," I said frantically. "I saw Dad."

Janet looked at me for a moment, and I swear I saw her eyes glistening with unshed tears.

"Maybe you need to go back into the hospital again, just for a little while until they sort your medication out," she said.

I opened my mouth to agree with her, but before I could speak, the doorbell rang.

"Ignore it," Janet said.

It wasn't a request, it was an order, and I felt a moment's rebellion. It was enough of a moment that, when the doorbell sounded again, I ignored the look I got from Janet and yelled for the person to come in.

"James?" a voice said as the front door opened.

"In here, Brianna," I called back.

14

Brianna walked into the room to find Janet glaring at her, and me just standing there, staring into space, most likely looking as lost and confused as I felt. If the whole situation weren't so sad, so pathetic, I think I would have laughed.

"And you are?" Janet demanded, raising an eyebrow at Brianna.

Brianna ignored her, her focus on me. "James, what happened? Are you alright?"

I nodded mutely, trying to work out if she was real or another hallucination.

"Umm, hello?" Janet said, positioning herself between Brianna and me.

Of course. Brianna had to be real, or Janet wouldn't be able to see her, too.

"Now isn't a good time for a visit, lady."

Brianna turned toward Janet and made an obvious show of sighing. "Maybe it isn't a good time for you, but seeing as I'm James's probation officer and this is a court-mandated visit, it's a good time for me. Unless, of course, you would rather I have you arrested for trying to stop an officer of the court from doing their job?"

I knew I should have felt offended on Janet's behalf. She was my sister, and she was just looking out for me, but instead, I found myself feeling strangely proud of Brianna for standing up to Janet, something I had never really been able to do myself.

Janet made a huffing sound in the back of her throat. "Well, get on with it, then."

I bit the inside of my bottom lip to stop myself from smiling. I had never seen Janet back down to anyone before, and I had to admit that it was kind of nice seeing her in that position.

"Should we sit down?" Brianna said with a smile, turning her attention back to me.

I nodded, and we walked over to the low coffee table that was flanked by two armchairs. We took one each. Janet followed us at a distance. She hung around in the background as Brianna asked me various questions about my whereabouts since our last visit. I answered everything honestly. I had nothing to hide.

Throughout the questioning, Janet edged closer and closer to us until she was standing directly behind my left shoulder. She kept sighing, and I wanted so badly to turn and look at her, but Brianna held my gaze, and I knew she didn't want me to give Janet my attention.

I don't know if it was because I found I would much rather focus on Brianna than Janet, or if it was just that Brianna's presence made me feel brave enough to stand up to Janet, but I kept my focus away from my sister.

Brianna opened her mouth to ask me another question, but I didn't hear it because Janet spoke over her.

"James, be a lamb and let me sit down," she said.

Instinctively, I started to get up, but Brianna shook her head, and I relaxed back into the seat.

"This is a private meeting," Brianna informed Janet. "I haven't said anything about you being here because James hasn't objected, but I must intervene now if you're going to disturb us. I would like James to feel relaxed enough to be open with me, so if you would like to sit down, then you might find that you're better off going to another room until we're done."

"I'll wait right here, thank you," Janet replied curtly.

Brianna turned her focus back to me. "You seem ... distant. Is there something going on that I should know about?"

"No," Janet answered for me before I could speak.

"I was talking to James," Brianna said, not looking away from me for even a second.

"James, don't tell her anything. She's just looking for an excuse to have you arrested," Janet said, an odd note of panic in her voice.

"On the contrary, James, I'm worried about you, that's all. All of the terms of your probation have been followed, and I am asking you if you're okay, as a friend," Brianna said.

I sensed her answer was aimed at Janet, but she was looking at me, and I felt as though her reassurance was for me, too. I decided in that moment to trust her. I had to get my pills, and I didn't know what else to do. I didn't dare call Dr. Sellers and ask for more, and I didn't want to go along with Janet's idea that I should go to the hospital to get treated. But if Brianna agreed that was a good idea, then I would do it.

"I've lost my medication," I responded. "I called my therapist and requested some more, but it either didn't come, or I've lost that as well, and now I'm onto my second day without them, and I don't know what's real and what's not real anymore."

I knew I'd said too much, but at the same time, I felt so much better for getting it off my chest.

Brianna smiled at me and stood up. "Well, they can't just have vanished into thin air, can they? Let's go look for them."

"Don't you think he should go to the hospital at this point?" Janet demanded, discussing me with Brianna like I wasn't there.

"I see no reason for that," Brianna replied. "Missing meds can cause hallucinations and a sense of not knowing what's real. But as soon as we find the medication and James gets it back into his system, he'll be fine."

I stood up and turned to my sister. "Do you want to help search for them again?"

"Again?" Janet repeated with a frown. "I never looked for them. I had no idea your meds were even missing until you told Brianna."

I was puzzled. It concerned me that Janet said she hadn't helped me to look for my meds, that she didn't even know they were missing. Did I hallucinate all of that, too? I don't think I could have, because that was before I had even missed my second pill, but I supposed it could be a false memory.

"If the trash has been on your mind, then that's the place we'll start looking," Brianna announced.

She and Janet stared at each other. I had no idea what

was going on between the two of them, and I didn't have the energy to try to work it out, so I just stood there and waited for the two women to finish whatever the hell that was.

Janet looked away first.

Brianna turned to me and smiled. "Ready?"

I nodded and followed her out of the room. She led me toward the kitchen, talking back over her shoulder to me as we went.

Janet followed, but as we reached the stairs, she stopped. "I'll be in my room reading my Bible if anyone wants me," she announced and hurried up the stairs without waiting for an answer.

She was behaving awfully strangely, I thought, but I didn't question it too deeply. I just shrugged and kept walking behind Brianna until we reached the kitchen.

She went straight to the trash can and opened it. She put her hand in, and, within a second, it came back out holding a small package wrapped in brown paper. One end was ripped open, and I could see the boxes of tablets inside it. I could also see my name and address on the label.

"You found them," I said, relief flooding my body. I held my hand out, and Brianna gave me the bag. "Thank you."

I filled a glass with water, and, with a slightly shaking hand, I tore the bag the rest of the way open. I went through each box methodically, popping a pill from the blister pack in each one. I swallowed them all down and smiled at Brianna. "I know they can't be working yet, but I feel so much better just knowing I have them and have taken them. Is that stupid?"

"Not at all. In fact, it makes perfect sense," Brianna said. "It's like when you're in pain and you take pain meds, and it seems like the pain goes away the second you swallow them."

"Exactly that." I grinned. I thought for a moment, and when I spoke again, I was serious. "You do believe me, don't you? That I didn't purposely throw my meds away because I didn't want to take them."

Brianna nodded without hesitation. "I saw the relief on your face when we found them. That wasn't the expression of someone who didn't want to take their meds." She smiled. "Now, let's think about the original ones. Where do you usually keep them?"

"In a lockbox in my bedroom," I said. I felt color rush to my cheeks as I said the word bedroom. If Brianna noticed my sudden discomfort, she didn't show it.

"So, upstairs, I presume?" she said.

I nodded, and again, I found myself following Brianna across the house.

She went up the stairs, and it was only when she reached the top that she stopped and looked back at me. "Which way?"

"This way," I replied, getting out in front of her and leading her down the hallway to my bedroom.

I was so glad I had decided to take the lock off the outside of my door. I wouldn't have fancied trying to explain that one to Brianna, or to anyone, really. I stepped into the room, and Brianna followed me. I went to the closet, pulled the door open and showed her the lockbox.

She kneeled and pulled at the lid. It didn't open, and she looked up at me. "Does anyone else have a key to the box?"

I shook my head.

"Okay," she said, getting back up. "So, talk me through taking your meds. You come in here, unlock the box ..."

"Yes. And then I take my meds to the bed with me and take them one at a time like you saw me do downstairs. Then I lock them back away again."

Brianna headed for my bed and sat down on the side of it, her feet barely touching the floor in front of my bedside cabinet.

"Would you say you sit here?" she asked.

I nodded.

Brianna peered behind my bedside cabinet. She pushed her hand down between my mattress and headboard. "Jackpot." She smiled as she pulled her hand back, revealing the boxes of meds. "They must have slipped down there after you took them the last time."

I really didn't think that was what had happened. I would have known if they had fallen. I was obsessive when it came to my meds, and if I hadn't completed the routine of putting them away and locking the box, I would have been aware of it. Hell, I likely would have had an anxiety attack about it. And if I hadn't put the meds back, then why had I locked the box? Also, I was almost certain that I had already searched down there, where Brianna had just found the boxes, and they hadn't been there then.

That was the trouble, though. I was only *almost* certain, and I wasn't confident enough to state it as a fact and embarrass myself even more in front of Brianna. It would sound like Janet was right and I really didn't know what I was doing.

"Yes, they must have," I said, instead of voicing my thoughts. "Thank you."

I took my meds, pulled out my key to the lockbox, and locked them inside. No sooner was my closet door closed than there was a rap on my bedroom door, and Janet marched in without waiting for a reply.

"Is this really appropriate?" she demanded. "A probation officer in the bedroom of someone she's responsible for?"

"Well, yes, it's perfectly appropriate under the circumstances," Brianna said.

I felt myself going red again, but Brianna showed no sign of any discomfort. I needed to relax and take a page from Brianna's book when it came to Janet, I thought to myself. I needed to just let her issues float away over my head and ignore them.

"So, did you find your meds?" Janet said.

"Yes, thank you," I replied.

"Where were they?" she asked.

"The emergency supply was in the kitchen trash can, and my normal ones were down there between my mattress and my headboard," I said.

Hearing it out loud, it did make me sound careless, but I wasn't. Not with my meds. And I hated the fact that I had let this happen.

"See, James? This is what I'm talking about," Janet said with an exasperated sigh. "You claim you're good with your meds, that you always take them, but that's clearly not the case, is it? You're hiding your meds so you have a reason to be noncompliant. And you know that what you're doing is wrong, that's why you contacted your therapist for an emergency supply to try to convince me that you're being responsible."

"I don't—" I started.

"I'm not saying this stuff to hurt you or belittle you," Janet interrupted. "I'm saying it because I'm worried about you. I think you need to be readmitted to the hospital. It doesn't have to be for long, just until you're back in the right headspace to want to be well again."

Her words made sense. But was she right? Was my subconscious hiding my meds from me and then blanking out the memory? I knew that was certainly possible. My childhood was proof of that. But, at the same time, I was still so sure that wasn't right. I didn't want to be crazy. I wanted to be a functional adult; I just couldn't find the words to express that.

"What do you think?" Janet snapped at Brianna. "As someone representing the court, do you think that my brother should be reassessed so someone can check he is safe to take care of himself?"

Brianna thought for a moment. "In a genuine case of noncompliance, I would completely agree with you that the patient should be hospitalized until they are in a more stable place mentally. However, I'm not sure this case is that straightforward. I don't think James is intentionally not taking his meds." She turned to me, her gaze steady. "James, what do you think? Do you feel like a short stay in the hospital could help you?"

"I don't think so," I said honestly. "I want to stay on my meds and be normal. But I don't want to miss a sign that something isn't right and risk me hurting someone."

"Okay, so for now, why don't we just leave things as they are? You've been doing really well, and I see no reason to think you might be a danger to yourself or others," Brianna said.

"That's easy for you to say," Janet snapped. "You don't have to live with him."

"And neither do you," I said with sudden clarity. "I appreciate your help, but if you're worried that I'm going to hurt you, feel free to go back to the city and leave me alone."

"I didn't mean it like that," Janet said, a sugary sharpness in her tone. "I'm just concerned about you, James, that's all."

"Right," Brianna said. "If you're concerned for James, then you'll accept his decision. Forcing hospitalization on someone who doesn't need it isn't good for them. It can actually be harmful."

Janet moved closer to me, then smiled warmly and squeezed my hand. "We wouldn't want that, would we? I guess we'll have to get by on our own with the good Lord's help, just like we always have, James. Don't worry. You'll always have me on your side."

Her words were the same as always, but for the first time, I was left wondering whether that was really such a good thing.

15

I lay in bed trying and failing to drift off to sleep. A few days had passed since my issues with my meds, and I was feeling much better and back to my normal self again now that they had kicked back in. I had hopefully learned from my mistake, and I was always super careful whenever I took any of my meds to make sure they went back in the right place.

Janet was still at the house, fussing over me one moment and berating me the next. I really couldn't figure her out. I flitted between believing she had my best interests at heart and believing she was only here to torture me.

I tried to avoid her for the most part, and when that didn't work, I just went along with whatever she said. It was easier that way. It saved us arguing. There was only one thing I stood up to her about, and that was whenever Janet slighted Brianna.

Of course, Janet relished that and decided that I had a crush on Brianna, which meant that whenever she wanted to wind me up, she'd start in on her, knowing I'd bite. And I did. Every single time. But I couldn't help it. Brianna was sweet and helpful, and she smelled like vanilla. She didn't deserve Janet's poison. And yes, if I was totally honest with myself, I thought that maybe I did have a little crush on Brianna. How else would I remember the color of her eyes and the scent of her skin? Why would I have noticed the way the little hollow in her throat moved when she swallowed, or how she always brushed her hair back off her face when she was annoyed?

As I lay there thinking about Janet and Brianna, I knew that sleep was going to elude me for quite a while longer, and I decided that I was finally feeling up to reading through some more of Mom's journal. I slipped out of bed and went to the chest of drawers. I opened the bottom drawer and pulled out the journal. Then I got back between the covers, ready to duck beneath them and hide the journal if Janet turned up for some reason.

I began to flick through the journal. I wasn't looking for any day in particular—I just kept stopping whenever a word or phrase caught my eye, and I would read a passage or two until the account became mundane, and then I would move on once more.

My name jumped out at me, and I paused to read some of the entry I was mentioned in.

My heart is breaking for my boy. James is such a sweet child, and yet, in this house, he has become somewhat of a pariah. Everything that goes wrong somehow gets blamed on him, and it's got to stop. I know this, but I also know that if I speak out, it will only get worse for both of us. Of course, I'll get a beating, but that's nothing new, and if that was all I was risking, I would do it in a heartbeat, but it's not. James would get some of the blame, too, and they would treat him even worse than they do now.

At least, at the moment, it's just Cain who gets physical with him. I hope Janet doesn't turn on him, too. I know she will if Cain tells her to, though. Yes, James is her twin brother, but I'm her mom, and she thinks nothing of smacking me around when Cain tells her to.

Wait, I thought, screwing my face into a frown. Is Mom implying that Janet used to beat her up too, not just Dad? I wanted to believe my mom so badly because, in my mom's version of events, I am not violent or nasty; I am just a normal kid born into a dysfunctional family.

But could I seriously let myself believe that? Had my mind shut down my childhood memories so completely that I didn't even remember Janet being as bad as my father, or was my mom delusional like my father and Janet had always tried to tell me that she was?

I didn't think I would ever know the true answer to those questions. Mom was gone, Dad was gone, and even if Janet was willing to talk about those days—which she never seemed to be—what would I ask her that I didn't already know the answer to? In the end, asking Janet about this stuff would just get her annoyed again, and she would search the house until she found the journal and threw it into the fire like trash.

The truth was, I didn't know what to think, and I hated the uncertainty of it all. I knew Janet could be cold and quite cruel when she fixed her mind to it, but would she have gone so far as to beat up our mom? My instincts told me no, but when I added my father into the equation and imagined him urging Janet on, then somehow, it didn't seem as ridiculous. Janet would have done anything to make our father happy, and it certainly seemed that hurting Mom made my father happy.

I knew I needed more clarity, and even if I wasn't going to get black and white, yes or no answers, I might get something that would help me to at least decide which way to lean.

I flicked forward a few more pages, and a loose sheet floated out. At first, I was upset because I thought I had torn my mom's journal, but a glance at the loose sheet told me a different story. It was something she had obviously wanted to keep.

I recognized my handwriting at the top of the sheet of drawings, my name carefully written along with the date. It was all fairly standard childhood stuff. Except for the pictures. To say that they weren't the sort of pictures a normal child draws would be the understatement of the year. I had drawn pictures of violent scenes, fists flying, bloody droplets exploding from broken noses.

I supposed I might have started drawing shit like that because of living with my cruel father. But the most disturbing thing was on the other side. I couldn't force my eyes away. I ended up studying it intently.

The picture wasn't well drawn, but it was easy enough to work out that the two stick figures showed a man and a girl. Just in case there was ever any doubt in anyone's mind who these people were, I had scrawled "Dad" and "Janet" and drawn little lines pointing to the characters.

Now, drawing a picture of a dad and his daughter wouldn't be that weird. Even with them holding hands. He could be making sure she didn't run across a road and get hurt. What made the picture weird was that not only were my dad and Janet holding hands in the picture, but there were red love hearts floating around them in a way that it would make it clear to anyone that the drawing showed a couple in love. Except they weren't a couple, they were father and daughter, and this whole thing was sick.

I sighed loudly and closed the journal. So much for the loose sheet of drawings not giving me any answers. It had actually done quite the opposite. It had shown me exactly who I had been, and that someone had been dangerously crazy even then.

I didn't know why my mom would want to keep something like that page of drawings—maybe it was a reminder to her that I was indeed crazy. Or maybe it was her way of making sure she didn't end up like me. Maybe she kept it to hide it from my father and save me from a beating, and then she just forgot it was there.

It was another question I likely wouldn't get an answer to, but it wasn't a big question, and I could live with not knowing why my mom had kept the picture. I would also have to learn to live with the fact that I had indeed been an odd, violent child. Instead of letting that knowledge drive me crazy once more, I was going to use it for good. Anytime I even thought about missing a pill or doing something against the advice of my therapist, I would look at that picture and remind myself why I couldn't do it.

I knew that my brief spell of positive thinking might not last, but I also knew that it was a good thing, and, while it was there, I intended to grab onto it with both hands and not let it go.

16

I paused to think. Dr. Sellers remained silent, too, giving me a bit of breathing space. I liked that about him. When he asked me a question, he wanted me to think about the answer, and when I did, he didn't get mad at me for taking too long, and he didn't try to put words into my mouth.

"Yes," I said finally. "I do believe that Janet deserves the inheritance from my father more than I do."

I had opened up to Dr. Sellers about my inheritance and Janet wanting access to my bank account. I told him I had offered her half of everything, and she had claimed that she didn't want or need the money, that she just wanted to look out for me.

"And, in your opinion, do you think Janet believes that she is entitled to that inheritance too?" Dr. Sellers asked.

This time, I didn't need to think about my answer. It was there on the tip of my tongue, and I barely kept it in until the doctor had finished asking me his question. "Oh yes, without a doubt. She was always my father's favorite child."

"You sound as if that's a foregone conclusion," Dr. Sellers commented.

"Well, it kind of is," I said. It was the one thing I clung to from my childhood because I knew without a doubt it was true. "I mean, he beat me, and he loved Janet."

"So, do you feel like you should give Janet some of the inheritance because you feel like she is owed that?" Dr. Sellers asked.

"Yes," I said without hesitation.

It was the first and only time I had knowingly lied to Dr. Sellers. But I couldn't tell him the truth because that would be disloyal to Janet, and she didn't deserve that after always being there for me. The truth was, I had started to think that giving her half of the money would be the only way to get rid of her. I knew she was here for my benefit, to help me, but she was so overbearing, and I felt like she controlled every aspect of my life, or at least tried to. In some ways, I felt more like a prisoner with Janet than I ever had while I was in the hospital.

"Okay," Dr. Sellers said, and then he paused before going on once more. "And how do you think you will feel once you have given away half of the inheritance?"

"I won't regret it, if that's what you mean. I think I'll feel better knowing that Janet got her share," I said. "And it won't hurt that I will be doing something my father had the chance to do and decided against."

Before Dr. Sellers responded, I heard a muffled sneezing sound coming from outside my bedroom door.

"I'm sorry. Could you excuse me one second, please, Doctor?" I asked.

"Of course. Is everything okay?" Dr. Sellers replied.

"Yes, I think so," I said as I stood up from where I had

been sitting on my bed and moved toward the door. I pulled the door open to see Janet standing there. I waited for her to explain her presence, but she just looked at me, as though her standing there was completely normal, and I was the one acting weird. "What are you doing?"

She ignored my question, moved past me, went into my room, and sat down.

I sighed and lowered my cell phone from my face. "Janet? What are you doing?" I repeated. "I'm in the middle of a therapy session, and I'd appreciate some privacy, please."

She still didn't respond as such; she simply laughed softly.

I rolled my eyes, and rather than getting into an argument with her now, I was the one to leave the room despite it being mine. I was bringing my cell phone back up to my face when I became conscious of a presence behind me. I turned around quickly, half expecting to see the hallway behind me empty, but it wasn't. Janet was following me.

"Go away," I said.

She shook her head.

Before I could say more to her, I realized that I could hear Dr. Sellers's voice drifting up from my cell phone. I pulled it back up to my ear.

"James?" Dr. Sellers said. "James? Are you there?"

"Yes, I'm here," I said, glancing over my shoulder as I went into one of the guest bedrooms.

I shut the door firmly behind me, but I might as well not have bothered because seconds later it opened again, and Janet strolled in.

"Get out and leave me alone," I hissed, my hand over my cell phone.

Janet shook her head, still not speaking.

I turned my focus back to Dr. Sellers, who was talking away. I hadn't heard a word he had said, and now I was going to have to interrupt him. I felt rude, but what else could I do? I wasn't comfortable speaking openly in front of Janet, and I didn't want to lie to my doctor.

"I'm sorry, Dr. Sellers," I said, cutting him off. "Something's come up. I have to go. We will have to reschedule this."

"Wait," Dr. Sellers said before I could end the call.

I didn't have the heart to hang up on him, so I waited, even though I was afraid that he would say something that I didn't want Janet to hear.

"What's going on, James? Don't forget this therapy is court mandated. It won't look good for you if I have to report back to the courts that you cut our session short for no good reason."

"I just ..." I paused, trying and failing to come up with a suitable lie. I couldn't think of anything that would be acceptable to my therapist that couldn't come back to bite me in the ass. "I can't open up as I should because my sister is following me around the house and eavesdropping on our conversation. I would rather reschedule at a time when I can speak openly."

There was silence on the other end of the line for a moment, and then Dr. Sellers sighed. "How about we reschedule for the same time tomorrow, and you make sure you are somewhere that you won't be disturbed?"

"That would be great. Thank you, Doctor," I said.

I felt relief flood over me. It wasn't until that moment that I realized that, for me, this therapy was about much more than following the court's orders. This was about me hopefully finding a way to clear up my past and leave it behind so that I could have a normal future.

I thanked Dr. Sellers once more, and then I ended the call. I looked up at Janet as I stuffed my cell phone into my pocket. "There. Are you happy now?"

"Oh honestly, James, you need to grow up," Janet said. "I can't believe you did that. It's just like when we were kids, and you would run to Mom with some story and tell on me. I thought we were past that now, but clearly not."

"I had to tell him the truth, or I could have been arrested," I said. "Why couldn't you just do as I asked and let me have a bit of privacy while I was on the phone?"

"Because you can't be trusted with privacy," Janet said. "I know what you're like. You would have ended up saying who knows what, and then chances are you would end up straight back in the nuthouse. And when that happens, who do you think would get the blame?"

I didn't reply.

"Yes, that's right—me. It would be all, oh, poor James is ill, and Janet let him get taken advantage of."

"Wait," I said, holding up a hand. "What exactly do you think I was going to tell him?"

"Oh, I don't know." Janet sighed. "But considering you claim not to be able to remember the majority of your life, it could be anything, couldn't it? You always did have quite the overactive imagination."

I could feel the panic surging inside me. My heart fluttered, and my head spun. My stomach clenched into uncomfortable knots, and I felt as though someone had wrapped something around my ribcage and started squeezing it tightly. I could barely breathe, but I had to calm myself down enough that I could speak. I had to make Janet understand that Dr. Sellers was helping me, that he was different than the other doctors I had seen before.

"Oh, here we go," Janet said, rolling her eyes. "Someone has said something that little Jamesy doesn't like, so there's going to be a meltdown. You know this stopped being cute when you were, like, five, right? Now, it's honestly pathetic. I'm embarrassed for you."

Her words cut me like a knife—a blunt, rusty knife that dragged over my skin, inflicting the maximum amount of pain.

"Well? What have you got to say for yourself?" Janet demanded.

I couldn't understand why she was so angry with me, but her anger was doing nothing to calm me down. In fact, it was pushing me closer to having a complete meltdown. I could feel the panic attack hanging around, waiting for me to drop my guard completely so that it could take over. I fought it, breathing deeply, closing my eyes. After a few deep breaths, I was still very much in a bad place, but the panic attack had retreated slightly.

I could hear myself wheezing as I breathed where my throat had closed up. Janet was staring at me expectantly. I knew if I didn't reply soon, she would take it as a victory, and I couldn't stand the idea of her thinking she was in the right with this.

"I ... just ... want ... some privacy ... in my own ... house," I managed to rasp out.

"Yes, that would be nice, wouldn't it?" Janet replied. "Do you think I don't want that, too? Do you think I enjoy following you around making sure you don't show yourself up? God, James, look what happens when I leave you to speak for yourself. You can't even form a sentence properly."

I refused to give her the satisfaction of wheezing out another sentence, but if I could have spoken normally, I would have told Janet that this was a result of her eavesdropping, and without the added stress of her listening in on my calls, this wouldn't have happened. At least I thought that was the case.

"Look, I'm sorry," Janet said. "I didn't mean to be so harsh, but it hurts me when I'm doing so much to help you and you throw it back in my face."

I found I could breathe more normally again as the anger left Janet's face and she stopped attacking me. I still waited a moment before I attempted to speak. I guessed part of me was hoping that Janet would say more, that she would really open up to me, but she remained quiet until I couldn't bear it any longer.

"I've never wanted to make you feel like I was throwing your help back in your face," I said. "I just want some privacy during my therapy sessions. You must know that it's hard enough to open up to someone when it's one-on-one without trying to do it with someone else listening in."

Janet pushed herself up straight and came over to me. She put her hand on my shoulder and gave it a gentle squeeze. "I know what you're saying, but I can't just stop having your back. I'm making sure that therapist doesn't go manipulating you and putting silly ideas in your head, that's all."

I flashed her a quick smile, feeling better now. "Don't worry about that. I'm the one who does all of the talking, so it's not like he can manipulate me anyway, but thank you for caring."

"Of course I care. I've got your back always." Janet

smiled, and then she removed her hand from my shoulder and left the room.

It was only once she was gone that I realized that she had apologized for maybe being too harsh in her words during my panic attack, but not for actually inducing the panic attack in the first place.

17

The past few days went by in pretty much the same way with Janet and me. She was constantly trying to control me, even down to changing the order I placed for groceries so that she was in charge of what meals we ate. When I asked her about it, she went quiet. But I pushed her for an answer, and she said that I hadn't put any real food on the order, just potato chips and sweets. I wanted so badly to tell her that wasn't true, but I didn't have the confidence to do it. Every time I went to speak up, a little voice inside me asked me if I was certain she was wrong. It made me doubt myself so much that, in the end, the answer was no, I wasn't certain that she was wrong.

The more I thought about it, the more I realized that it was a good thing that Janet seemed to be taking over more and more aspects of my life. After last week, with my lost medication and the general confusion I felt even after it reappeared, I could hardly complain and insist that I was capable of taking care of myself. However, even though it was for my own good, Janet's constant mothering made me uncomfortable, especially because she made no secret of the fact that helping me was a nuisance to her.

I could hear her coming along the hallway, and I braced myself. I kept my back to the kitchen door, pouring myself a cup of coffee just to have something to do with my hands so Janet wouldn't see them shaking if she went on for too long.

"Coffee?" I said as she entered the room.

"Yes, please," she said. "That's what I was coming for. You must have read my mind." She laughed softly.

I waited for some sort of barb about how I could read her mind when I couldn't even sort my own out, but nothing came, and I realized Janet had genuinely been making a joke. I laughed with her, perhaps a little too late, but better late than never, right?

I grabbed another cup and filled it, and then I moved toward the kitchen table where Janet had sat down. I sat down opposite her and pushed her coffee toward her. She smiled her thanks, and I decided that now was a good time to tell her about this afternoon while she seemed to be in a fairly good mood.

"I've got a telephone appointment with my solicitor later today," I said. "Actually, in about fifteen minutes."

Janet raised an eyebrow.

I went on. "I thought it was time I arranged with him to have our father's assets divided equally between us, like I said I would."

"No, no, no. I told you, I don't want the money. I have my own money. I don't need handouts from you or Dad or anyone else."

"But you were so keen to be added onto my account," I said, cringing inside, waiting for her to start yelling at me, but she didn't, she just smiled sadly.

"Like I told you at the time, James, I only want access to your account so I can make sure you're not wasting money and that no one is taking advantage of you," she said. "I think we both know that you're not going to be able to get a job like a normal person."

I ignored the dig. It didn't matter what I said, she would continue to speak about me in that manner, and when I called her out on it, she would forever say I was being too sensitive.

"So, this money has to last you your whole life. I want to make sure you don't spend it all too quickly and end up with nothing."

I could understand her concern if there wasn't a lot of money, but there was more than enough for both of us and any children we might have to live on for the rest of our lives, their lives, and probably their children's children's lives. This wasn't about Janet looking out for me with my spending. It was about her taking control of my life. It was one more area she could boss me around in, but if she got her way and could monitor what I spent, maybe she would be more relaxed with the day-to-day stuff. I thought for a moment and then nodded.

"Okay," I said.

"Okay, what?" Janet asked, narrowing her eyes slightly.

"Okay, I'll ask my solicitor to add you to my account instead of asking him to divide the assets," I said.

"I think that's for the best," she said.

"It's almost time for my appointment," I said, standing up. I finished the last bit of my coffee and took my cup to the sink. I was suddenly filled with a confidence that came from knowing that, for once, I was in charge. I turned to look at Janet. "Stay here."

"What?" she said, frowning.

"You heard me. Stay here. I am making a private phone call, and I have no intention of having a repeat of the other day," I snapped.

"Okay. I'll stay right here," Janet said. For a moment, she looked quite cowed, but then her usual haughty expression returned, and when she spoke, her voice once more held its obvious contempt. "I'll start on the dishes, seeing as I'm the only one around here who seems to think they don't just magically wash themselves."

I bit my tongue to keep from telling her not to be such a drama queen. The only dishes waiting to be washed were the two cups we had just used and a glass from the orange juice I had at breakfast. It wasn't like there was a mound of pots. Still, I kept quiet. I had won one battle with Janet, and I had no intention of getting into another one so soon, at least not over something so petty. If it made her feel better to moan about something that didn't matter in the big scheme of things, then she could get on with it.

My cell phone rang right on time, and I took the call.

"Hello, Mr. Bryant," I said.

"It's Larry, remember? How are you, James?" he replied.

"Not so bad, thanks," I replied. "And you?"

"Can't complain," Larry replied. There was a friendly tone to his voice, but when he spoke again, he was all business. "So, what can I do for you today? It says in my notes that you want to halve your inheritance with your twin sister. Is that correct?"

"It was," I said. "But things have changed since I made the appointment. I'm sorry."

"No, no. Don't apologize. The fact things have changed is a positive," Larry said. "Because I would have had to spend the next who knows how long trying to convince you that was a bad idea. What are you thinking instead?"

I decided to tell Larry the truth about what I wanted to do. While I wasn't naïve enough to think Larry cared about me on a personal level, I knew that he cared as my lawyer and that the best way to make sure things worked as I wanted them to was to be honest with him.

"I wanted to give my sister half of the inheritance because I am sick of her trying to control every aspect of my life, and I figured if I gave her the money that she is so jealous of me having, she would leave me alone. The thing is, she is insistent that she doesn't want half of the money—or any of it, in fact—rather she is insistent on being added to my bank account to keep an eye on my spending. Maybe I'm paranoid, but I don't think that would be a good idea. I am more than capable of not blowing my money without Janet babysitting me."

"Quite right," Larry put in. "She has no legal right to be on your account, and I most definitely wouldn't recommend that as a course of action."

"Good," I said. I had believed there was no legal reason for Janet to be on my bank account, but it was good to hear it being confirmed by someone who knew the law inside out. "I realize that, in theory, I could just tell her no, but quite frankly, she makes my life unbearable at times, and I know she would eventually wear me down. My plan is to open a second account and transfer a couple of thousand dollars a month into it. I am going to tell Janet that this is my monthly allowance and that is all I get to touch from the inheritance, that the rest is used for bills and so forth, but it's all done through solicitors."

"Okay," Larry said slowly. "So, we'll open an account and

have a standing order set up for $2,000 to go in on the first of every month. I will open it and start it off with $1,700. I think that's a good amount to make it look as though you've had your first payment and have spent a little bit, but not enough to make anyone think it's out of the ordinary."

That was a good plan, and the idea of having some money already sitting in there to make the lie look like the truth was something that hadn't occurred to me until Larry suggested it. I was more than happy to have him on my side.

"Thank you, Larry," I said. "How soon can you have it set up?"

"Give me around twenty minutes," he said. "Once it's done, I'll email you the details of the new account and the login for your online banking. I will then set up a second account, the one Janet will have access to, which I will also email to you. I will have a card and a PIN sent out today, and that should be with you within seven working days. Obviously, I will only be sending you one card. If your sister just wants to observe the account, then there is no need for her to have a card or a PIN."

I could hear the smile in Larry's voice as he spoke, and I felt myself smiling, too. He had found another way to trap my sister in her own lie, and I was loving it.

"That all sounds great," I said.

"With regard to Janet's login, would you like that login to only have access to view the account, or would you want her to be able to potentially transfer money and make online purchases and that kind of thing?"

I kind of liked the idea of Janet having a login that would only let her view the account—after all, that was what she claimed she wanted to be able to do—but I knew she was already going to be majorly pissed about this not being my main account. I wasn't going to give her another reason to argue with me. I mean, what could she do? The account was only going to contain pocket change. If she really wanted to steal it, she could have it.

"Set both logins up to be able to use the full extent of the account, please," I said. "I think her not being given a card and PIN will get the message across nicely without yet another argument about her login."

"As you wish," Larry said. "My email with all of the information on your new account will be with you soon. Is there anything else I can do for you today, James?"

"No, that's everything, thank you. And thank you for getting this all set up so quickly," I replied.

I ended the call and stayed sitting on my bed with my back against the headboard while I waited for Larry's email. Twenty minutes wasn't that long, but I knew it would be driving Janet crazy. She hated to be kept waiting—even two or three minutes was enough to make her angry.

I couldn't help but think I had won this battle. I had managed to find a way to both appease Janet and let her think she had what she wanted and also keep her away from the thing she wanted access to the most. Maybe I was getting better at learning to cope in the outside world, after all.

I was still feeling pretty good about myself when my cell phone pinged. I looked at my emails and found that, as expected, I had a message from Larry. I opened it and looked over the details, then downloaded the app for the bank Larry had chosen. Within minutes, I had the app on my cell phone, and I had tested both logins. I left myself logged in, and then I moved the app to my cell phone's front screen, so Janet wouldn't see that it wasn't the only banking app I had on there.

When I was confident that I had everything set up properly, I opened the small cupboard in my bedside cabinet and dug out a pen and a notepad. I tore a page from the notepad and jotted down the details for Janet's login, and then I put the notepad and the pen away. I stood up, put my cell phone back in my pocket, and then I went down to the kitchen.

I felt another moment of pride when I found Janet seated at the table, sipping a cup of coffee. She had stayed put like I had told her. I decided against mentioning it to her. It was enough for me that she had done as I had asked without me having to lord it over her.

I sat down opposite her and pushed the piece of paper across the table. "All sorted." I smiled. "That's your details to log into the app with."

"Thanks." Janet smiled. "Excuse me a second." She left the room and returned with her cell phone. She sat back down, and her focus flitted between the piece of paper and the cell phone.

I knew the moment she got logged in before she even spoke. I saw her eyes widen and her mouth open slightly, and then she stared at me in such horror that it would have been funny under any other circumstances, but I had to play this just right, and starting out with laughter was the opposite of that.

"James, where has it all gone?" she breathed.

I frowned, pretending like I had no idea what she was talking about. "What do you mean?"

"There's only just over $1,700 in here. What the hell have you done with the rest?" she asked.

"Relax," I said. "Jeez. It's not even $300. I bought groceries twice, and I bought—"

"What do you mean it's not even $300? Are you seriously

expecting me to believe that our father's whole estate came to just $2,000?" she demanded, the horror replaced by anger.

"What? No, of course not," I said. "But that's the amount I get per month, and it's only been one month since the payments started."

"Oh, I see," Janet said, visibly relaxing. "So this is like a pocket money account?"

"Yeah, I guess you could say that." I smiled. "All of the household bills and everything relating to taxes come out of the main account, and each month, $2,000 gets deposited into this account. Obviously, if anything goes wrong and I have a large expense or if I want to buy a car or go on vacation or something, I can request more."

"Request it? What do you mean?" Janet asked. "Isn't it in your other account?"

"Yes, but technically I don't have access to it," I explained, relishing the moment. "It's all taken care of by my legal team."

"Oh, that's a relief." Janet tilted her head at me. "At least now I can stop worrying about you blowing the lot in one go!"

I tried to smile, but suddenly my hard-earned victory didn't seem like such a big accomplishment. Hot shame flooded through me at Janet's words. Was it possible that I had gotten the whole thing wrong, and she really did just want to be able to keep an eye on me? Had I let my paranoia win again? Or was she every bit as good an actress as I was an actor?

It certainly seemed like my paranoia had won, and while I regretted that a lot, it was too late to do anything about it. I wasn't about to backtrack and tell Janet the truth. I knew for a fact that would cause an argument. One in which she would scream at me and not let it go; then I would have another panic attack ... I really didn't have the energy for that.

No, I would just have to live with the guilt of lying to the one person I should be able to trust. Maybe that was more like the moment when I started to learn how to cope in the real world. The moment when I learned how to lie to my sister. This was something I'd never been able to do well, even as a child.

18

I was sitting on my bed, waiting for my call with Dr. Sellers, when there was a noise from in the hallway. Angry, I stood up and threw open the door. Had Janet learned nothing since she cut short my last session with my therapist? I opened my mouth to demand she stop eavesdropping, but then I saw that she had her coat on and was pulling a wheeled suitcase behind her.

"Are you leaving?" I asked.

Janet nodded. "I got a call from my agent. I've landed a new role, a big one, so unfortunately, I can't let you take up any more of my time and energy. I've been praying for this role, and now it's mine. You understand why I have to do this, don't you?"

I knew from experience that what Janet wanted, Janet got. It wouldn't matter if I told her I didn't understand and begged her to stay. Just like it wouldn't have mattered if I had told her I didn't need looking after and she could leave. She would come and go as she pleased, as was her nature.

"Of course, I understand," I said. "Go knock 'em dead."

She flashed me a quick smile. "Goodbye, James. Don't be getting in any more trouble, okay?"

"I won't," I replied, although that could be a lie, for all I knew. It just felt like the right thing to say. I didn't remember the last time I had gotten myself into trouble, so I couldn't guarantee anything, really.

Janet pulled me in for a stiff hug that I returned equally stiffly. She air-kissed my cheek, then turned away from me and headed for the stairs. Within less than a minute she was gone, and all that was left was a sweet whiff of vanilla in the air where she had stood moments ago.

I felt a flicker of unease. Would I be okay without Janet keeping me right? I knew I would be. I had been just fine before she came, but I still felt a bit anxious. I swallowed my worries. They had no place in reality, and that was where I wanted to be.

My cell phone ringing stopped me from getting too caught up in my worries, and I ducked back into my bedroom and picked up my phone from the duvet. I checked the screen as I sat down on the bed. It was indeed my therapist, and I took his call.

As we went through the usual few opening questions about how I was feeling and whether I was taking my meds properly and everything like that, it occurred to me that not only had my brief sense of unease moved on, but that I felt only one thing about Janet's departure now—relief.

I was relieved that I could take a phone call in peace. I was relieved that I could be responsible for my medication once more and not be classed as irresponsible if I was so much as one minute late to take it. I was relieved that I could once more do my own shopping and cooking and generally do my own thing. Of course, with that relief came a rush of guilt. How could I think these awful things about my sister?

But even as the guilt burned its way through me, I also reminded myself to change the details on my accounts so that grocery money came out of the new account, just to keep up appearances if Janet kept checking.

"James?" Dr. Sellers said. "Can you hear me?"

I realized that I had completely drifted off into my own little world, and I hadn't heard a word he had been saying. "I ... yes. Sorry. I was a million miles away. What were you saying?"

"Perhaps it would be more useful to talk about what is on your mind?" Dr. Sellers said. He made it sound like a question, but I was pretty sure it wasn't optional. It was fine anyway. It wasn't like Janet's departure had to be a secret.

"There's not really much to say," I began. "I was just thinking about Janet, my sister. She left to go back home."

"Oh, I see. Are you worried you'll have problems coping without her help, or is it more of a case of missing her company?" Dr. Sellers asked.

"Neither," I admitted. "This is going to make me sound like a terrible person, but all I feel is relief. I feel like I can get on with my life in my own way now without her interfering. But then I think of all she's done for me, and I feel guilty for being pleased she's gone."

"And what did she do for you that you don't feel confident that you could do yourself?" Dr. Sellers asked.

I thought of the things Janet did—reminding me to take meds that I hadn't forgotten about, redoing grocery orders I had already completed. Everything I could think of seemed to undermine rather than help.

"Well, nothing, if I'm honest, Doctor. But knowing that

doesn't make me feel any less guilty about being happy she's gone."

"Are you close to your sister?" Dr. Sellers asked. "Or were you before any of this happened?"

"We were never close in the conventional sense, but Janet is the only person in my corner. She always has my back," I said almost automatically.

"Right. So, is that why you feel guilty about being happy to see her leave?" Dr. Sellers asked.

I opened my mouth to say I wasn't happy to see Janet leave, but I closed it again. It would be a lie, and if I couldn't be honest with my therapist, then who could I be honest with? "I don't know. Maybe."

"I could be a little off the mark here, but when you told me that Janet is always in your corner, it sounded like a stock answer to me, like it was something that you are conditioned to say whenever you are asked about her." He paused for a moment. "So, let me ask you this: Do you think Janet is always in your corner and always has your back?"

I opened my mouth to say yes, but then I closed it again. Was it true? Or was it just something that Janet always told me rather than something with any real meaning behind it?

"Umm, well, I guess Janet says it a lot," I said finally. "But that doesn't mean it can't be true, right?"

"No, of course not," Dr. Sellers replied. "But I find it very contradictory to everything else you've told me about her."

"You do?" I asked.

"Most definitely," Dr. Sellers replied. He paused for a second. "Well, that's our time for today. Why don't you think some more about your relationship with Janet and try to decide for yourself whether she truly has your back or whether she simply tells you that she has it. We can discuss it more fully in your next session."

"Okay. Thank you, Dr. Sellers," I said, and then I ended the call. I lay back on my bed, looked up at the ceiling and sighed.

Dr. Sellers pointing out the contradiction in Janet's words and her actions had made me question my relationship with her more deeply than I had before. In the past, I had always pushed my doubts about her to one side, telling myself that I was being paranoid. But Dr. Sellers wasn't paranoid, and he seemed to think that Janet was bad news. He didn't come right out and say that, but he didn't have to. I could read between the lines.

Maybe Janet was hindering my recovery. She certainly wasn't helping it, but I honestly believed she was just sort of there alongside it. But if she was slowing down the process, I definitely needed her to keep away until I found myself once more.

Somehow, that awareness made me feel ready to face the past in a way I had never been able to consider before. All I really knew was, as Janet put it, that my violent tendencies had reached a level the family could no longer cope with. But now I was no longer content to accept Janet's word that it was better I didn't remember the exact details of whatever it was I had done to get sent away.

And if Janet wasn't really in my corner, how could I be sure that the story she told was even close to the truth?

19

I didn't want to rush into anything. Once I knew what I'd done to get sent away, I wouldn't be able to go back and unknow it; there was always a chance that it would be too much for me to handle. After all, my mental health still hung in the balance.

Even so, my desire to learn the truth intensified over the next few days to the point that I knew I would go completely mad if I didn't find out soon. I needed to hear it from someone I trusted, and I knew that that person was no longer Janet. I had just about decided that I should call my therapist, but then someone else popped into my mind whom I figured I could trust—Brianna, my probation officer.

She was much more likely to know the ins and outs of what I had done, whereas my therapist most likely only had access to the bare bones, if that. Once I'd thought of Brianna, I knew she was the right person to ask, so I called and asked her to come over today for lunch. When I realized it sounded like I was asking her on a date, I quickly explained that I had some questions about my case. She agreed to come, so I obviously hadn't scared her off too much.

I made a cheese and ham pasta salad, and it sat waiting for us in a bowl in the fridge. The table was set for two, and I kept telling myself I was only nervous because I was about to learn something big about myself.

The doorbell rang, and I jumped. I laughed at myself, but I cut off the laughter short when I heard the shaky, nervous quality it held. I hurried to the door and opened it.

Brianna stood on the doorstep. "Hi," she said.

"Hello," I replied, stepping to one side, and gesturing for her to come in. "Thank you for coming. May I take your coat?"

Brianna smiled at me as she wriggled out of the black and gray checked coat she was bundled up inside.

I closed the front door, and then I took the coat and hung it on a hanger beside mine in the front closet.

"I hope you like pasta salad," I said, heading for the kitchen and gesturing for Brianna to follow me.

"I love it," she said.

I felt a bit better hearing that, and when we arrived in the kitchen, I pulled out Brianna's chair like a gentleman.

She thanked me and sat down.

I took the bowl from the fridge and a large serving spoon from the drawer and placed both on the table. "Help yourself. Would you like anything to drink?"

"Just a glass of water, please," Brianna said.

I nodded and grabbed two glasses. I filled Brianna's with water and my own with soda, and then I sat down opposite her. I was pleased to note she had helped herself to a large portion of the pasta and was already tucking in, so she hadn't just been humoring me when she said she liked it.

"Where's your sister?" Brianna asked when I was seated.

"She went back home," I said as I helped myself to some pasta.

"Good," Brianna said with conviction.

I glanced up at her.

"Sorry. I shouldn't have said that. But there was something about her I didn't quite like. She gave me a bad feeling, that's all."

"It's funny you should say that," I said. "I have always described Janet as the one person who has my back, the one person always in my corner. It came up with my therapist, and he pointed out that despite me saying that, everything else I had told him about Janet contradicted the idea. He really made me think, and I realized that I say those things because Janet always says them. And now I guess I'm questioning my whole relationship with her."

"Well, that explains why you called me to ask your questions instead of asking Janet," Brianna said.

"Yes," I agreed. "I wanted to hear the answers from someone I trust, and right now, I'm not sure Janet is that person."

"Fair enough," Brianna said. She stopped eating and looked at me. "If I can answer your questions, I promise you that I will. I will be honest in my answers, but first, I need to be sure that you've thought this through and that you're ready to hear the truth."

I was as sure as I could be that I was doing the right thing. As I nodded, a memory came to me, not one I had so much repressed as just something I hadn't thought of in a while. It was a memory of my first conscious day in the hospital, and the orderly had taken me to the day room to sit with some of the patients. A lot of them were clearly sedated, but some were lucid, and I remembered how they had whispered and pointed at me, saying I was a killer. Obviously, they had been delusional.

"I'm sure," I said. "It's not like I've murdered anyone, right?"

I laughed, but my laughter froze in my throat when I noticed Brianna's horrified expression. Dread flooded my system. It was true. I had killed someone. Somehow, just the thought of it meant I could remember now. Not the actual killing, but the doctors from my early days in the hospital, how they would try to get me to feel remorse. But how could I be expected to feel remorse for something I didn't remember doing? It would be like being sorry for something I hadn't actually done.

"I did kill someone," I said quietly as an awful clarity dawned. "Right?"

Brianna shifted in her seat and nodded.

"I ... I just ..." I stopped, took a deep breath, and started over again. "I can't believe that it's possible to do something so terrible and not remember doing it."

"Do you really not remember it at all?" Brianna asked.

"If I did, I would have said so. And I certainly wouldn't have been joking about it just now. The first year or two of my therapy revolved around various therapists trying to get me to talk about the 'incident,' as they called it, to say I felt remorse. I used to tell them that I couldn't feel remorse for something I didn't remember doing. They told me I would have a shorter stay in the hospital if I just admitted to remembering what I had done. If I remembered, I would have spoken up then."

"What's the last thing you remember before waking up in the hospital?" Brianna asked gently.

It was the first time I had been asked that question in years. I didn't want to lie to Brianna, even accidentally, so I took a moment to make sure I remembered everything correctly.

"It was a school day. I'd been to all of my classes, and I was going to meet my girlfriend. She was the same age as me, but she went to an all-girls school. They finished later than us, and I would have to wait around for her. We had arranged to meet down by the river, and the last thing I remember was walking there."

Brianna put down her fork, her lunch finished. My own food sat before me, mostly untouched. Brianna picked up her glass and sipped her water. I couldn't read her expression, but when she put the glass back down and spoke, she sounded normal, not like she was suddenly afraid of me or angry with me or anything. I guessed that made sense—I was the one who didn't remember what I had done, not Brianna. None of this was news to her.

"I could never quite believe that someone could murder another person and then just wipe it from their memory. I always thought you were lying, that you were thinking you could save your skin by pretending it didn't happen. But you genuinely don't remember it, do you?"

"Not a bit of it," I said. "Will you tell me what happened, please?"

"Are you sure?" she asked. "I don't want to tell you anything that's going to upset you and slow down your recovery."

"I need to know," I said. "I'm ready."

"Okay," Brianna said. She watched me for a moment, and our eyes met.

I held her gaze as confidently as I could.

She nodded. "I don't know every little detail. I only know what was in the police reports, so I have no idea what happened before the police arrived. They found you at the river with Terri dead in your arms, strangulation marks on her neck. The autopsy confirmed she had been strangled. You were catatonic, just sitting there, cradling Terri, staring out at the river. You remained like that for two whole days, and then you woke up in the hospital."

I sat sipping my soda. I remembered Terri, of course I did. Her freckled face came to mind. How could I have forgotten her freckles? That had to be why I had that panic attack before; the delivery driver had reminded me of Terri. All of these years, I'd assumed she had turned her back on me because I ended up in the hospital. But no. I killed her. That was why I never saw her again. No, that couldn't be true. I couldn't be a killer. Could I?

"James? I know it's a lot to take in," Brianna said quietly. "Are you okay?"

Definitely not, but I didn't want her to think she had done something bad by being honest with me, so I forced myself to nod, swallowing down the panic attack welling up inside me.

"I just don't get it," I said. "I don't feel like a murderer. If anyone had asked me, I would have said I wasn't capable of that, that I would sooner be the one being killed."

"Maybe the therapy and everything worked," Brianna said. "Maybe you've changed a lot."

I nodded, but that didn't feel right either. I couldn't have killed Terri, of all people. If it had been my father, I might have seen how it could have played out that way, but Terri? No. I loved her.

"Maybe you're right," I said with a sigh. "And maybe not

being able to remember the murder makes it hard for me to associate myself with the word 'murderer.' But it doesn't make sense. Why would I have killed Terri? She was the love of my life. I get we were just kids, and it probably sounds stupid now, but at the time it sure felt that way, you know?"

Brianna nodded.

I went on, feeling a bit better now that she seemed to be getting what I was saying. "I spent almost a year after I woke up thinking Terri would come to visit me soon. I tried calling her cell phone, but it was disconnected, and eventually I accepted that she didn't want a nutjob for a boyfriend."

I was quiet for a moment, thinking, and then something else occurred to me. "Wait. I remember everything after I woke up in the hospital. Or at least I think I do. Yet I don't remember there being a trial. Surely if they thought I'd killed someone, there would have been a trial."

"There was a trial," Brianna said quietly. "But you were deemed mentally unstable and not well enough to attend. Your lawyer made a deal with the DA to keep you in a secure hospital where you could be treated rather than send you to prison."

I blew out a soft whistle through my teeth, and we both sat in silence for a few moments.

"There's one thing I don't understand about the case. Well, two, actually," Brianna said eventually, flashing me a smile, which faded so quickly I thought that maybe I had imagined it. "But the second one is new. If you were down by the river, why weren't there any witnesses to what happened? It's always busy down there."

"We had a spot," I said with a smile as I remembered Terri and me cuddled up together in our own secluded spot where we could watch the world go by. "It's probably overgrown now, but back then, there was a patch of shrubbery right by the stone bridge. There was a small gap that if you squeezed through, you came out in a clearing. I found it by accident one day when a ball I was playing with rolled in there, and when Terri and I got together, I knew it would be the perfect place for us to be alone. No one else knew about it, to my knowledge."

"Then that gives me a different question. How did someone know where to find you and then to call the police?" Brianna asked.

"I don't see how anyone could have stumbled upon it by accident," I told her, glad to have her here to unravel the truth. "Was it a kid who called the cops?"

"I don't know. That all adds to the mystery. The call came from a public payphone, and they never traced the person who called," Brianna said. "But we know they didn't witness the actual murder. They reported seeing a boy who looked out of it with an unconscious girl in his lap."

"Probably thought we were on drugs or something," I mused.

"That would explain why they didn't attempt to offer any help on the scene. The police appealed for the person to come forward, but they never did. Eventually, the police stopped trying to find them. The case was solved, and they didn't want to waste resources on tracking down someone who had done nothing more than place a call to the authorities."

It made sense. But I still didn't understand how that person found us in the first place. They couldn't have spotted us unless they were trampling through the shrubbery.

This whole thing had made one decision easy for me. I wanted to start my proposed course of hypnotherapy as soon as possible, so I could get to the bottom of these strange events and find out what had actually happened. That thought reminded me that Brianna had said there were two things she didn't understand about this case.

"What was the other thing?" I asked.

"Huh?" Brianna said, seeming to have been pulled back from a million miles away.

"Earlier, you said there were two things you didn't understand. One was the lack of witnesses. What was the other thing?"

Brianna smiled, and I was sure she blushed a little. She looked at me and then down into her glass. "I can't fathom how you, this sweet person I am getting to know, is the same person who supposedly strangled a teenage girl with his bare hands for no apparent reason."

"Well, I wish I could help you, but none of it makes any sense to me," I said. "But you said *supposedly*. Does that mean you don't believe it to be true?"

"I don't know," Brianna said. "But I do believe what you've told me today. You genuinely don't remember what happened, and the more I hear about this spot you two had as teenage sweethearts, the more unlikely it all sounds. Look, please don't get your hopes up, okay? But I'm going to investigate this a bit more, to see if I can help you piece the truth together."

I nodded, not trusting my voice. I suddenly had a huge lump in my throat. This was it. This was what having someone in your corner actually felt like.

20

I sat looking at the two things in front of me: my cell phone and a box of old school reports I had found. I had been through them all, and once again, there was nothing to suggest that I was ever violent. If anything, I was described as quiet and shy.

There was one report left for me to read, but I didn't think I would have time before Janet called for our weekly check-in that she insisted upon. That was why I kept glancing at my cell phone and feeling dread in my stomach. I wasn't sure I could handle Janet right now, but I didn't have a choice. If I didn't take her call, she was likely to over-react and have the police come around to check that I was okay.

As if on cue, my cell phone vibrated into life, the screen lighting up with Janet's name in big letters. I hit the answer button and brought the phone up to my face. "Hey," I said.

"What sort of greeting is that?" Janet asked.

She said it in a light tone of voice like she was joking, but I had fallen for this one before and laughed, and then she'd denied that she was joking, and everything became an issue. This time, I didn't respond, and I heard Janet sigh.

"I'm sorry, am I keeping you from something important?" she asked sarcastically.

"Well, now that you mention it, I was in the middle of reading something," I replied honestly, hoping that she might take the hint and cut our call short.

"I'd like to think I'm a little bit more interesting than whatever book you're reading, unless it's the Bible," she said.

"Of course, and no, it isn't," I replied.

I didn't want to tell her about what I was really reading, so I let her think I was reading a book. I wasn't lying. She was the one who had said it was a book, and I just didn't want to contradict her and risk making her mad.

"So, how are you doing?" Janet asked. "Are you remembering to take your medication?"

"Yes," I said.

It was the truth. I hadn't missed a single dose. That was part of the reason why the fact that I was still losing my mind was so fucking annoying. I was doing everything right, yet I was still suffering. How was that fair?

"Why do I feel like there's a 'but' in there?" Janet said.

I sighed. "I don't know. I swear I'm taking my medication properly, but it doesn't seem to be working anymore. At least not properly. Do you think I should ask for a higher dose?"

"No," Janet said. "Not unless you want to go back into the hospital while they reassess you."

"Oh no, I didn't think of that. That's the last thing I want. Don't worry, I'll just have to get used to it all," I said.

"Why? What's happening?" Janet asked.

I wasn't going to tell her, but now I had started to talk about it, I knew I might as well tell her everything. She would only peck away at me until I did, and besides, maybe it was a good thing to tell her because she had already just saved me from making a big mistake.

"Some weird things are going on. I'm hallucinating like I do when I don't take my meds," I said. "But it's not just that. Things keep disappearing from where I've put them and then reappearing somewhere odd. And it gets worse at night. I swear I hear noises that sound like someone moving around, and I find lights on that I know I switched off, doors open that I know I closed."

"Is it possible that the noises and the things moving around are all a part of your hallucinations?" Janet asked.

"I wondered that myself at first," I said. "But it feels different. Don't get me wrong, in the midst of a hallucination, it feels so real, and it scares the life out of me. But once I get myself together, I know it isn't real. These other things don't go away no matter what I do, which makes me think they have to really be happening."

I had tried everything I could think of to find an explanation for what had been going on recently, and I'd failed miserably. On the plus side, I'd discovered the box of my school reports while I was trying to locate the source of the strange happenings in the house. Of course, I didn't tell Janet that part.

"You don't think ...?" Janet said. "No, it's silly, ignore me."

"No, come on," I said. "If you've got a potential explanation for this, please tell me."

"Well, from what you've said, it sounds kind of like the house might be haunted," Janet said.

Was she for real, or was she just trying to trick me into believing her so she could laugh at me for being gullible? I wasn't sure, but as crazy as the idea was, it would explain things. I didn't think it could be my father's ghost, though. I was sure I would feel the malevolence oozing out of the walls if his spirit were hanging around. That left one other person. I decided to take Janet's statement at face value and see what she thought of my theory.

"You don't think it could be Mom's ghost, do you?" I asked quietly.

"What are you talking about?" Janet said. "You have to be dead to be a ghost. You know that, right?"

"Obviously," I said.

"And obviously," Janet said, "Mom isn't dead."

I frowned. What was Janet playing at? She had to be trying to spare my feelings, but it wasn't working. "I appreciate you trying to make me feel better, but it's okay. I'm not going to fall apart. I know Mom died when we were kids."

"You really believe that, don't you?" Janet asked quietly. "James, surely you know it's not true. Mom didn't die. She left because she couldn't cope with your behavior any longer. Dad told us all about it."

"She died." I shook my head despite Janet not being able to see me. "I know she died."

"I'm sorry," Janet said. "But think about it rationally for a minute." She paused, as if giving me time to do just that. "Was there ever a funeral or a wake for Mom?"

"Well, no, but ..." I started.

"Did we get any bereavement cards?" Janet pressed on. "Flowers?"

"No, but ..." I started once again.

"Did we ever go to a cemetery and see her grave?" Janet asked.

"No," I said, my voice barely above a whisper, and my whole world began to reel.

It hit me that Janet was right. None of those things had happened, and they would have. My mom wasn't dead. It was a lie I had constructed to protect myself from the truth —that I had pushed Mom away.

"What did I do to make her leave?" I asked.

"Oh, James, it wasn't just one thing. It was just ... well, everything, really. The way you were with all of us," she replied.

If I had somehow misbehaved enough that Mom had left her family because of me, it would certainly explain why my father hated me so much. But then again, it seemed like my father had hated me from the moment I was born.

"Do you hate me, Janet?" I asked quietly, afraid of her answer. "Because I sent her away?"

"No, of course not," Janet said quickly. "I know it wasn't your fault. You were ill. It's not like you chose to act that way. Besides, to be honest, Mom was never really much use for anything. She was always taking to her bed; she found her life too much to cope with. And, again being totally honest, not much changed when she left. We still had Dad, and he was the only one who made the effort with us anyway."

That wasn't how I remembered things at all, but up until five minutes ago, I had been convinced that my mom was dead, so I couldn't rely too much on that memory. I didn't want it shattering though, so I just kept quiet.

"Mom isn't dead, and Dad didn't die in the house, so that rules those two out," Janet said. "But the house itself dates back to the 1800s, so I'm sure plenty of people died there over the years. Maybe one of them wants the house back now."

"That's not funny," I snapped.

"Oh, come on, lighten up." Janet giggled. "I'm joking.

Well, at least about them wanting the house back. I'm starting to think there's some truth to the idea of the house being haunted, though."

I didn't want to think about the house and the weird goings-on anymore. I already regretted telling Janet about them, because once she got a bee in her bonnet, she wouldn't leave it alone until it was out and angry, and someone else got stung. There was only one way to get her to drop it, and that was to bring up her favorite subject —herself.

"So, enough about me. How are you, Janet?" I asked. "How's the play going?"

I listened and tried to be enthusiastic as she told me all about the role and how great she was and how much the director liked her. I reminded myself that despite what my therapist and Brianna thought, Janet wasn't the enemy, she was my sister, so I told her that I was proud of her. She thanked me, and that pretty much wrapped up our conversation.

I put my cell phone down on the table in front of me, and then I thought better of it and slipped it into my pocket, the only place I could be sure no ghost could move it.

Could a ghost really be causing these problems? Even as I tried to write it off as a stupid idea, it clung to me. There was no denying that the theory explained the weird things that had been happening lately.

I checked the time and saw it was about fifteen minutes before my next dose of medication was due. I stood up and went to the sink. I grabbed a clean glass and half filled it with water; then I went back to the table and picked up the box of school reports.

I headed up the stairs toward my room, ready to take my

medication and then sit on my bed and go through the last report.

As I reached the top of the stairs, I felt the icy fingers of fear grip my heart. My bedroom door stood open, and I was certain I had left it closed.

21

I didn't know if it was inappropriate to ask Brianna if she wanted to stay for dinner when she came to do her check-in. If it was, she obviously didn't mind because she said yes. I made us Polish sausages, then fixed mashed potatoes and gravy as a side dish. I was worried it wouldn't be sophisticated enough for Brianna, but I had invited her to stay on a whim, and it wasn't like I had all the ingredients for a restaurant-style meal just lying around the kitchen. I need not have worried. Brianna ate the lot, and she told me how much she enjoyed it.

Now we had finished dinner, including a large bowl of chocolate ice cream each, and we had moved to the living room with some drinks—a tonic water with ice and lemon for Brianna and a lime cordial with tonic for me. We had been chatting about general stuff. It made it easy to forget that Brianna was my probation officer and not just a friend.

In a sense, remembering that Brianna was only here because she was my probation officer upset me. But, as I reminded myself, her duty to her job had long since been fulfilled, and she was still here. Perhaps our friendship wasn't so one-sided after all.

"I've been looking into your case," she said.

So that was technically work talk, but at the same time, she had to care about this—dare I even think she might care about me?—or she wouldn't be spending her time with me when she was off the clock, and she wouldn't be looking deeper into my case.

"Okay," I said, not really sure what else to say.

There were a million questions I wanted to ask, but I was afraid of the answers. Did Brianna think I was a psychopath? A cold-blooded killer? Did she think I was beyond redemption?

"I don't know if I'm being naïve because I really like you and I want you to be innocent, but honestly, the more I read about what happened with your case, the more I doubt the official findings," Brianna said after a moment.

She really liked me? I felt my heart swell. I really liked her, too, but for now, I had to know what she meant about the case.

Was it possible that the police and the experts had all gotten it wrong?

Was it possible that I didn't remember killing Terri because it hadn't actually happened?

I didn't want to get my hopes up too far only to have them dashed again, but I couldn't help but wonder.

"How come you think they might have gotten it wrong?" I dared to ask.

"Well, there were no witnesses, and forensics found none of your DNA under Terri's fingernails or anything like that, which they would have expected to find, given that she was strangled. The ligature marks on her neck only prove she was strangled, not who strangled her," Brianna said. "As far as I understand it, there's absolutely nothing to confirm whether or not you killed her." She paused. "Or if it was simply that you found her dead."

I waited for her to go on. If this could still go either way, there had to be another reason why she was willing to believe me.

"I just ... well, from getting to know you, it doesn't seem that you fit the normal profiles of a killer. And, besides, to me at least, it all looks a little bit too convenient, doesn't it? Instead of launching a full investigation, blame the mentally ill kid who can't remember what happened," she said. "It's a nice easy win for the DA, and it makes citizens feel safer knowing that the police are so quick to get bad people off our streets."

I looked at her, amazed at how clear it all seemed. "For the record, I certainly don't feel like I'm capable of killing someone," I said. "And even if I was, why would I have killed Terri? Why not my father, who mercilessly abused me day in and day out? Or why not one of the kids at school, who made fun of me when I went into a world of my own?" I questioned, for the first time. "Why would I have chosen someone I actually liked and who liked me in return?"

Brianna nodded. "Yeah, that's another thing that didn't really add up. At the time, it seems that even Terri's parents were skeptical about you being responsible for her death," she said.

"It wouldn't be the first time I've gotten blamed for something that probably wasn't my fault," I said with a sigh. "Maybe I just have one of those faces that seems easy to blame."

"I don't know about that. I like your face," Brianna said

with a smile. Then her cheeks flushed pink, and she quickly hurried on. "What else have you gotten the blame for?"

I was happy that she had told me that she liked my face. But I could see that she was embarrassed by her comment, so I didn't draw any more attention to it.

"I thought my mom died when I was a kid," I told her. "And I've only just found out from Janet that it isn't true. She didn't die; she left us. And Janet told me she left because I was violent and nasty to her. That I drove her away with my behavior."

"What a terrible thing to say," Brianna said, looking genuinely shocked.

"It's not really her fault. It's what my father would have told her since the day Mom left, and she would have believed anything he said. She's mentioned things about me being violent as a child, but unbeknownst to her, I found my mom's old journal. I've read it cover to cover, and there is nothing there to suggest that I was ever violent toward my mom. It was clear from what I read that my father was violent toward her. Maybe even that Janet was too, if my father egged her on. But not me. Never me."

Brianna reached out and put her warm hand on top of my coolish one. She left it there for a moment and squeezed my fingers before she moved it away.

It felt nice to have contact with another human being, especially one so pretty, who smelled amazing and whose touch made my skin tingle.

22

When I opened the front door and saw Dr. Sellers standing there, I smiled and gestured for him to come in with a sweep of my hand. He smiled back and wiped his feet on the welcome mat, although he didn't leave so much as a speck of mud behind, and then he stepped inside and started down the hall.

I closed the door, moved around him, and led him to the living room. "Would you like a cup of tea or coffee?"

Dr. Sellers sat down in an armchair. "No, thank you, James."

I sat down on the couch opposite him. "Thank you for coming."

"Of course," he replied. "Whatever is best for the patient. Now, how have you been feeling?"

It was the question most of our sessions started with. I thought for a moment.

"Strange," I finally answered. "In some ways, I feel much better, but other ways, I feel quite a bit worse."

Dr. Sellers nodded at me to go on.

"I've been misplacing things and finding them in some strange places," I replied, toning down slightly the things that made me feel worse. I didn't want to discuss the possibility of the house being haunted with Dr. Sellers. "And I feel better because of these old things I found. School reports mostly, but my mom's old journal and some of my drawings, too. And there's nothing there to insinuate I was violent as a child."

"The misplacing of objects could possibly be a side effect of your medication," Dr. Sellers told me. "It can make you— a little bit fuzzy-headed, for want of a better term."

I thanked the doctor for his suggestion. I didn't think it was that, though. Not with everything else going on, too, but I didn't dare tell him about the rest. Not yet. He was here to do some hypnotherapy to try to unlock my hidden memories, and I didn't want to say something that might make him think I wasn't mentally strong enough for that right now.

"May I see the things you found?" Dr. Sellers asked me.

I nodded. I trusted Dr. Sellers, and I knew he wouldn't try to take them away from me. I also wanted to hear his thoughts on the matter, and to see whether he noticed something I had missed.

I hurried up to my room and retrieved my school reports, my drawings, and my mom's journal, and when I came back into the living room, I handed the stuff to Dr. Sellers and sat quietly while he looked through it all.

When he had finished, he smiled at me. "I have to say that I rather agree with you. There is nothing here to suggest you had any violent tendencies."

While I felt relieved and wanted to be able to take his word for it, I had to know more. "What about the drawings?" I asked. "Some of them are pretty weird."

"Some kids are pretty weird," Dr. Sellers said with a smile. "It doesn't necessarily mean anything except that you had an overactive imagination."

I felt as though he was holding something back from me, but I didn't ask what it might be. I didn't want to sound paranoid. Instead, I just nodded.

"In my opinion, the school reports and your mom's journal paint the picture of a lonely boy with some anxiety issues," Dr. Sellers said. "It sounds like you had panic attacks as a child. It also seems that your imagination sometimes took over, and some of the schoolwork you produced wasn't necessarily on the topic the work had been set to cover. But none of that points to a child being violent."

"I don't think my father ever liked me very much," I said. "But Mom seemed to care about me. And yet, she was the one who left me."

"I'm sure she had her reasons for doing what she did," Dr. Sellers said.

I realized that he didn't believe that. Not really. He was as disgusted as I was at the thought of someone making an escape for herself while letting her children stay with a monster in the way that she had.

"Now, should we make a start?"

I nodded, my mouth dry. I felt nervous. Dr. Sellers smiled reassuringly, and I felt instantly better. I smiled back at him.

"Okay, just a few things to go over before we get started. If you seem too disturbed or agitated by what we're doing, I will move us on to safer ground. If you seem like you're too far gone for that to make a difference, I will awaken you immediately. If you decide you want out of the trance before I see your distress, you can think your way out of it easily enough, or you can use the safe word—banana—and I will wake you up. Does that make sense?"

I nodded again. And if I was being fully honest with myself, I trusted Dr. Sellers to know if I needed out of there more than I trusted myself.

Dr. Sellers smiled at me. "I need you to relax. Listen to the sound of my voice, and as you do so, feel each muscle in your body, and actively relax it. Let's start with your feet and move upward."

I did as Dr. Sellers said, relaxing my feet, then my calves, and then my thighs. I listened to his voice, and I was aware that I could no longer make out his words. Instead, I could just hear the sound of his voice. I didn't panic, though. I knew what I needed to do, and I kept on doing it. I relaxed my stomach and chest muscles, and then I moved onto the muscles in my hands, and the ones all the way up my arms.

I sit on my bed, my back pressed against the headboard, my knees drawn up to my chest. Tears roll down my cheeks and soak into the knees of my pajamas, but even as I sob, I make no sound. Terror has rendered me silent.

I want to call out for my mom, but I don't dare do it. Besides, even if she heard me, all that would happen is she—and I— would endure my father's wrath. It's not like she could stop him. Calling out to her would only mean that she was punished, too.

It didn't seem fair that Mom might get punished for something she didn't even do, just like it's not fair that I'm getting punished for something that I didn't do. As soon as I saw the scratch on my father's car as I walked up the driveway after school, I knew I was in trouble. The fact that I had been at school and couldn't possibly have caused the damage was irrelevant. It would still somehow be my fault.

The second I stepped inside, my father was there, yelling in my face, plastering me with a layer of spittle and enveloping me in a cloud of stale coffee and cigarette breath. He'd dragged me up the stairs and along the hallway by one arm, me crying all the way. He had thrown me into my bedroom, slammed the door, and pulled the bolt across. And then he had told me that he would be back soon to teach me a lesson. His threat had turned my blood cold.

I can hear his breathing as he paces in a circle outside my bedroom door. I'm not sure what he's doing, but if I had to take a guess, I would say he was psyching himself up for what is coming. The thought fills me with horror, as I am sure it's his intention.

Then the door to my bedroom opens, and my father walks over to the side of my bed. This is so much worse, and I wish he would go back to the pacing. In his hand is a thick leather belt. The buckle end swings loose of my father's hand, and before I really register the movement, the belt sails through the air and smacks down across my shins.

The stinging pain of the leather is enough to make me cry out, but it is nothing compared to the agonizing pain of the buckle hitting my shinbone, and now the tears that run down my face are as much from the pain as they are from my fear of my father.

"Stop crying and take it like a man," my father yells, and then the belt is raining down on me, hitting my arms, my head, my face. I am screaming and screaming, and the pain is so bad I think this might be the beating that kills me.

"James, it's okay."

It was a male voice, but it wasn't my father's, and it sounded like it belonged to someone who cared about me, the tone soft and gentle.

I dared to lift my head and open my eyes. I was sitting on my sofa, my knees drawn up, and kneeling on the floor in front of the sofa was Dr. Sellers.

I began to relax slightly as it came back to me. The terror with my father wasn't real. Well, it was—it was likely one of the suppressed memories from my childhood—but it wasn't happening to me right now. It was just a half memory, a snapshot of the past.

I loosened my death grip on my knees and lowered my feet to the floor, sighing in relief as I did so. I was aware that a layer of sweat covering my body was cooling off, leaving me shivering in spite of the warmth in the room.

"I ... I'm sorry," I managed to say as my heart began to beat at a more normal pace.

"You don't have to apologize," Dr. Sellers said. "Do you need to take one of your sedatives?"

"No," I replied. "I feel okay now. It's just the scene that played out with my father has me feeling drained and like I can't be bothered to do anything."

"I can understand that. Emotional trauma is often more tiring than physical trauma simply because we can heal physical trauma so much more quickly."

"It hurts too much," I blurted out. "I never want to do that again."

"Don't rule anything out completely, James. You never know when it might be our only option," Dr. Sellers said kindly enough. "For now, we'll go back to the more standard therapy and see if you start to feel better."

I nodded.

"Something of note did come to my attention during this session," Dr. Sellers said. "James, I don't believe for one moment that you were ever a violent child. It's clear to me from your reaction just now, and from the papers I have looked through, that you were a victim of your father's abuse. Your mom's journal and your school reports certainly back up that theory."

"Thank you," I said. "It means a lot to me that you should say that."

"It's the truth. Everything about this screams that your father was gaslighting you," Dr. Sellers said. "There was emotional and psychological abuse along with the physical."

"So I'm not crazy?" I asked, convinced I'd missed something.

"No, you're not crazy," Dr. Sellers said. He made a show of standing up and looking at his watch at the same time. "That's our time up, James. Believe it or not, we made really good progress today, and I am confident that you will only continue to improve with time."

"Thank you, Dr. Sellers," I said.

I stood up and walked the doctor to the door, where we finalized a time and date for my next appointment and said our goodbyes until the next session.

Once Dr. Sellers had gotten into his car and driven away, I closed the door and started back toward the main body of the house. I was smiling as I walked.

I wasn't crazy. I never had been. It was my father making me think I was crazy. It was the first time I had even dared to let myself consider the idea of me not being the problematic one in my family, but it was really starting to seem like it might just be the case.

23

The time between my last appointment with Dr. Sellers and this one had flown by. It had been three weeks since the painful attempt at regressing me, and we hadn't revisited the idea. I had a feeling that Dr. Sellers would ask about trying again, and who knew? Maybe I would say yes because I was feeling stronger now. I thought maybe I could do it. I could sure try.

I glanced at my watch and saw we had less than ten minutes left in the session, and I really needed to talk to Dr. Sellers about the one thing that was still hindering my progress.

"I don't think my medication is working anymore," I blurted out.

I tried not to hear Janet's voice in my head saying that they'd take me back to the hospital to reassess me. If they did that, then so be it. I hoped they wouldn't, but I had to sort out my head. If that meant being reassessed and getting my medication changed, I would put up with it to feel better in the long run.

"You don't?" Dr. Sellers said with a raised eyebrow.

I shook my head.

"What makes you think that, James?"

"Well, over the last couple of months, every time I first fill my prescription, I'm fine. More than fine. Good even. I clean the house, talk to Janet and my friend Nick, and check in with my probation officer. But then I feel like I go downhill for a day or two, and before I know it, I'm having full-on panic attacks and hallucinations again. Is that normal?"

"It can be if the dosage is too low or if something triggers an attack. Do you think that might be the case here? Is something triggering you?"

"No," I said. "I did consider it the first time it happened, but it happens all the time. It's happened when I'm in, when I'm out, when I'm busy or when I'm bored."

"Okay." Dr. Sellers looked thoughtful. "I'm not sure why the medication isn't working as well for you as it should be. But don't worry. I intend to find out, and when I do, then hopefully we can do something about it," he said. "Let's start with a blood test to make sure your body is absorbing the medication the way it should be."

I waited while the doctor opened his bag and pulled out a needle and several empty syringes. I rolled up the sleeve of my thin sweater and held out my arm to Dr. Sellers. I looked away for a minute while he took the blood, and by the time it was over, I looked back, surprised that it hadn't hurt at all.

Once our time was up and Dr. Sellers had left for the evening, I made and ate my dinner, took a shower, and then decided to have an early night.

As I lay in bed waiting for sleep to take me, I realized I did the right thing talking to the doctor about my medication. He was going to fix it for me without hospitalizing me again, and it felt good to realize that I made the responsible decision even though I knew I might not have liked its consequences.

Later that night, for the first time in ages, I was smiling gently to myself as I drifted off.

24

I had just finished getting dressed when I heard my doorbell ringing. I frowned as I went downstairs to answer the door. I had no idea who I would find there. Dr. Sellers and I didn't have another session until next week, same with Brianna. *Please don't let it be Janet*, I couldn't help but think.

I got to the door and pulled it open. "Hi. Is everything okay?" I gasped, surprised to see Dr. Sellers. "Have I got the wrong day? I thought it was—"

"No, no, nothing like that," Dr. Sellers interrupted me. "There's just something I'd like to discuss with you, and I didn't want to wait another week. May I come in?"

"Yes, of course," I said, remembering my manners.

He led the way to the living room, and I shut the front door and followed him. We both sat down, and I offered him a drink, an offer he had never taken me up on before, and today was no different.

"May I see your medication?" Dr. Sellers said. "Not your sedatives. Your main pills."

"Sure," I said, standing back up. "Excuse me for just a second."

I went out to the kitchen. I didn't keep my pills under lock and key now that Janet was no longer at the house trying to take over dispensing them to me. I grabbed the bottle from the cupboard, returned to the living room and handed it to Dr. Sellers, then sat back down.

He opened the bottle and tipped it up, spilling a tablet out onto his palm. He nodded. "As I suspected."

"What is it, Doctor? Is there something wrong with my pills?"

Dr. Sellers put the loose pill down on the end table, and then he put the lid back on the bottle and stood it beside the lone pill. "Yes. I got your blood test results back late last night, and I had a look through them this morning. Your blood levels imply you are taking a 200 mg tablet per day. But you were prescribed 600 mg."

"Yes, 600 mg," I agreed. "But I swear I'm taking the full pill."

"I figured you were; otherwise, you wouldn't have been so surprised that your tablets don't seem to be working as effectively," he said. "The fact that you feel okay for a while after filling your prescription means they aren't sending you the wrong pills. That time you have when you feel good again is when you are getting the correct dosage of your medication. The hallucinations and so on slip back in when you go onto the lower dose, which, by the way, are identical except for one thing." He beckoned to me, and I leaned closer as he picked my pill back up and pointed to it. "See here? Where the brand name is?"

I nodded.

"See the tiny dot beneath it?"

I screwed my eyes up, and eventually, I saw it. "Yes, but I would never have seen it if you hadn't told me to look for it."

"Yes, in my opinion, it should be more obvious because that's how you can tell the pills apart. The ones with one dot are 200 mg, two dots are 400 mg, three dots are 600 mg, and so on."

"That all makes sense," I said thoughtfully. "Apart from one thing."

"What's that?" Dr. Sellers asked.

"How are they changing at some point through the month?" I asked.

"Well, that's the question, isn't it?" Dr. Sellers said. "Do you have any regular visitors other than myself and your probation officer?"

"No," I said. "My sister was here for a while, but she's been gone for over a month now. And my friend Nick visited me once. But the only regular visitors are you and Brianna."

"Brianna? Is she your probation officer?" Dr. Sellers asked.

I nodded.

"And does she know where you keep your medication?"

"Yes, I think so. I keep it in a cupboard in the kitchen, and I'm sure I had to take some during one of her visits. We usually sit at the kitchen table, so she would have seen where I got them from. But do you really think a probation officer would do something like that?"

"Well, my instincts say no, a probation officer would never meddle with anyone's pills, but what other option is there? I know it wasn't me. It wasn't you. And no one else comes around regularly. Having said that, I won't be reporting her until I am one hundred percent certain."

I hated the thought I could be sabotaging myself and

then blocking out the memory of doing it, but I hated the thought of Brianna doing this to me even more. And the idea of her being reported and losing her job killed me a little bit inside, even if her actions dictated that she deserved it.

"But what if it is me?" I asked. "What if I'm switching up my pills and then blocking out the memory?"

"It's possible. But you've come a long way, and I don't think you are in a place mentally where you would self-sabotage like that. However, let's keep an open mind and assume that you could be doing this. Let me think for a moment."

After a few minutes, Dr. Sellers smiled. "Yes, that'll work nicely. Instead of filling your prescription at the pharmacy like usual, I will bring you a week's worth of your pills when I come for your session. We will examine each pill together, so we know they are all correct, and then I want you to keep those pills on your person at all times. If they still get exchanged, then we know it's you doing it and blocking out the memory. And if they don't get exchanged, problem solved."

And we'll know it's Brianna doing it, trying to make me para-noid, I thought. Why would Brianna do that to me? I honestly thought she liked me, but now I wasn't so sure. I didn't even know if I could trust her. And if I couldn't trust her with something as simple as my medication, then what was to say she wasn't lying about looking into my case?

No, I couldn't let myself go off down that rabbit hole. At least not yet. Brianna was innocent until proven guilty. I, for one, knew all about that. I was going to have to find a way to give her the benefit of the doubt while at the same time not letting myself get my hopes up too much when she talked about my case.

"James?" Dr. Sellers said, pulling me out of my thoughts.

I realized I hadn't spoken since he had suggested the new plan. "Sorry. I was just thinking. Yes, that would work."

"Then that's what we'll do. For your next dose, take three of those and then throw the rest in the trash. I have sessions all day, but I will drop the correct pills off this evening, and we will check them all as we have discussed. Is that okay?"

I nodded. What choice did I have if I wanted to stop having hallucinations? I had to trust someone. I had once thought that someone was Brianna, but maybe I had been wrong, and it had been Dr. Sellers I should have been putting my trust in all along.

Or maybe it was time to finally start trusting myself and my own instincts. That was going to be much harder than anything I had ever done before. Much harder.

25

Three weeks had passed since Dr. Sellers changed the way my medication was dispensed to me, and true to my word, I kept my pills on my person at all times. The only time they weren't in my pocket was when I showered, and I always made sure to lock the bathroom door with my medication in there with me. I wasn't paranoid enough to think Brianna stood watching the house and would sneak in while I was showering and switch my meds. It had just become a habit to move the meds from my jeans pocket to the edge of the sink and then into the pocket of my pajama top, something I had never worn before, but did now simply for the pocket.

In that time, my meds had been correct, and I felt much more stable again now that I was taking my correct dosage each day. At that point, it probably seemed bizarre that I still didn't want to think that Brianna had been messing with my meds, messing with my head. It was the logical explanation, but it wasn't the only explanation. I hadn't mentioned my alternative theory to Dr. Sellers yet because I wanted to play it out a little longer and make sure there were no holes in my logic. I might have been the one to mess with my medication, and then, knowing that I would instantly be caught, I could have simply stopped doing it.

I knew it sounded lame, but I didn't want to think of Brianna as an enemy. Especially not after she had been so good to me. Despite that, I knew there was a better-than-average chance that she was responsible for my meds being tampered with, and while I still felt that fluttering in my stomach at the sight of her, it wasn't the same. I had to remind myself that a crush was one thing, but if I couldn't trust her—which I seemingly couldn't—then I couldn't let myself get too close.

Every time she had been around since Dr. Sellers told me to keep my medication on me, I had been hyper-aware of my meds in my pocket, and I kept touching the pocket whenever Brianna left the room, just to make sure they were still in there and she hadn't somehow managed to get them away to switch them. How she could have gotten my medication out of my front jeans pocket without me noticing her doing it, I don't know, but I needed to be certain, and that meant checking.

I also couldn't help thinking about what she had said about me perhaps being innocent. Had she really found evidence? Did she really believe that? I didn't think so anymore, because if she believed I was innocent, why was she trying to make me crazy? I figured she might be saying those things to try to get me on her side so that I was easier to manipulate. But if that was the case, what was her end game? What did she want to manipulate me into doing? She had never asked anything of me, and I couldn't think what I might be able to do that she wouldn't be able to do herself. All I knew was that I still had to keep my guard up, and wait to see if she dropped any sort of bombshell down the line. Something that would make me shudder at the thought of doing it, but something that I might be willing to do anyway if Brianna had molded my mind enough.

All these thoughts meant I could feel myself starting to edge toward an anxiety attack. I had to calm myself down; Brianna was due here any minute. The last thing I wanted was to have a mental breakdown in front of her and end up telling her why. I had to make more of an effort to focus on the good things I had going on. For example, if Brianna was responsible for messing with my meds, she now knew that wasn't possible anymore. I had come out on top with my sanity intact.

The doorbell rang. I took a deep, calming breath, and then I went to the door and opened it. Today, Brianna was wearing a yellow blouse over white capri pants, and it was hard not to notice her obvious attractiveness. Just like it was hard to ignore the butterflies in my stomach at the sight of her. But I couldn't think like that. I couldn't quite bring myself to think of her as the enemy, but I could no longer think of her as my cute friend. I had to keep it cool and professional and think of her as nothing but my probation officer.

Brianna stepped inside and went to the kitchen like she always did on her visits.

I shut the front door and hung back for a second, wondering if I would catch her in the act of looking through the kitchen cabinets for my medication. I waited for a count of twenty—long enough for her to start looking, but not long enough for her to have finished her search—and then I crept along the hallway as silently as I could. I stepped into the kitchen, ready to catch Brianna red-handed. Instead, I caught her sitting at the kitchen table and smiling at me as I came in.

Her smile faded into a frown when she saw me. "Are you okay? You seem—I don't know. A little off, I guess," she said.

"I have a headache," I lied as I sat opposite her.

She made a sympathetic clicking sound in the back of her throat. She shifted in her seat and crossed her legs, then put her hands on the table.

I quickly felt my pocket. My medication was still there, and she couldn't get it without her hands being beneath the table, so I felt safe for a moment.

"How have you been other than your headache?" Brianna asked.

"Fine, thank you. My medication is working well, and everything is just as it should be." I smiled when I said it, but I sensed it wasn't a very convincing smile. It sure didn't feel like a real smile.

Brianna smiled back, but it wasn't her usual happy smile that lit up her whole face. This smile seemed confused, like her lips were doing what they thought was required, but her heart wasn't in it. Was it because my smile had been weird, or was she pissed because she could no longer switch out my meds?

"Anything to report?" she asked.

I shook my head slowly as if I were thinking about it, but nothing had changed since this time last week when we'd spoken. "Like I said, everything is good. My bills are all being paid on time, I have a good handle on buying and preparing my food, my meds are working, and I am still having my weekly sessions with Dr. Sellers."

"And how do you feel those sessions are going?" Brianna asked. "Do you feel like they are helping you?"

This was new. She never normally asked about my therapy beyond making sure I hadn't missed any sessions.

"Dr. Sellers is helping me a lot. He's got my medication right for what feels like the first time in a long time. He's enabled me to see that my father's actions were only ever a reflection of him, that none of what he did to me was my fault."

I stopped, but then I realized I wanted to tell her everything. There was nothing here she could use against me, so why not? "And we tried a session of regression therapy. I'll be the first one to admit that I'm not in a hurry to repeat it, but it's helped me to know that my childhood memories are all still there. They're just locked away where I can't be harmed by them."

"Wow, that sounds brilliant," Brianna said. "Between you and me, you got extremely lucky with Dr. Sellers. He's one of the best therapists we use. Too many of them take shortcuts for state-mandated therapy, but Dr. Sellers actually cares about his patients."

"Yes, I get that impression," I said. "I think that's why I find myself opening up to him."

"And is that why you open up to me?" Brianna asked, looking down at the tabletop. "Because I care about you too, you know."

"I know," I said, my hand going to my jeans pocket and finding my pills still there.

When she spoke this way, she was so genuine. It was why

suspecting her was so hard. Again, I was left with a blank when I tried to think what sort of end goal she could have by manipulating me.

She looked back up from the table, her eyes holding mine for a moment. "So, tell me this, then, James. Why do I feel that you are acting strangely today? It seems like you don't really want me here. Have I done something to offend you?"

"No. You haven't done a thing." I felt guilty that I had made her feel uncomfortable and unwelcome, another feeling that was at odds with logic. *Oh, fuck logic*, I thought. *Listen to your gut. What does that say?* I knew what it said. Brianna cared about me. Maybe she even liked me as more than a friend. And there was no way this woman was trying to send me back to crazy town. "I'm sorry. I'm always a bit spaced when I have a headache."

I didn't like lying to her, but it was better than attempting to explain the truth when I didn't even really understand it myself right now.

"I have some news, but maybe I should leave it until next time when you're feeling a bit better?" Brianna said.

"No, no, I'm okay," I said. "Besides, you can't say something like that and then not tell me."

This time when I smiled at her, it felt real, and the smile I received in return was Brianna's usual smile. It faded slightly as she kept looking at me.

"It's not exactly good news, James," she said. "In fact, I might call it weird."

"Go on," I said, intrigued now.

"Well, I've been trying to find your mom. I thought you might want to rebuild some sort of relationship with her. Here's the thing, James. I can't find her."

"It's okay," I said. "Thank you for trying."

But it wasn't okay, and I was trying to hide my disappointment and confusion. Not so much at the fact that Brianna couldn't find my mom, but more at the fact that I had been expecting something bigger than that, but I didn't know what because my memories were all fuzzy on what had happened to Mom. Still, it was sweet that she had tried, and I didn't want her to think that I didn't appreciate it. It also forced me yet again to wonder how I had ever questioned whether or not Brianna was on my side.

"No, you don't understand," she said. "I don't mean I lost track of her trail. I mean I couldn't find a single trace of her since the last time she used an ATM when you were eleven. I have had two highly rated private investigators look into it, and both of them have come up empty, too."

I let that sink in, and then I locked eyes with Brianna, searching her face. She was telling me the truth right now. I was certain of it. And that meant only one thing.

My heart raced as I whispered, "I was right, wasn't I? My mom dying wasn't a delusion. It was true." I could barely contain my thoughts, and it caused another moment of confusion, and my brow furrowed. "But I was led to believe she had left because that was something else my father could blame me for."

"Yes, but there's more to it than that," Brianna said. "If she had died in an innocent manner, her death would have been recorded, and I would have found that record. And even if I didn't, one of my investigators would have. I am sorry, James, but your mom was never reported missing, dead, or any of it. She just ceased to exist. It makes me think perhaps your father had something to do with it."

I kept trying to make sense of what she was telling me.

"He blamed me for her death so that I would be so eaten up with guilt that I wouldn't ask any questions. He used my paranoia to keep his secret," I said, as the past started to click into place. "Which I suppose is why I'd always thought she died, but then Janet told me she had gone away, and that Dad blamed me for that, so I thought I'd always been wrong. Of course, Janet would have believed whatever he told her, so I guess in the end I just didn't know what the truth looked like."

"I can certainly understand you feeling that way," Brianna agreed. "The only problem is, I have no evidence of any wrongdoing whatsoever, and I don't know how to go about finding it, especially now that your dad has passed away. I could go to the police with my suspicions. I have a few friends on the force who would take me seriously, but I don't think I have enough for them to launch a murder investigation. Because, as painful as it is to consider, it is possible your mom *did* leave. Although I highly doubt it was because of you. Maybe she left because of how your father treated her, and she made sure she disappeared properly and couldn't be found."

"I know that's a possibility in theory, but it doesn't feel right to me," I said. "I don't think my mom would have up and left me with that monster. I don't even think she would have left Janet here with him, and Janet would have wanted to stay. But I get what you're saying. How do we prove that?"

"Exactly. Other than your sister, who I don't know would cooperate, you're perhaps the only person who can give us something to go on. If you can face trying, that is."

I nodded for her to go on. Whatever it was, I would do it because now everything was starting to make a certain sort of sense, and I didn't want to let this trail fade away without finding what it might lead to.

"So, try to ignore everything your father or Janet said about your mom not being around anymore. And then focus on the time she disappeared. I know you won't have the exact day—"

"Actually, I do," I interrupted her. "I have her journal. She never missed a day, so she went missing the day after the last entry she wrote."

"Okay," said Brianna. "That's good. Can you think of that day? I know it's hard, and I know your mind has buried these memories for a reason. So, if you don't think you're strong enough to cope with them yet, don't go digging too hard."

"It's okay. I can do it." I had to do it. I had to know what happened to my mom. I had to know if that bastard really had killed her.

I felt my stomach knotting as I forced my thoughts back to the last day I ever saw my mom. I felt a pain down the center of my head as my mind fought with itself, half of me needing to know the truth badly enough to risk the pain, the other half so intent on protecting me that it didn't care whether I ever learned the truth.

I could feel the memory tickling the edges of my mind, and I forced myself to move closer to it until I could reach out and grab it, and then suddenly, I had it, and it was all unfolding before me, every last nightmarish detail.

I felt a sharp pain in my stomach, a rush of nausea overtaking my body. I was covered in a sheen of sweat, and I could feel a panic attack threatening to engulf me. I couldn't let it, though. Not this time. Not when I was so close to the truth.

I screwed my eyes closed and balled my hands into fists.

They were so tight that my nails split the skin of my palms, but I barely registered the sting of the cuts.

Instead, I felt a different pain, a deep pain that took my breath away. And then, just like that, I took myself there. I was inside the memory of the last time I had seen my mom.

26

As the reality of the memory engulfed me, the panic attack hit me with its full force. I was too immersed to fight it—fighting it would mean I would have to come back to my present self, and I was so close to finding answers that I decided to let the panic attack happen. I told myself it wouldn't be as bad as usual; it would be like it was happening to someone else.

The decision made, I relaxed and stopped fighting. The last physical sensation I felt was lunging up from the table and lurching to the living room and half sitting, half collapsing onto the couch. I could feel my chest constricting as I wheezed, fighting for breath. My heart pounded so quickly that I thought it might explode, and I could feel the thumps of my pulse bouncing through my head and neck.

"James?" Brianna said as she sat down next to me. "Please don't do this to yourself."

I ignored her plea and plunged on, finally facing my memory, embracing it so that it became the present. As I slipped away, I felt warm arms wrap around me. They comforted me and made me feel safe, yet my hand moved to my pocket and patted it. My medication was still there.

I was sitting at the top of the stairs, reading a book. I liked sitting on the stairs—it meant that I got to avoid being in the living room, where my father most often resided when he wasn't working, and I also got to avoid being in my bedroom. I didn't mind being in my bedroom as such, but I was in constant fear of being locked inside. Also, I liked it on the stairs because I could hear what was going on in pretty much any part of the house without having to creep closer and risk being caught snooping.

Sitting there, I didn't just get bits of idle gossip—although that was fun, too—I got a heads-up if anyone was arguing, or if my father was in a particularly bad mood. Knowing these things in advance was important to my survival. If I knew my father was on the warpath, I could keep myself out of his way and avoid becoming a scapegoat, for the most part.

I turned the page and continued reading, engrossed in the story of Moby Dick. I had barely covered the first paragraph on the new page when I heard a scream that made my blood run cold. It was my mother's voice, and it was filled with pure terror. The screaming came from my father's wing of the house, and before I even had time to think about what I was doing, I was up and running toward his rooms.

As I ran, the scream came again, but this time, it was different. I could still hear the terror in it, but it was quieter, and I could also hear the shaky quality that pain could bring to a person's voice.

My mom must have fallen and hurt herself. She could be lying on the ground with a broken leg or something, and as much as I didn't want to see her hurt like that, I knew I couldn't just ignore her cries for help. And I wasn't about to go and get my father—he was likely to find a way to blame me for the accident and then waste time beating me instead of helping my mom.

I was in my father's wing now, and I could tell that the sounds were coming from his office. I was really glad that I hadn't gone to find my father. If he caught my mom in his private office, a room off-limits unless he summoned us, he wouldn't have helped her— he would have made her pain worse.

I reached the office door and paused. I could still hear my mom, her screams now quiet whimpers that somehow sounded even more pain-laden than before. I could also hear something else —a dull thudding sound.

I pushed the door open, and for a second, the world stood still. My mother stood before my father, cringing away from him, begging him with her eyes to leave her alone. My father, the very picture of rage, his face red, the veins in his neck standing out, raised his fist.

As time started to move again, my father slammed his fist down into my mom's face. The thudding sound came again and then the whimper as my mom's knees buckled and she tumbled to the floor. I knew then what I had been hearing. The thudding was the sound of that monster punching my mom in the face.

She was lying down now, and I wanted to beg her to get up. I wanted to scream at him to leave her alone, but nothing came out. My voice was as frozen in terror as the rest of me. I was shaking, my brain already trying to deny what I was seeing, trying to tell me that the streaks of blood on the floor were nothing more than rose petals, that my mom was just taking a nap, and that my father wasn't kicking her in the ribs.

Except he was. And this time, the sound that I heard wasn't a dull thud, but a brittle snapping sound. My mom screamed in agony, and that scream broke my paralysis.

I spoke up.

"Stop!" I shouted, taking a step into the room. "Leave her alone, you bastard!"

My father turned and stepped toward me, his face contorted like a demon, his eyes so full of rage he barely looked human.

I felt a warm rush of liquid on my thighs and smelled the acrid odor of ammonia as my father reached out for me.

And then I stood banging on the inside of my bedroom door. I had no recollection of how I came to be in my bedroom. All I remembered was my mom on the floor, my father kicking her, and then him advancing on me. Was it possible that all of that was nothing but a twisted nightmare?

The cold, damp patch on my crotch told me otherwise. It was no dream. It had all happened. After my father grabbed me, I didn't know what he did, but he obviously locked me in here. I didn't think he'd beaten me this time. I wasn't sore anywhere except the sides of my hands, and I thought that was probably from banging on the door, desperate for someone to let me out.

I rattled the doorknob, but of course, the door didn't open. Tears of fear and frustration ran down my face. How long had I been in there? Was I ever going to be set free? Was my mom okay?

I went back to banging the sides of my fists on the door. I watched in a sort of horrified fascination as each thump of my fists left behind a smear of blood. I must have been locked in here for a long time for my fists to be missing their skin that way.

I blinked and looked around. I was still in my father's house, but I was downstairs, and I was no longer a small child, but a fully grown man. I was back to myself, pulled out of my memories. The panic attack was over, but its aftermath had left my body shaking.

I slowly became aware of warm arms wrapped around me, a hand stroking my back, and a quiet whispering voice telling me over and over again that everything was going to be okay. Brianna must have held me through my panic attack, making sure I was alright.

I smiled slightly at the thought of her being there for me, and I wrapped my arms around her and clung to her tightly. I would have loved to stay that way forever, but of course, I knew that I couldn't. Brianna would think I had lost the plot if I refused to let go.

I straightened back up, and we released each other. I quickly tapped my pocket, relieved to find my pills were still there. Why wouldn't she have taken them when she had an easy chance? Perhaps because she knew there could be no doubt about who had taken them in that situation.

"Are you okay, James?" Brianna asked.

I nodded, although I wasn't sure if I was.

She reached out and took one of my hands in both of hers. She squeezed my hand, but then she didn't release it, she took it into her lap and held it between her warm palms.

"What did you see?" she asked me finally. "If you can bring yourself to talk about it, of course."

I didn't particularly want to talk about it, but I didn't want Brianna to think I was hiding something from her. If she wasn't stealing my pills and she was still on my side, then she might be able to help me if I told her the truth. If she was stealing my pills, I had to convince her that I wasn't onto her until I got more information about why she wanted to keep me ill.

"My father," I started. "He was beating my mom."

Brianna squeezed my hand again.

"He always beat my mom, I was used to seeing shit like that, but it never got any easier to watch, you know? Besides, this time it was different. It wasn't just a backhander or a shake that would rattle her head on her neck. This was a full-blown attack. It was brutal." I paused for a moment as I felt the panic starting to spread through me once more.

"It's okay," Brianna said. "If you don't want to tell me any more, I understand."

"No, no, it's not that. I want to tell you all that I remembered," I reassured her. "I just need a minute, that's all."

We sat quietly until I felt ready to go on.

"I wanted to make him stop, but I was frozen," I went on. "Eventually, I came to my senses when my mom was on the floor and my dad kicked her so hard, I heard one of her ribs crack. I called out for him to stop hurting her, and he came for me next." I paused again, fighting to slow down my breathing and ignore the fluttering palpitations in my chest.

"Oh, my God. No kid should have to see something like that," Brianna said. Tears were shining in her eyes.

I shrugged because I didn't know what else to do. In the midst of the horror of my memories, I wanted so badly to kiss Brianna, but I kept thinking about my pills; then I wondered what would happen if I kissed her and she didn't want me to. I forced away the desire for Brianna. I had more than enough messes in my life without creating my own new ones.

I told her how I had lost a whole chunk of time, but when I came back to myself, I was locked in my room and pounding on the door. "Nothing on my body hurt except my hands, which made me think that I had been there a while and that my father had refrained from hurting me. My mind shut it down before I got out of the room, so I don't know what happened next."

"What do you think happened?" Brianna asked, her voice so quiet I had to strain to hear her.

"Knowing what I know now, I think he killed her and

told people she left because of me so they wouldn't be suspicious that she was missing," I said.

"That's what I think happened, too," Brianna agreed, her voice louder and slightly surer of herself now. "And I think that so-called fake memory you have of your mom being dead wasn't so much a fake memory as it was a tiny fragment of the memory of what actually happened."

"I don't know how to feel about this," I said, sighing deeply. "It's kind of a relief to know my mom didn't hate me enough to leave the whole family because of me. But it's awful in another sense because she died, was murdered, and we didn't even have a funeral or do anything to say goodbye to her."

"Maybe you and I can have a ceremony for her once you've finished your probation," Brianna said.

"I'd like that," I said with a smile. I thought for a moment, and the smile faded. "So, what happens next? I mean, it's good to have some closure about what happened to my mom, but it's not like it changes anything. I'm not being accused of her murder, and even if we could prove that my dad murdered her, what use would it be? He's dead. They can't punish him."

"I know," Brianna breathed. "If we found some concrete evidence, your dad could still be found guilty after his death, but what would that achieve? I just wanted you to know that she didn't leave because of you. I genuinely believe your mom loved you and Janet, and that she was too scared of your father to do much to protect you both."

I nodded. That sounded about right, except that Janet had never needed protection from my father. Not really. She enjoyed the attention she got from him. Or maybe she didn't.

Maybe she just went along with it so she didn't get a beating, and maybe my mom knew that.

"The thing is, I don't think that's the only time you've been blamed for something someone else has done," Brianna said.

"Oh, it isn't," I agreed. "I don't remember much of my childhood, as you know, but what I do remember of it, I could tell you a hundred things Janet did that broke the rules, and that I got the blame for."

"That's not what I meant," Brianna said. "I think all siblings lay the blame on each other. This is more serious than that."

"Go on," I urged when she stopped talking and looked down into her lap.

She looked surprised when she saw our clasped hands lying there, but she didn't pull away. Instead, she looked me in the eye and kept her grip on my hand. "I don't think you killed Terri. I think whoever did it knew enough about you to know you were the scapegoat for things in the past, and they knew that they could manipulate you into believing that this bad thing was your fault. They perhaps didn't bank on you being found catatonic and ending up in the hospital, though."

"Are you serious?" I asked. "You believe I didn't hurt Terri?"

"Yes," Brianna said, without hesitation. "But again, the problem is, there's no evidence of what happened."

Brianna believed that I wouldn't hurt anyone, let alone Terri. There was no way this woman was fucking with my medication. Unless she had a sick plan to drive me nuts by convincing me of my innocence and then dropping the truth on me later.

But that didn't feel right.

Why would Brianna do that? Why would she be doing any of this if she didn't genuinely believe in me? Surely, she wouldn't want to sit here and eat lunch with me, hold my hand, or chat for hours after her shift had ended if she thought I was capable of murder.

"It's enough for me that you believe me," I said.

"No, that shouldn't be enough. The very system that is meant to protect innocent people has devastated your life," Brianna said, and I could hear the anger at this injustice in her voice.

I didn't reply because I didn't know what to say. How was I supposed to tell her that, in some ways, being sent to the hospital and away from my father had likely saved my life?

"And even if you don't care about that, think of this: Whoever killed Terri is still out there. They're mocking you, mocking the system, mocking Terri. And they might kill again, they might have already killed again ... and we might be the only people who can even attempt to find out who they are and stop them."

I didn't care if some stranger was out there laughing at me. But I did care if they were laughing at Terri. And I certainly cared if they were going to hurt someone else. It would make me guilty if I knew there was someone out there who might kill, and I just sat back and did nothing about it.

"I hear you," I said. "But what the hell can we do about any of this? We have no real evidence to get the case reopened, and I still have no idea what happened between my walking to the river and coming to in the hospital. Plus, I can't think of anyone who might have wanted Terri dead."

Brianna squeezed my hand again, as if in encouragement. "You have to keep trying, James. Keep delving into your past and forcing yourself to remember, even when it hurts so much you don't think you can do it anymore. That's the only chance we've got of discovering the truth of what happened."

"Even if I can do that, it's not evidence," I countered. "You said so yourself. A jury won't believe me. They'll think I'm just saying whatever it takes to get away with murder."

"I know," she replied. "We will have to hope you remember something that could be used as evidence."

"That's a big hope," I said.

"Yes, it is. But it's all we've got."

27

I kept flicking through the pages of my journal. Where the hell did my money go? Since I had opened the account that I had given Janet access to, I had noted everything I spent from it. When I started, I didn't even know why I was doing it, but it felt like the right thing to do. Now I was glad I had, as it gave me some answers.

The amounts for each bill were all neatly printed in the journal on the days they came out of the account. There was also the time I treated myself to a new mattress.

I had added up all of those figures, and I should have been left with well over $4,000 in the account, but there was nothing in it. In fact, it had been ten dollars overdrawn, which I had fixed by calling my lawyer and having an extra ten dollars transferred. He had asked me if I wanted to stop Janet's access, when I had explained to him that money was going missing from the account, but I said no.

I wanted to give Janet a chance to explain. Maybe she had once again decided I was incapable of looking after money and had siphoned it off into another account to keep it safe from me. Or maybe she had had some sort of emergency and needed the money.

I knew I was right about the money going missing. I had double-checked my figures more than enough times before I had called my lawyer, and then I had him double-check my accounting. I would have to stand my ground with Janet if she tried to play innocent.

I picked up my cell phone and scrolled through my contacts until I found Janet's name. I selected it, hit call, and waited for her to pick up.

"What is it?" Janet said, rather than hello, as she took my call.

She sounded tired, and I knew she often got irritable when she was tired, so I steeled myself for her to start moaning at me.

"Hi, Janet, how are you?" I started, unable to stop myself from getting a dig in about her impolite greeting.

She sighed loudly. "I'm busy, James, that's how I am. Seriously, what do you want?"

"Well, I'm a little bit concerned about money going missing from my account. More than $4,000 is missing, which I know I haven't spent. I wondered if you knew anything about that."

"Yes. I spent it," Janet said, sounding surprised that I had even asked her about it.

"You spent it?" I repeated. "So, essentially you stole it."

"Oh, don't be so dramatic," Janet snapped. "And stop being so miserly with our money, for goodness' sake."

It wasn't lost on me that she had just described my money as *our* money, but it didn't seem important enough to argue about. But stealing money from my account was different. I was almost certain that if I hadn't called to confront her, she never would have mentioned it unless it was to say I must have spent it and she needed more control over me.

"I would hardly say I was being miserly, Janet. If you think back to the conversation we had the day I gave you access to that account, I offered you half of everything and you refused, saying that you didn't need it and I did. You said you only wanted access to my account so that you could make sure I was being responsible with my money."

"Where do you get these fanciful notions from?" Janet said with a soft laugh. "That conversation never happened, and you must know that somewhere deep down. You said you were adding me onto that account because I deserved the money as much as you did. I argued with you at first, but you insisted, and now what? You're mad at me for doing what you wanted me to do in the first place?"

Was that what had happened? No, it couldn't have been, because if it was, why would I have even opened that account? I would simply have given her half, and I wouldn't have needed an additional account. I wasn't going to let it go, but I also was not going to have the argument with Janet until I was absolutely certain I was right.

It had never even occurred to me the conversation might go this way. The worst thing was, if Janet had just said she had spent the money and not tried to make me out to be the bad guy, I would have let it go. But I was getting damned sick of taking the blame for everything bad everyone around here did, and I wasn't going to do it anymore.

I flicked back through my journal, trying my best not to get stressed out as I searched for the evidence I needed. I knew roughly when we'd had the conversation, and I soon found the right day.

"James? What are you doing? I'm busy here, and if you've

only called to have a go at me and make me out to be a liar and a thief, I'd really like to get on."

"Give me a minute," I stated. It came out firm, more like a demand than a request.

Janet sighed, but she stayed on the line.

I found the entry and skimmed through it until I found the relevant part. I read it; then I read it again to be sure I was right before I spoke up.

I've finally spoken to Janet about the inheritance. She insists that she doesn't want or need the money and that she only asked about being put on my bank account so she could be sure I'm not wasting money or being taken advantage of.

I am kind of pissed at her for always assuming the worst of me, but I'll pick my battles, and this is one I can do without. I am going to set up a billing and everyday expenses account and add her to that and see if she keeps her word.

"Janet, you're lying. I have proof of the conversation we had. You know what was said, and I feel like you're trying to gaslight me," I said, confident now that I had the proof I had been looking for.

"Oh, that's a good one," Janet sneered. "In case you forgot, you've just got out of the fucking nuthouse. I don't need to make you crazy. You got there all on your own."

I bit my tongue. I didn't want to take her bait. No, I was not falling for any more of her shit. When I was sure that I could say what I needed to say calmly and rationally, I took a final deep breath and forced myself to keep my voice even and reasonable as I spoke.

"Janet, you had your chance, and you've chosen to use my generosity against me. I will be revoking your access to that account, and when the whole estate's value is finalized, I will see that you get half of the money, just like I originally told you I would," I said.

"But if you do that, who will oversee your spending and make sure you're doing okay?" Janet asked.

"I will," I replied. "Because, believe it or not, I'm not the one who has frittered away $4,000 with no explanation. I am more than capable of taking care of my own finances."

"Oh, James, that's amazing. I'm so proud of you," Janet said, her voice suddenly warm and enthusiastic.

I tried to remember the step I had missed to bring us from our argument to this point, but I couldn't. I was genuinely starting to think I wasn't the only one with mental health issues. Maybe Janet was schizophrenic or bipolar.

"Umm, what?" I said after a few moments, when I still hadn't managed to make any sense of what Janet had said. I must have misheard her.

"I'm so proud of you," Janet repeated. "Look, I'm sorry I had to trick you and lie to you, but I needed to know for my own peace of mind that you would notice if your money started to go missing, and you did. And you stayed calm and rational while you confronted me."

"Are you saying this was all some sort of test?" I asked.

"Yes, I suppose I am," Janet admitted. "But don't worry because you passed with flying colors. It's up to you whether you want to take me off your account, but either way, I don't want a penny of the inheritance, and I certainly don't want half. Let's call the $4,000 my share, huh?"

"Yeah, sure," I said, still trying to get my head around what she was telling me. "The $4,000 is yours to keep."

"Thank you, darling," Janet trilled. "You see? This is why I am always on your side, even when no one else is. We just get each other, don't we?"

"Yeah, I suppose we do," I said, although I wasn't sure that was true at all.

Half of the time, I didn't know what the hell was going on in Janet's head, and even when I did, I never fully understood her motivations. Still, it was easier to agree with her.

She was still going on about how she had my back. I didn't really think tricking me that way was the action of someone who had my back, but I was getting tired, and I didn't want another argument.

"I'm sorry, but I have to go; my dinner is almost ready," I lied. I hadn't even decided what I wanted to eat, let alone started cooking it.

"Oh, I'll let you go, then," Janet said. "Bye, James, take care."

I ended the call and took a deep breath, which I let out slowly. I would never understand Janet. I shook my head to clear my thoughts, then opened up my email and began drafting one for my lawyer.

Hi, Larry,

I hope my email finds you well. I have a quite urgent matter I would appreciate you taking care of for me. As I'm sure you recall, we recently set up a new account that my sister has access to.

After some additional developments, would it be

possible to put some sort of tracking on her login? I don't want the login to be blocked, nor do I want it to show up as anything different to Janet. I just want to be informed any time she logs in to the account, so I can keep an eye on her movements.

Thank you in advance,
James Owens

As I hit send, I nodded to myself. It would be ideal if I could have a way to track Janet's movements on my bank account because I had a feeling that, despite her words today, she would still be all over it.

I had barely covered two steps when the lights went off. With the heavy velvet drapes closed, I was plunged into darkness.

I told myself not to panic, but it was hard not to. My heart was racing, and I could scarcely breathe as I edged forward. The lights came back on, flickered twice, then solidified. I gave a shaky laugh. The electricity in this place was probably as old as I was, and it had decided to have a moment. Instead of creeping around the house in a state of panic, I should be focused on calling an electrician to come over.

Still, the electricity didn't explain the movements of my oven gloves from one room to another, or the crashing sound.

After leaving the dining room, I continued my search upstairs. I forced myself to go into my father's wing, needing to get it over with first. I peered into his bedroom; nothing. His bathroom; nothing. I took a deep breath and opened his office door. I expected to feel a rush of emotion as I saw the place I had recently remembered with such horror, but I felt nothing. Maybe I was finally broken. And maybe that wasn't such a bad thing.

I backed out of the office and closed the door. There was nothing to see there.

I made my way back to the stairs, passing them, and moving into the side of the house with my room in it. I was peering into the unused guest rooms when I first heard what sounded like someone whispering. I ignored it, knowing it had to be my imagination.

I could still hear it, even when I told myself I couldn't, so I stopped to listen properly. It sounded like multiple people having a whispered conversation, but I couldn't make out any words. I had no idea what the sound could be, but I knew it wasn't really anyone whispering. There was no one here—I was sure of it now, although I was still checking the last few rooms.

Finally, my search was complete. I could be confident that I was the only person in the house. I went back downstairs and checked that the front and back doors were locked. They were, and the keys dangled from the locks where I had left them. I went back to the kitchen. I noticed that the whispering sound seemed to follow me, and wondered if maybe I was developing tinnitus or something similar.

I went to the living room and collected my oven gloves; then I came back to the kitchen and slipped them on. I pulled the casserole from the oven, breathing in the savory waft of air that came from the oven as I opened it. I put the casserole down on the side and scooped some onto a plate, figuring I'd save the rest for the following day. I sat at the table and dug my fork into a piece of sausage. I blew on it a few times and put it in my mouth.

Instantly, I knew something wasn't right. The sausage itself tasted okay, but the gravy had a bitter taste and a strange, almost powdery texture. I stopped chewing and spat the mouthful into a napkin. My heart raced again as I poked at the casserole with my fork. I knew it was impossible that my food had been tampered with, but I couldn't help but think it had been poisoned or drugged. How else would gravy get such a taste and texture?

Was I being paranoid, and there was actually nothing wrong with the food? Either way, I wasn't about to risk it. I had more than enough problems to contend with. I stood up and scraped the plate into the trash, followed by the leftovers I had planned to eat tomorrow.

I ran hot water into the sink and added dish soap; then I began to wash the dishes. I didn't think I would be able to eat now, but my stomach growled as I worked. When I finished the dishes, I went to the fridge and looked inside, but instantly, I closed it again. If the casserole had somehow been tampered with, then anything in my fridge could have been tampered with, too. It was easy enough to open a Tupperware or pull something out of an open packet.

Instead, I opened the freezer and pulled out a ready meal. I checked over the box and the carton inside several times until I was confident it was untouched; then I read the instructions and set the meal in the microwave. While I waited, I dried the dishes I had just washed and put the plate and cutlery back out on the table, ready for my new dinner.

If I looked at the situation logically, I was sure I could find an explanation. I thought for a moment. The only scenario I could come up with was that someone had sneaked into the house earlier and hidden themselves away somewhere. They had then moved my oven gloves to distract me, made the crashing sound to attract my attention, and then, while I was searching the house, they sneaked into the kitchen and tampered with my dinner.

The beeping of the microwave interrupted my theorizing. Once more, I sat down at the table, and this time I poured macaroni and cheese onto my plate. I began to eat it. There was no bitterness, no powdery feel. It was hardly a culinary delight, but at least I felt safe eating it.

I went back to my theory as I chewed. While it did make sense in a way, there were still so many unanswered questions. Like, who would do such a strange thing? And why?

No, it couldn't be that. There was just no reasonable explanation.

So that meant it was either something supernatural, like Janet had suggested, or I was more paranoid now than I had ever been. Usually when I was being paranoid, everything had a sheen across it, like it was too shiny, but this felt real right down to the most mundane details. It was dull enough to be the truth.

But was I ready to believe that my house was haunted? Wasn't that as crazy as believing that someone broke in just to freak me out? I sighed. I wasn't getting anywhere with these questions. Maybe this should remain a mystery. I was taking my medication, I hadn't been poisoned, and I would just have to try to put everything else out of my mind.

As I raised the last forkful of macaroni and cheese, I paused. My mouth dropped open in shock. "What the fuck?"

The table I was sitting at was moving. It was rattling on the floor, as though it were involved in an earthquake, but nothing else in the room moved. I wasn't being paranoid now. There was no way in hell I was imagining this. I could see the table moving, hear its legs tapping the floor as they came up and then back down again.

I pressed my hand flat on the table, and it stopped moving. I lifted my hand away slowly, and it stayed down. Crazy or not, I was becoming more open to the idea of this all being something supernatural. I didn't believe for a second that it was my mom—she wouldn't come back and try to scare me. Her presence would be warm and friendly, just like it was when she was alive. I guessed it could be my father—he would take great delight in trying to scare me— but whatever it was, it didn't feel malevolent enough to be my father.

trampling through shrubs and undergrowth until I reached the edge of the grounds. I would find a hotel, I decided. I had no money on me, but maybe, if I could contact my lawyer from the hotel, he would help with funds.

I was only one step from leaving the property when I remembered my stupid ankle bracelet. It was well past my curfew, and if I left the property now, I would be arrested for violating parole. I could go to prison. And I had a hard time believing that any judge would buy my story about what had driven me from the house. Even Brianna might think I was lying.

I couldn't leave, and I certainly couldn't bring myself to go back into the house. I didn't know what I was going to do. My meds were kicking in hard again now that the adrenaline was leaving me, and I could barely keep my eyes open, let alone devise a sensible plan.

I backed slowly away from the front gate, my mind still sharp enough to make sure I didn't get arrested. I felt something catch the back of my ankle, but I was too slow to right myself, and before I knew it, I was falling. I landed in a tangle of twigs, right in the middle of some sort of shrub. Sharp pieces dug into my back, my ass, the tops of my legs. But I noticed it was warmer than it was on the outside of the shrub. I decided to stay where I had landed for a second, until I was a bit warmer.

Within seconds I knew I had made a mistake. Lying down in the warmth of the middle of the shrub combined with my sedative to send me right to the edge of sleep. I told myself I had to get up. I could maybe go and sleep in the garage or something. But no amount of telling myself what I needed to do was enough to make me do it. My body was no longer obeying my commands.

My eyes began closing, and I forced them open, but I didn't have the energy to do any more than that. The garage might as well have been in another city for how far away it felt, and when my eyes started closing again, I had no strength left to open them.

Instead, I used the last bit of wakefulness I had left to snuggle down deeper in the shrubbery, ignoring the scratches from its little sharp branches, just wanting to be hidden from the house. I managed to force one eye halfway back open to check whether the shrub concealed me and the house from each other. Satisfied that it did, I breathed a sigh of relief and stopped fighting my meds. I let my eyes close, and when sleep came over me in a wave, I didn't fight it; I rode it deep down into the oblivion of darkness.

29

A hand touched my shoulder, and I jumped awake. I knew instantly I wasn't in my bed—whatever I was lying on was hard and bumpy, and I was freezing cold. I reached for the duvet but found nothing.

"James?" a voice said. "Are you alright? What are you doing out here?"

Out here? What did that even mean? And who was out here with me?

As I sat up, the events of last night came flooding back to me—fleeing from the ghostly happenings inside the house, remembering my curfew at the last minute, and finally, curling up in a shrub, too exhausted to feel the cold or anything at that point.

"James," the voice said again, and I realized that it was real and that it belonged to Brianna.

"I'm okay," I told her. "I just ..." I trailed off. I didn't know what I had been about to say. Instead of trying to form words, I focused on taking action. I pushed myself to my feet, disentangling myself from the shrubbery until I was standing up free and clear of leaves and twigs, although I was sure a few still clung to me.

"What happened?" Brianna asked. "Why are you out here?"

I knew I had to tell her something. She wasn't going to believe I just fancied a night sleeping in a bush. I decided I might as well tell her the truth. It probably didn't sound much more believable, but it had happened, so if Brianna didn't believe me, that was on her. At least I wouldn't have to feel bad about lying to her.

"Honestly, I'm not completely sure what happened," I said. "At the time, when it was happening, I was convinced my house was haunted. Now, I know that sounds crazy, but I have no rational explanation for it, either. There was banging and footsteps and laughter, and a voice saying my name over and over. The voice was the worst. It kept echoing back to me, and I thought I would go mad, my own name echoing all around me and inside my head." I stopped talking for a moment as the feeling of panic began to grip me once more.

Brianna put a warm hand on my cold arm. "It's okay," she said quietly. "Let's get you inside."

She took a few steps toward the house, but I hung back. I didn't think I was ready to go in there. I didn't think I would ever be.

Brianna paused and looked back at me. She held her hand out to me, and, reluctantly, I took it. Even as she led me toward the house of horrors, I couldn't help but be conscious of the feeling of her hand in mine and how our skin touching sent shivers through my whole body.

"Why didn't you go back inside once you'd calmed down?" Brianna asked.

"The combination of the spent adrenaline and the sedatives I'd taken knocked me clean out," I said. "I almost left the grounds; then at the last minute, I remembered about being tagged. I think that spike in adrenaline was the last thing my body could handle. I passed out where I landed, and I stayed that way until you came along."

"I'm so glad I looked for you. I know I'm early for our appointment, so you wouldn't have been in any trouble if you had been out somewhere, but the front door was ajar, so I figured you were maybe doing a bit of weeding or something."

I opened my mouth to respond, but I noticed we were almost back at the front door, and I closed it again. I felt sweat erupt over my body, and my breathing became ragged. I felt my hand tighten on Brianna's, but I made a conscious effort not to squeeze too hard.

She didn't try to pull her hand away. Instead, she smiled at me. "Come on, James. I swear it'll be okay."

The last thing I wanted to do was go back into that house. But it was bad enough that Brianna had found me in a bush in the garden, without me refusing to go inside as well and having a total meltdown in front of her.

I swallowed hard, nodded, and willed my feet to carry me forward. Brianna led me inside, and I breathed out a sigh of relief. The feeling of being watched, that intense, horrible feeling from last night, had gone, and the house felt normal once again.

I must have imagined it. That was the only explanation. How could a place feel so toxic one moment and so peaceful the next? I wasn't sure how I felt. Was it better to think that my house was haunted by a spirit who seemed to want to break me? Or was it better to think that I was perfectly safe from supernatural entities, but that my mind was breaking?

Brianna led me down the hallway and pushed open the kitchen door. She gasped. "What the fuck?"

I wanted to know what she had seen to get that kind of reaction, but she was blocking the small gap she had made.

"I'm sorry about the language," she said as she glanced over her shoulder at me. "But seriously, James, you weren't kidding about what happened, were you?"

"No," I managed to reply. I cleared my throat and went on. "So, does that mean you believe me?"

Brianna shrugged. "I would love to find a rational explanation for this, but unless you're lying to me, which I don't think for a second that you are, I can't imagine what could have happened in here."

She finally pushed the door far enough open so that I, too, could see into the room. My jaw dropped at the state of my kitchen. I had lived through last night, and I still wasn't expecting the level of destruction I saw. Plates, cups, bowls, and glasses were smashed all over the floor. On top of the smashed pieces, milk and broken raw eggs ran. My cupboards were all open, and some of the contents had spilled out into the mess. The drawers were at various levels of open, except for the cutlery drawer, which was on the floor, its contents spread across the floor, adding to the chaos.

"Why do you believe me?" I blurted out.

"Don't you want me to believe you?" Brianna asked.

"Of course I do. But I was here for this last night, and even I was starting to wonder if I had dreamed it," I said.

"Firstly, I believe you because you've never lied to me before, and I'm hoping you aren't going to start now.

Secondly, look at this mess. How could anyone create this much havoc without being covered in eggs and milk and God knows what else?" She paused and gave me a half-smile. "The only things you're covered in are mud and leaves."

I looked down at myself. "I should go and shower. Why don't you wait in the living room?"

"You go ahead. I'll start cleaning up."

I shook my head, ready to protest.

But Brianna turned and put her finger over my lips. "Really, it's fine."

The feeling of her finger on my lips sent shivers running through my body. I was taken aback by the undisguised lust on Brianna's face as she looked at me. I had always thought the attraction I felt for Brianna only went one way. Now I thought I might have been wrong about that.

I stepped back slightly.

Brianna's hand fell away from my mouth, but her eyes stayed firmly fixed on mine.

I wanted to look away. Needed to look away. But I had already moved back a step. That had taken all the willpower I had left, and I couldn't bring myself to break our eye contact, too. That was going to have to be on Brianna.

She stayed in place, her eyes searching my face.

If she didn't look away soon, I wasn't going to be able to stop myself from kissing her. I had kept my feelings for Brianna at bay because she had never given me such a clear sign that she wanted me. But now she had, and if I didn't make a move, I knew she would think I didn't want her. My thoughts started to tumble, and I was frozen to the spot, unsure of what to do.

I was saved from having to decide when Brianna's cell phone beeped loudly in her pocket, making us both jump.

Brianna laughed awkwardly. "Sorry," she said as she retrieved her phone.

"It's okay," I said, meaning it. "Make yourself at home while I go and shower."

I turned and hurried away before she could respond because, in my mind, I could see her asking if she could join me in the shower and me saying yes and her in my arms, my mouth on hers. But I couldn't let that happen. Now that I wasn't pinned by her gaze, I remembered why I couldn't. I had to keep her at arm's length in case she was the one who was stealing my pills.

The idea seemed more ridiculous the more I pondered it, but it was still the only rational explanation I had come up with.

I sighed as I went into my bedroom. I pulled the pills out of my pocket and checked them again. They were all there, exactly as they should be. I took out the ones I needed to take first thing in the morning and placed them on the bed. Then I put the box on top of my chest of drawers.

I picked up my morning pills and went into the bathroom with them, placing them on the small shelf over the sink. I peeled off my dirty clothes and put them in the clothes hamper in the corner. I looked in the mirror above the sink as I brushed my teeth. I was a little pale, but otherwise okay. It was hard to believe that it was less than twelve hours after I had been terrified out of my house by ... well, by something.

I let go of the thought. If I didn't, I was going to make myself crazy.

I finished brushing my teeth, and then I took my pills

and started to run the shower. Once the water was hot, I stepped under the spray. I turned up my face, letting the water hit my skin like small needle pricks. It felt refreshing, and I stayed that way for a while before I washed my hair and body.

I rinsed off; then I stood beneath the spray once more, enjoying the feeling of the water on my skin. Eventually, I turned the shower off and grabbed a towel. I felt so much better now, energized, almost invigorated, and I told myself that, no matter what happened, I wasn't going to let this stupid house scare me again.

I finished rubbing my hair dry, wrapped the damp towel around my waist, and headed back to my bedroom. The door was slightly ajar. I was sure that I had left it closed. Steeling myself, I remembered the promise I had just made to myself, and I took a deep breath and opened the door wider.

I was waiting for something to grab me, or for the obscene laughter and whispering to start up again as I entered the room, but, instead, I saw Brianna. She stood with her back to me, looking out the window. Instinctively, I looked at the chest of drawers where I had left my pills. They were still there, exactly as I had left them.

"Brianna?" I said softly. "What are you doing up here?"

Brianna turned around and smiled. I felt her eyes roaming over my bare chest, and I knew that my towel wasn't hiding how hard I was, yet I didn't care. I wasn't embarrassed or ashamed.

"I missed you," Brianna said, her voice low and husky. "Is that okay?"

I nodded, not quite ready to trust my voice to sound normal.

Brianna smiled again, and then she walked toward me. She didn't stop even when the gap between us was almost closed. She reached out and hooked her hand into my towel and pulled me roughly against her, and then she tilted her head up, and her lips found mine.

I wrapped my arms around her, holding her close, kissing her every bit as hungrily as she kissed me. I could taste the sweetness of her lips, smell the coconut scent of her hair. She was into me and on me. She was consuming me whole, and I loved it.

Brianna pulled away before I wanted our kiss to end. For a second, I thought I had done something wrong, that I had somehow misread the signals. But then I saw the smile on her face, the way her lips curled up at the sides. She looked me in the eye as she pulled her top over her head, only breaking our eye contact for the seconds it covered her face. Still looking at me, she reached behind and opened her skirt, letting it fall to the floor and then kicking it away.

She stood before me in a matching black lace bra and panties. I reached for her, and she shook her head, giggling and dancing away. I couldn't help but smile as she undid her bra and slipped it down her arms. She teased me with it before dropping it to the floor, and this time when I lunged for her, I caught her and pulled her into my arms once more.

Brianna allowed me to hold her, and as we kissed, she walked me toward my bed. I felt it hit the back of my legs, and I stopped. Brianna reached down and pulled my towel away, throwing it onto the floor with the rest of her clothes. She moaned as her hand ran up the length of my cock, and I moaned with her, her touch awakening me in ways I had forgotten I could be awake.

Brianna put her hands on my chest and pushed me.

Caught unaware, I went to take a step back, but found that I couldn't because of the bed. I fell backward onto my ass on the bed. Brianna grinned down at me. She pushed her panties down and kicked them away, and then she climbed onto the bed, straddling me.

This time, there was no stopping for either of us. We were a tangle of limbs, our hands and mouths kissing and caressing, groping and nibbling. When I knew I wasn't going to be able to hold myself back any longer, I slipped inside Brianna, and we thrust our way to a mutual orgasm that left me feeling heavy and sated and utterly delicious.

Afterward, we held each other as our breathing leveled out. I tried to think of something to say, but the truth was, the situation needed no words, and I just relaxed. I heard Brianna's breathing deepen, and I knew she had fallen asleep. I closed my eyes, snuggled closer, and drifted into sleep beside her.

I WOKE up and stretched and yawned. I winced slightly as I opened my eyes and the sunlight streaming in the window got to me. I rolled onto my side so that the sun was behind me, and that was when I saw that the other side of the bed was now empty. I looked at the floor and saw her clothes were gone.

I wondered lazily if she'd left me a note somewhere saying when she would be back. I understood that she probably had other appointments to deal with today, but surely, she would be back tonight. She couldn't have walked away after what we had just shared. Even if she thought it was a mistake, she would want to tell me that.

The thought fizzled out and my heart sank when I glanced in the direction of my chest of drawers and saw that my medication was gone. I shook my head, refusing to believe it, even while knowing that I had no other choice. How could I not believe it when I could see it right there in front of me? I still had to be certain, though, so I got up, went to the bathroom, and looked around. I hadn't left my medication in there, like I had been hoping. There was only one hope left, and even as I went through the laundry hamper and found my dirty jeans, I knew my medication wasn't going to be in the pocket. I was right.

My pills were gone and so was Brianna.

I clung to one last hope as I went back to my bedroom and got dressed. Could Brianna be downstairs? Could she have woken up, decided to make us lunch, and thought I might want my pills with food? I knew it was ridiculous. Even as long shots went, it was unrealistic at best. But it gave me something to cling to, so I went downstairs. I called Brianna's name and got no answer.

I looked into the kitchen. The only sign she had been here at all, and wasn't a figment of my imagination, was the fact that the room was spotless. She had cleared up the mess. I went to the window and looked out. Brianna's car was gone. That confirmed it. There was no more hope, no more what-if. She had left.

Brianna had seduced me so that she could sneak my pills away. But why did she want to play mind games? And why had she done it, when it was so obvious that she had taken my pills?

I had no answers to those questions, but I couldn't help wondering if there was something more going on. On the surface, it was something that only had one rational explanation, yet so many irrational things had happened since I came back to the house that I couldn't help but still not fully accept it.

Despite that, I knew I had to accept it. And so, when I called my therapist and asked for some extra pills, I told him I had accidentally dropped the box into the garbage disposal. I didn't know why I was protecting the woman who had seduced me, played mind games with me, used me, but something told me it was the right thing to do, and I was going to listen to my gut.

It had now been over twenty-four hours since we had sex, and I still hadn't heard from Brianna. I had tried calling her, but her cell phone went straight to voicemail. I didn't want to call her office because I knew that those calls were recorded, and I certainly wasn't going to embarrass myself by having a permanent record of my rejection saved somewhere.

So I tried to put Brianna out of my mind and concentrate on the movie I was supposed to be watching. I had no idea what was going on, and I would have gone to bed if it weren't for the fact that it was barely nine o'clock. I picked up the remote control and began flicking absent-mindedly through the channels.

I jumped to my feet when the doorbell rang, dropping the remote onto the couch cushion beside me, and leaving the TV playing a rerun of *Friends*. I hurried to the door, sure it was going to be Brianna with an explanation for everything. I needed to know that I had been wrong, that she wasn't playing mind games with me.

I pulled the door open and frowned at who I saw standing there.

I saw not Brianna, but a police officer and a man in a

dark suit who I assumed to be some sort of detective, likely the police officer's boss.

"Um, hi," I said, unsure what else to say.

"James Owens?" one of the men said.

I nodded.

"I'm Officer Peters, and this is Detective Lapley. May we come in?"

"I ... Yes," I said, standing aside and letting them enter.

They nodded to me as they passed by, and Officer Peters took off his hat.

"Go on through to the living room, second door on the left."

The men followed my instructions, and I closed the front door and followed them. I debated offering them a cup of tea or coffee, but I wanted to know why they were here first. I had done my time. I didn't need police officers coming to my door to check up on me.

"What can I do for you?" I asked.

I picked up the remote control and muted the TV. I motioned for the men to take a seat, and they sat on either end of the couch, and I took the armchair.

"When did you last see Brianna Caldwell?" Officer Peters asked me.

I had certainly not expected that question. I mean, sleeping with your probation officer might be against the rules, but surely it wasn't illegal.

"Yesterday," I said.

I was careful to answer the question without giving more away than I had to.

"She came to visit you, correct?" Officer Peters said.

"Yes. She's my probation officer," I said.

I was sure that wasn't giving too much away. They must

already be aware of that. Why else would they be here if they didn't at least know that much?

"What time did she leave here?" Peters asked.

"I don't know," I said.

It was true. I had no idea. I had been asleep when she sneaked out. But I was nervous, and I felt like my nerves were showing. I was conscious that being visibly nervous might make me sound as though I were lying.

"You don't know?" he echoed.

"No," I said. "I don't mean to be rude, Officer, but do you note the time of every little detail of every day in case someone asks you about it later?"

"Listen, Mr. Owens," Detective Inspector Lapley said. It was the first time he had spoken, and Officer Peters made no effort to interrupt him, confirming my earlier notion that he was in charge. "I suggest you try harder to remember the details. Brianna Caldwell is missing, and your house is her last known location."

30

"Brianna is missing?" I said, shocked. "What do you mean?"

"I mean *missing*. Gone. She didn't return to the office yesterday. She hasn't been in today, and none of her appointments after this one yesterday were completed," Detective Lapley said.

"With that in mind, it's important that you think really hard about what time Ms. Caldwell left here yesterday," Officer Peters said. "Assuming she left here at all."

I was a little embarrassed to realize how slow on the uptake I had been. They weren't here to try to find out if Brianna and I had sex or to try to fill in her calendar. They were here because I was a suspect in her disappearance.

"She left," I said. "Feel free to search the house if you think you might find her here, but I assure you that you won't."

"Right." Officer Peters stared at me. "You've learned the hard way about not leaving evidence."

I felt anger flare up inside me, but I swallowed it down. I

wasn't entirely sure what was going on, but I knew enough to know that losing my temper with the police officers sent to question me wasn't going to help my cause. I was innocent of any wrongdoing, and this time, I wasn't going to let anyone convince me otherwise.

"My appointment with Brianna was at 10 a.m.," I told Detective Lapley. "I didn't check the time when she arrived, but I have no reason to doubt that she was on time; in fact, I believe she made a comment about being a little bit early. She asked a few questions, and then she left. I don't think she was here longer than half an hour."

"Right. That's about standard for a parole meeting. But Ms. Caldwell's colleagues are under the impression that she normally spends longer than that here with you," Detective Lapley said. "You wouldn't be trying to give us a false time-line, would you, Mr. Owens?"

"No, I most definitely would not," I said. "I can't speak for Brianna's colleagues. I have no idea what they think, and I don't know if Brianna spends longer here than she does with her other parolees. But I know this: I didn't do anything to her, and I have no idea where she is."

"Can you prove that?" Detective Lapley asked.

A wave of panic spread through me. I felt as though I was going to be sick. It was happening. They were going to pin this on me, and whatever had happened to Brianna, I would go down for it. Detective Lapley must have known as well as I did that I had no way of proving I wasn't involved in any foul play with Brianna. Except ... maybe there was a way after all. I almost smiled when the answer hit me, but I stopped myself at the last second.

"No, but you can," I replied.

"Excuse me?" Detective Lapley said with a raised eyebrow.

"I take it you know the car Brianna drives? The make, model, color, all of that?" I asked.

Detective Lapley nodded.

"And you, no doubt, have scouted around enough before knocking on my door to know that her car is not on my property. Correct?"

"Yes, but that proves nothing," Officer Peters put in. "You could have moved the vehicle."

I lifted my pants leg and showed the men my ankle monitor. "This records my movements, right? Pull up my surveillance record, and you will see that I haven't left the property at all in ... well, I don't know how long exactly ... but certainly not yesterday or today."

I could tell by the look the two men exchanged that I had given them enough to go on for now. I could also tell they still didn't completely believe in my innocence, but they had no reason to arrest me or even to question me further. I believed that if I hadn't previously been convicted of murdering Terri, they wouldn't even suspect me.

The two men stood up, and I followed suit.

"That's everything for now, Mr. Owens; thank you for your time," Detective Lapley said.

"Of course," I replied as I followed them to the front door.

They stepped out, and I stayed on the doorstep.

Officer Peters turned back to me. "We'll be in touch if we need anything more from you, Mr. Owens. I trust that won't be a problem?"

"No, of course not. I really hope you find Brianna, and if I can help in any way, I won't hesitate to," I told him.

He nodded, and they walked down my driveway to where they had left their car.

I didn't go back inside until I had watched them drive away.

I debated calling Brianna, but I decided against it. There were enough missed calls on her cell phone that, if she had it on her, she wouldn't be able to miss them. She either wasn't with her cell phone, or she was choosing not to call me back. Plus, I figured that if the police found her cell phone, they might think it was strange that I had tried to call her right after they left. Still, I was worried about her.

I didn't think this was part of a game. There was no way she would get two police officers—one, a detective at that— to go along with a game. What if none of it was a mind game? What if Brianna was addicted to pills, and she had taken some of mine and then crashed her car somewhere? It didn't feel right as a theory. And, as much as there was no other explanation, Brianna taking my medication didn't feel right to me.

I had thought about nothing else, really, and I still had no logical explanation for everything that had happened. I stretched and yawned, and that was when I noticed it was suddenly almost midnight. I stood up to head up to bed, but I realized I was hungry, so I went into the kitchen first. I poured a bowl of sugar puffs, added milk, and sat down to eat.

I must have been even more worried than I realized because the cereal tasted strangely bitter, almost coppery, like my mouth was flooded with the taste of adrenaline. Ignoring the taste, I ate the rest of the cereal. I stood up and went to the sink to rinse the bowl. As I rinsed, the ground beneath me seemed to lurch, and I grabbed the edge of the sink for support. The ground wasn't really moving, I was having a dizzy spell, but it didn't change the fact that I felt like I might go sprawling onto the ground at any given moment.

I took deep breaths until the dizzy feeling passed. Well, the feeling didn't really pass, but it did ease enough that I dared to stand unaided. It was definitely time for bed. I was stressed and overtired, and a good night's sleep would make me feel a whole lot better.

I made my way out of the kitchen and along the hallway. I went up the stairs to use the bathroom. When I came back out, I was sure I saw someone at the top of the stairs, a figure silhouetted against the darkness.

A shudder went through me, and for a second, I was paralyzed by fear. I finally snapped myself out of the stupor and put my hand around the corner of my bedroom door, flicking on the light.

It didn't illuminate the entire hallway, but it produced enough light to chase the shadows away, and I saw that there was nothing there. I laughed at my fear. It was a shaky laugh, but it was a laugh all the same, and I ducked into my bedroom on legs like jelly.

I removed my clothes, took my pills, and got into bed. I had barely lain down when I heard footsteps running along the hallway toward my room. I flinched, waiting for the door to fly open, but nothing happened, and the footsteps were gone as quickly as they had come. I felt the same surge of anger I had felt before, and this time I didn't swallow it back.

"Oh, just fuck off and bother someone else!" I shouted.

I closed my eyes, desperate to fall asleep, so that if there were any more noises, I wouldn't hear them, but with my moment of strength came a rush of adrenaline that kept my heart racing and left me unable to even contemplate sleeping.

I couldn't hear the footsteps anymore, but I realized that they had been replaced by laughter, a sound that echoed around my room. With the laughter came the whispering, my name repeated over and over again at various pitches and volumes until it felt like the whole room was screaming for me.

I wanted to run, but I didn't think I would be able to move, and, besides, where would I go? One night spent in a shrub was more than enough. Instead, I lay on my left side, my head pressed on the pillow and my hand holding the other side of the pillow over my right ear, blocking out the sounds as best I could.

It wasn't a great solution, but it must have worked to some extent because, when I woke up a couple of hours later, the sounds had stopped. I stayed still for a moment, listening. Still, I heard nothing. Content, I closed my eyes again and pulled the duvet tighter around my shoulders. There was some resistance, and I ran my hand down my back to see what the problem was. I felt something that shouldn't be there, and fear gripped me for a second before I laughed softly. I had nothing to fear.

It had to be Brianna. She had come back to me. I rolled over, ready to pull her into my arms. Instead, I found myself looking into the empty eye sockets of a skull. I closed my eyes quickly, telling myself it was my medication making me hallucinate, nothing more sinister than that. I kept my eyes closed for a few seconds, but I didn't dare to keep them shut for too long. I had to know what the hell was in my bed with me.

I opened my eyes. Even though I was expecting the skull

this time, it still came as a shock, and I gasped in a terrified breath. Then I looked lower down the bed and saw it wasn't just a skull; it was a full human skeleton.

And it was dressed in my mom's favorite dress from my childhood.

The thing in my bed was my mother's corpse.

A scream ripped from me, and I pushed myself backward. I fell from my bed, landing hard on my back, but I barely registered the pain. I kept scrambling backward, not taking my eyes off the bed, sure that at any moment the skeleton would come after me, grinning its forever grin, watching me with its forever-empty eye sockets.

Tears ran down my face, and panicked sobs ripped from my throat with each breath. I kept scooting backward until I was in the hallway, and then I finally got to my feet. I started to turn toward the stairs, but as I did, I was overcome by a wave of nausea. I changed direction and ran for the bathroom instead. I didn't pause to close the door; I just threw myself on my knees in front of the toilet. I managed to lift the lid just in time as my sugar puffs came back in a hot, congealed mess of sour milk.

The sight and smell of the partly digested cereal made me retch again, and this time, hot, yellow bile seared my throat. I reached up, groping blindly along the toilet until I found the flusher. Once the mess was gone, I stopped retching. I wiped my mouth on a piece of tissue; then I sat in place for a moment.

My body was shaking, partly from fear and partly from the cold. I was covered in a sheen of sweat that had turned cold as it exited my pores. My breathing was still erratic, a mix of gasps and sobs.

Finally, I pushed myself to my feet, the seared feeling in

my throat forcing me to do something. I wasn't sure that my legs would hold me, but they did. I sipped cold water directly from the faucet until my throat felt a little bit soothed; then I swilled my mouth and spat water into the sink.

After that, I shut off the faucet and put the toilet lid down. I sat down on it while I thought about what the hell I was supposed to do next. I couldn't go anywhere. A glance at my watch told me there were still almost four hours before my curfew lifted and allowed me to leave the property. I was too cold to go outside. I knew if I tried that again, I would make myself sick, and I had enough problems without adding pneumonia to them. I couldn't go back into my bedroom. What if that ... *thing* ... was still there?

Every instinct was telling me it was a bad idea, but I knew I had to go back into my bedroom. For one thing, I was naked. For another, my medication was in there.

I stayed on the toilet lid until I became so cold that I had no choice but to move. I edged out of the room and swallowed hard as I moved closer to my bedroom. The door stood wide open, just how I had left it. One more step, and I would be looking directly into the room. I took a deep breath, and I took the final step. I tried not to look at the bed, but of course it was the first place my eyes went.

My jaw dropped when I saw my bed empty except for the tangled, sweat-soaked duvet. I had imagined the whole thing. No, not imagined. Dreamed. Yes, that had to be it. It had been nothing but a bad dream, a nightmare of the very worst kind.

A laugh came from me. A high-pitched laugh that sounded on the verge of hysteria. I didn't like that sound at all. It was the sound a person made when they were right on the edge of crazy. I screwed up my mouth tightly, stopping any further sound from escaping my lips, and then I stepped into the room.

I went to my chest of drawers and pulled out a pair of underwear and some socks. I put them on the top of the unit next to my pills as I went to the closet. Nightmare or not, I wanted out of this room. I would gather my clothes and get dressed in the bathroom.

I opened my closet and grabbed a T-shirt and a pair of black tracksuit bottoms. I turned back toward the rest of my stuff, and that was when I saw it. The piece of paper on my bed. I frowned and moved closer.

I stopped as soon as I was near enough to read the words. They were written in an untidy scrawl I didn't recognize.

Not even a goodnight kiss for your mother?

31

I felt fear slam back over me like a wave. I backed away from the bed and made for the door, pausing only long enough to grab my underwear, pills, and cell phone. I sprinted from the room, and I didn't stop running until I was downstairs.

I didn't know why, but I felt safer in the living room. I didn't question it. I didn't want to question it because then I would have to accept that feeling was stupid, and I wouldn't feel safe anywhere.

I pulled on my clothes, and then I sat on the couch, my elbows on my knees and my head in my hands, as I tried to work out what the hell I was going to do. The trouble was, no matter how much I tried to convince myself that this was a genuine haunting, there was a little voice inside my head that insisted I was losing my mind and imagining all this stuff. And when I tried to convince myself that I didn't believe in ghosts and that I had to be losing my mind or having some sort of adverse reaction to my medication, that same little voice told me I was mentally fine and that I had been on my meds long enough to know I wasn't reacting to them. It had to be a ghost.

Until I could decide which of these scenarios was correct, I wasn't going to be able to work out what my next steps might be. I had to call Janet and find out once and for all if she was in my corner or if it was all just words. If it was true, she would come here like I was going to ask her to and help me to decide if I was being haunted or going mad.

I picked up my cell phone. It was still really more night than morning, but if I didn't call her soon, I would chicken out, and I couldn't face another night of indecision. If Janet wouldn't come, I would call my therapist and have him section me if I had to.

I found Janet's name, hit call, and waited, listening to the ringing sound.

"James? Is everything okay?" Janet said. Her voice was thick with sleep, her words slurred, and I barely understood her at first. I listened as she yawned. "What's happened? What's wrong?"

I didn't even know how to begin to explain, but I knew if I didn't, she was likely to end the call and not come.

"I ... something's happened, Janet," I said. "Something bad."

"Like what? Are you hurt?" she asked.

I could hear the urgency in her voice, and it soothed me slightly. She did care about me. It gave me the confidence to go on.

"No. I'm not hurt. It's not that kind of bad. It's ... look, you know you said you thought maybe the house was haunted? Well, I think you're right. Either that, or I'm losing my mind. Things have been happening here. Things I can't explain. I've heard footsteps, laughter, people whispering my name.

My kitchen was trashed. And it all came to a head last night. I mean tonight. I woke up, and there was a fucking corpse in bed with me, and ..." I was starting to let hysteria overtake me, my words getting faster and faster as I babbled away.

Janet finally stopped me. "James, calm down," she said, her voice low and soft, the voice a person would use on a small child.

I knew I should be annoyed that she was being so condescending, but I found that I was just grateful that she wanted to make me feel better.

"Everything is going to be okay. I promise."

I took a moment to calm myself down so that when I spoke again, I didn't sound hysterical.

"I don't see how it can be okay if I'm here alone. I don't know what's real anymore. What I'm trying to say is, would you come back and stay? Just until we can work out whether the house is haunted or if I'm losing my mind."

"Wow," Janet said. "After all these years, you're finally admitting you actually need me."

I hated the smug tone in her voice, but I hated being alone and feeling terrorized more, so I forced myself to ignore the smugness and just tell her whatever she needed to hear to get her here.

"Of course I need you. I apologize if I've ever given you the impression that's not true," I said. "You're my sister, and everyone needs their family."

"Especially the members of the family who fight your corner," Janet agreed. "Of course I'll come. Can you sit tight until I get there in a couple of hours? Will you be okay?"

"Yes," I said, feeling better already for knowing that she would be coming. "Thank you."

"See you soon," Janet said.

She ended the call, leaving me holding my phone and feeling calmer than I had since I woke up to find that Brianna had left me.

I TENSED up as I heard a noise coming from the hallway. I had managed to get myself into some sort of order, had taken my meds, and had even made and ate breakfast, but now it seemed that the house—or my mind, one of the two—was ready to throw me back into disarray.

I jumped and got to my feet as I heard a noise that sounded like a door slamming.

Before I had a chance to move, the kitchen door started to slowly open, and I backed away. My back hit the counter at the same time Janet appeared in the doorway.

I breathed a sigh of relief.

Janet entered the kitchen and dropped into a chair at the table. "I could murder a mug of coffee. Please tell me you have a pot on."

I moved aside so that Janet could see the coffee machine behind me, the jug full. She grinned, and I poured us both a cup. I sat down opposite her and sipped my drink. Janet did the same and made an "ahh" sound. She blew on the top of her cup, casting tendrils of steam around her face.

"How did you get in?" I blurted out after a moment as it occurred to me that Janet didn't have a key.

"Through the door," Janet said, looking at me as though I really had lost my mind.

"The door was locked," I said.

"No, it wasn't," Janet said.

I started to stand up.

"It is now. I locked it when I came in."

I sat back down. I knew that door had been locked. Or did I forget to lock it?

"What?" Janet said after a moment of me frowning.

"I just ... that door was locked," I said, shaking my head.

"Clearly, it wasn't," Janet said. "Or do you think I can walk through walls these days?"

"No, of course not." What exactly did I think was happening here?

"I know from what you said on the phone earlier that you're having a hard time deciding what is real and what isn't. I get that, but you can see that I am real. Touch my hand." She pushed her hand toward me.

I hesitated, but I knew she wouldn't rest until I did as she said, so I touched her hand. It was warm from her mug.

"See. I'm real. So, unless you think I died and no one told you, and then my ghost turned up here, you need to accept that you forgot to lock the door."

Of course, Janet had to be right. She was here in front of me, and there was no way she could have gotten in unless I had left the door unlocked, as she had claimed. I decided it was the shock of hearing something out in the hallway before I realized it was Janet that had gotten me all riled up.

"I must have," I said eventually. "I'll have to be more careful in the future."

Janet nodded. "To be honest, you're probably okay out here, but it's always best to be safe, right?"

"Right," I agreed.

We finished our coffee, and Janet smiled at me and stood up.

"I'm just going to go upstairs and unpack my bag," she

said. "And then I'll come down, and you can tell me more about what's been going on here."

I nodded.

Janet picked up her purse and got up. As she passed, she rubbed her hand over mine. "It's a big step, you know, finally admitting that you need me."

She left the room, not waiting for an answer. I was glad because I was already starting to regret calling her.

I LAY in bed trying to go to sleep. The house was silent. Of course it was. It was typical that, from the moment Janet had arrived, not one thing even remotely out of the ordinary had happened. Even my taste buds seemed to be pleased she was here, my food tasting less bitter than it had in days.

The silence, while welcome, wasn't really helping. If nothing happened, how would I know the truth? Did the lack of action mean that I had a shy ghost that wouldn't manifest itself around Janet? Or did it mean that I was going crazy being on my own all the time, so I felt slightly less crazy while Janet was here, and that was why the hallucinations stopped?

I was more than aware that this train of thought was doing nothing to help me fall asleep. I debated taking a sedative, but if something *did* happen, I didn't want to sleep through it. I wanted to be able to show Janet what I saw.

I forced myself to stop thinking about my dilemma. Instantly, Brianna's face filled my mind instead. Normally that would have made me happy, but tonight, it just made me even more stressed. Had she been found? Would anyone notify me if so? Would it look suspicious if I called to check in on her, or would it look more suspicious if I didn't?

My mind wouldn't stop whirring. It passed from topic to topic, spinning away, keeping me awake despite the fact that I was exhausted.

When I finally fell asleep, my sleep was fitful, full of half-dreams and dark images that kept my heart racing and stopped me from fully relaxing.

I felt a warm hand shaking me awake, and I was glad to be pulled out of my nightmarish slumbers.

"What's wrong?" I asked when I opened my eyes and saw Janet standing beside my bed, her eyes full of tears, her mouth twisted in fear. I sat up quickly. "Janet, what happened?"

"I ... I saw something," she said.

"What?" I demanded.

She sat down on the edge of my bed, facing me. "I don't know what, exactly. I woke up and became conscious of someone standing over me, watching me. But when I turned my head to the side, obviously expecting to see you, what I saw was ... well, it sounds crazy ... but it wasn't human."

While I was impatient to hear the rest, I resisted the urge to hurry her up, letting her take a minute to tell her story in her own time.

"It was vaguely human in shape, but it was all wrong. It was too skinny, more like a skeleton than a person. But—and I know this sounds crazy—it was wearing a yellow dress with these tiny white flowers on it. That much I could see even in the dark."

The more Janet explained, the faster my heart beat. I didn't know if I was more relieved that I wasn't crazy, and that Janet had seen things too, or more scared that my house

really was seemingly haunted. Never did I expect my mom to
haunt me this way.

"That's her. She was in my bed when I woke up the night
I called you," I said. I saw a shiver go through Janet and felt
as though it was going through me, too. "I think it's Mom.
That dress. It was her favorite."

"We already talked about this, James," Janet said. "Mom
isn't dead."

I opened my mouth to argue with her, but then I remembered that Brianna had told me about Mom most likely
being murdered and that Janet still believed my father's story
about Mom leaving. In that moment, it didn't seem like the
right time to convince her otherwise.

Janet whispered, "Maybe it was a demon trying to make
you think it's Mom."

"What?" I asked. "Why?"

Janet shrugged. "I don't know. To make you trust it? To
scare you? Who knows? But I know now that you were right.
This house is haunted, possessed, or something. I should
have taken you more seriously when you first told me about
the weird goings-on. Demons are nothing to mess around
with."

I knew that was the closest I would ever get to an apology, and for Janet, that was a big deal, so I smiled and
squeezed her shoulder. "Let's not worry about the past. Let's
worry about how the hell we get rid of this thing. Assuming
there is a way."

"We need a pastor to come and bless the house and exor-
cise any spirits or demons."

"Isn't that just something they do in movies?" I said with
a frown.

"No, of course not," Janet said. "The Catholic Church just

likes to pretend that exorcisms aren't a thing anymore, and besides, they aren't the only ones who do them. Don't ask me why. But my pastor will be happy to help cleanse the house. And, let's be honest, it won't hurt for you to meet her. You clearly need Jesus."

What the hell was that supposed to mean? I wanted to know but not badly enough to ask.

Janet stood up abruptly. "I'll call her at nine. I won't be able to sleep now, so you might as well have a lie-in." She closed my bedroom door on her way out.

Now that she had seen the same thing I had, which surely proved that I wasn't going crazy again, I found I was finally able to relax. When I fell asleep this time, it was a deep and restful sleep.

32

It was almost lunchtime when I finally woke up. I felt rested for the first time in what felt like years, and I whistled as I went down the stairs after showering and getting dressed for the day. I had a session with my therapist at 2 p.m., and I wanted to grab some lunch before he arrived.

I went into the kitchen and set about making Janet and me some sandwiches. I peered into the fridge and decided on cheese and pickle. Still humming, I spread pickles on the buns and then added the cheese. I took the plates to the living room, where Janet sat watching a talk show.

She looked up and smiled when I came into the room. I handed her one of the plates, and she frowned slightly as I sat down.

"What's wrong?" I asked. "Don't say you don't like cheese and pickle."

"Of course I like cheese and pickle," Janet said. She grinned at me. "What sort of monster doesn't like cheese and pickle?" She turned serious again and went on. "I'm just ... I don't know. You seem different today."

"I guess knowing that whatever is going on here is real, and that I can't be crazy because you've seen it too, has cheered me up somewhat," I agreed.

Janet smiled, but it was strained, and it didn't seem to reach her eyes.

It occurred to me that maybe she was scared after her experience last night. The first time I experienced anything even close to what she had seen, I ran from the house and spent the night in a bush, so I definitely understood where she was coming from. I decided to change the subject and see if I could make her feel better.

"Have you heard anything from your director or anyone yet? They must be missing you," I said, knowing Janet loved nothing better than talking about what a star she was, although I personally had seen no evidence of this.

"No, and I don't expect to either," Janet said.

Her tone of voice told me I should leave it and move on to an even safer topic, but her answer had piqued my curiosity, and I couldn't help but probe.

"Why not?" I asked. "I thought they would at least want to check in and see if you had a return date in mind yet."

"A return date?" Janet said with a humph. "I don't have anything to return to. I quit the play to come and look after you."

"Oh. I'm sorry, Janet. I didn't know," I said.

Janet shrugged. "Don't worry about it. Family first and all that."

It seemed strange that they would let their leading lady go just like that, and I began to wonder how much of what Janet had said before was even true. It was certainly possible that she was hiding the fact that she hadn't even gotten the part.

I was saved from having to work out whether she wanted me to thank her, commiserate with her, or neither of the two, when the doorbell rang.

"That could be your pastor," I said.

"No. She's not coming until tomorrow," she said. "Didn't you say you had an appointment with your therapist today?"

"Yes, but it's a little early for that," I said.

I popped the last of my sandwich into my mouth and got up. I walked to the front door as I chewed. I pulled the door open and smiled when I saw Dr. Sellers standing there.

"Good afternoon, James," he said, stepping inside and moving down the hallway. "I'm early. I hope that's okay."

"Yes, of course," I said, closing the front door and following Dr. Sellers toward the living room.

"Janet, this is Dr. Sellers, my therapist," I said as we entered the living room. "Dr. Sellers, this is my sister, Janet Owens."

Dr. Sellers extended his hand to Janet, and she shook it.

I gestured for Dr. Sellers to sit down, then I tried to catch Janet's eye to get her to leave us alone, but she seemed to be avoiding my gaze.

"I've heard a lot about you," Janet said to Dr. Sellers.

"All of it good, I hope," Dr. Sellers said with a smile.

"Well, James seems to think you're good," Janet said. "But I tend to judge people as I find them, so we'll see. I'll let you know after this session if I think you're any good or if you just use psychobabble to flummox people and try to sound clever."

"Janet," I said, my shock making me sound angry.

"It's okay," Dr. Sellers said, smiling at me. "People who don't understand how therapy works are always quick to write it off. Luckily, I don't take much notice of what unqualified non-patients think of me or my methods."

Janet's cheeks flushed red. She looked down into her lap for a moment, her fingers plucking at her skirt. Finally, she looked up and forced a smile at Dr. Sellers. "Well, let's get started, then, and see if you can change my opinion."

"Your opinion is of no interest to me. Now, you must either leave, or James and I must go to another room. Therapy is confidential between a patient and the therapist," Dr. Sellers said.

"I'm sure James would want me to stay. Right, James?" Janet said, looking across at me.

It was starting to get embarrassing, the way Janet refused to leave the room. "No, but thank you for the offer," I said, forcing myself to smile like this was all perfectly normal and not in the least bit strange. "I will get more benefit from my session if I don't have to hold back."

"You don't have to hold back in front of me," Janet replied.

"Janet, please, just go," I said.

"Fine," Janet said with a sigh as she stood up. She gave Dr. Sellers a look so full of contempt I was surprised he didn't say anything. "Just remember who is on your side in all of this, James, okay?"

I nodded, wanting her to go. She finally left the room, and I breathed a sigh of relief.

"I'm sorry about that," I said to Dr. Sellers. "She gets overprotective sometimes."

"Not to worry," Dr. Sellers said. "How have you felt since our last session?"

"Good," I said. "There was an incident where I thought I was hallucinating again, which is how Janet came to be here.

I called her, and she agreed to come and take care of me. But then she saw the same thing as I did, and I realized I wasn't hallucinating after all."

"So, looking back, was there anything that would have tipped you off to this being real?" Dr. Sellers asked.

"It felt real. My hallucinations usually have a slightly surreal feeling to them that I can identify if I don't let myself panic. But this didn't. In theory, I knew it was real, but it was something so ridiculous, I suppose you would say that I didn't believe it could be real."

The door opened, and Janet poked her head around it. "It's not that ridiculous. My pastor said—"

"Have you been listening at the door?" I snapped, cutting her off.

"Oh, you make it sound so sordid," Janet said, rolling her eyes. "I want to make sure your therapist isn't filling your head full of nonsense, that's all."

"As opposed to a pastor," Dr. Sellers muttered.

I knew he had spoken too quietly for Janet to hear him, and I suspected he didn't intend for me to hear him either, so I ignored his whispered statement and turned my focus to Janet.

"Janet, please," I said. "Give us some privacy. Dr. Sellers is helping me, not putting ideas in my head."

"If you say so," Janet said, pulling her head back out of the room. "But call for me if you need me, okay?"

"Okay," I said, knowing that I wouldn't be calling for her, but also knowing that she wouldn't go away until I had agreed. I waited until the door closed and a few seconds passed; then I turned back to Dr. Sellers. "I'm sorry about that," I found myself saying again.

"It's okay," Dr. Sellers said.

He smiled, but the smile seemed strained, and I felt like I had to say something more, something to make him understand that Janet was just being ... well, Janet.

"She means well," I said. "She wants to make sure I'm okay."

"Well, the best way for her to do that is to let you get help from a professional," Dr. Sellers said. "Her reluctance to do so makes me question her motives, if I'm honest. It's almost as though she doesn't really *want* you to get better. Maybe she enjoys feeling useful taking care of you. Or maybe she likes the attention."

"Maybe," I said, with a shrug. The conversation was making me uncomfortable. I didn't think Dr. Sellers was entirely wrong, but I felt I should defend Janet.

The door to the living room flew open, and she strode in once again. "Do you see what I mean now, James? About putting ideas into your head? Of course I want you to get better; then maybe we can both get on with our lives."

"You were still listening," I said.

It was a stupid thing to say. But I didn't know what else to say. I was starting to wish I had called Dr. Sellers and either put this appointment off or gone to his office.

"Ms. Owens, you need to go upstairs or leave the house so that James and I can have a private, uninterrupted therapy session," Dr. Sellers said.

"Don't you dare tell me what to do in my brother's house," Janet said, fixing her attention on Dr. Sellers.

"Ms. Owens, this therapy is a court-mandated treatment, and I will not have you disturbing our progress," Dr. Sellers snapped. "You will kindly do as I say, or I will call the police and explain that you are interfering with an activity the courts have ordered, and you will be arrested. Which option would you prefer?"

Janet ignored him and looked at me. "I'll be upstairs in my room if you need me." She didn't wait for an answer. Instead, she stormed out of the room, leaving the door wide open behind her, a final petty gesture.

Dr. Sellers waited a moment, then stood up and crossed the room. He looked up and down the hallway, and, seemingly satisfied that Janet had indeed gone upstairs, he came back into the room, shut the door, and sat back down. "Is she always so overbearing?"

I didn't reply because I wanted to be loyal to Janet, but at the same time, I didn't want to tell an outright lie.

"James, you can tell me the truth. I'm not going to make trouble for your sister, I just want to try to understand the dynamic at play here. It seems to me that Janet likes to be in control of what goes on in your life."

I decided to tell Dr. Sellers the truth, but the part that at least made Janet look like she cared a bit about me. "She can be a little bit overprotective. But she is on my side, Doctor. She's done a lot for me, including possibly ruining her career."

"How so?" Dr. Sellers said with a raised eyebrow.

"She's an actress. She recently got the lead role in one of those plays that attract a lot of critical attention and can make or break a person's acting career. She walked out during rehearsals to come and take care of me."

Dr. Sellers looked at me quietly for a moment. "James," he said, "I hope you don't mind, but whenever I start working with a new client, I do a bit of research into their families and close friends. Nothing sinister; I just like to check out their social media profiles, that kind of thing. It's mostly to see what type of people my clients are surrounded by, and to maybe get a feel for who may be a healthy influence or an unhealthy influence."

"I don't mind," I said.

"Good," Dr. Sellers said. "From your sister's various social media profiles, I learned she was an actress, so I had a look to satisfy my own curiosity and to find out if I had seen her in anything. I read something about the new play she was in, and I made a mental note to see it. Then, when I went to buy tickets, I found an article about your sister."

I waited, wondering what on earth Dr. Sellers had found out about Janet.

He brought his cell phone out of his pocket and tapped away on the screen. After a few seconds, he handed it to me.

I gasped. The headline told me everything I needed to know. My sister hadn't left her prestigious role to come and take care of me. She had been fired. Weeks ago.

I looked up at Dr. Sellers in shock. I skimmed the article, but it didn't really elaborate on the situation, and I handed the cell phone back, my head reeling.

"I'm sorry. It's not easy to learn that a family member you thought you could trust has been lying to you."

"It's kind of the story of my life, Doc," I said.

"That doesn't make it easier," Dr. Sellers said.

"No," I agreed. "But, to be honest, I was starting to suspect something was going on concerning the play. Firstly, I didn't think Janet would drop it to come and look after me, but I told myself I was being paranoid. But then I asked her why she wasn't keeping in touch with the production people, and she said she had quit the play, and I don't know ... I guess I didn't quite believe that. I wanted to, so I told myself I did, but something felt off."

Dr. Sellers nodded. "I believe that you would be a lot better equipped to decide for yourself what is real and what is a hallucination if you learned to trust your gut instinct."

I nodded. I knew that made sense.

"Okay, let's work on that for the rest of this session. To be honest, I am not comfortable doing any sort of hypnotherapy knowing your sister might burst in at any moment and ruin it," Dr. Sellers said.

I nodded again, and the rest of the session flew by. At the end of it, I was starting to think that maybe I could trust my gut instinct.

Just before he left, Dr. Sellers handed over my next week's worth of pills. "Keep these on you at all times. I'm not saying Janet will do anything to them, but I'd be lying if I said I trust her one hundred percent not to."

I wanted to be able to tell Dr. Sellers confidently that he should trust her, but I couldn't because I had to admit that at least a part of me thought he was right.

After I saw Dr. Sellers out, I went to the kitchen, where I poured myself a glass of juice. I headed back to the living room and was surprised to see Janet sitting there.

"That went well, didn't it?" she said.

"What?" I asked, confused by both her sudden presence and her question.

"Your session with Dr. Sellers, silly," Janet said, with a tinkling laugh. "I'm so glad he let me sit in. I feel like I learned a lot about your triggers. Seems it all stems from a lack of confidence and self-belief."

"What the hell are you talking about?" I demanded. "Dr. Sellers didn't let you sit in on the session. He caught you listening at the door and threatened to have you arrested."

"James, James, James," Janet said, her voice slow and

patient like she was talking to someone of below-average intelligence. "Listen to yourself. Do you really think the police would come and arrest me for listening in on a conversation? And do you really think a professional doctor would believe that might be the case?"

"Well, no. But ..." I trailed off.

It did sound ridiculous when she put it like that. But it had happened. Dr. Sellers had told me to listen to my gut instinct, and it was telling me that I was right about this. But was I? Or had I hallucinated that part of the session?

"Okay, then," I said to Janet. "Tell me what we talked about. Not in general terms like you did earlier. Be specific."

"I can't remember his exact words, but he talked about how trusting yourself would help you to learn the difference between reality and your hallucinations. And that you had to learn to trust your gut instinct because it was there solely for us to use to assess a situation, but that a lot of us don't know how to listen to it anymore." Janet smiled at me. "Is that enough detail, or do I need to go on? He also said about asking yourself if this is likely or not and—"

"Okay, you can stop," I said sharply, cutting Janet off.

I sat down on the settee and began to think. I was so sure I had been right about the way I remembered things, but the more I thought about it, the more surreal it seemed. As if Janet would have been listening in at the door to our session. And as if Dr. Sellers would have threatened to have her arrested for something like that. No, I had to have imagined that part. Which meant that I could have imagined the part where there was only Dr. Sellers and I present for the rest of our session. Janet could have been there.

"So, now you believe me, it shows you're still struggling with knowing the difference between fantasy and reality,"

Janet said, her voice soft and gentle. Kind, even. "Do you think that for now it might be best if I keep hold of your medication and dole it out to you?"

I thought again. I had a vivid memory of Dr. Sellers telling me to keep my medication on me at all times. He had said he was suspicious of Janet. But that had to be fake, right? My gut instinct told me he had indeed said that, and that I should heed his advice.

I smiled at Janet. "No, it's okay. I'm better when I am in control of my meds. Thank you for the offer, though."

She nodded.

What else could she do, really, except wrestle my medication away from me? I made a mental note to be damned sure it never left my sight. I had made that mistake once with Brianna. I wasn't about to make it again with Janet.

33

W e had finished dinner, washed and dried the dishes, and were finally sitting down to relax when the doorbell rang. Janet and I exchanged a glance, and I shook my head, telling her I had no idea who it could be. I stood up and headed for the door, wondering if it could be Brianna.

I had been thinking about Brianna a lot since my therapy session earlier that day. Despite everything, my gut instinct told me that Brianna hadn't touched my medication. That led me to think that if she had no interest in taking my medication away, she hadn't seduced me to distract me. Did that mean she actually liked me? I was starting to think so. But then where had she gone, and why hadn't she been in contact with anyone? None of it made sense.

I pulled the front door open, and my heart sank when, instead of seeing Brianna standing there, I saw Officer Peters and Detective Lapley.

"Good evening, Mr. Owens," Detective Lapley said with a

smile that seemed practiced rather than genuine. "We were wondering if we might have a word with you."

"Have you found her?" I asked as I stepped aside and let the two policemen enter.

"No," Officer Peters said. "And here's the strange thing. Everything points us back here to you. It seems that after coming here, Brianna's trail goes cold, and no one has seen or heard from her since."

I wasn't an idiot. I knew how this must look. I also knew that Officer Peters hadn't asked me a question. Instead of falling into the trap of babbling to fill the silence, I pointed to the kitchen door. "Do you mind if we do this in the kitchen? My sister is here."

Detective Lapley nodded and made for the kitchen door.

Soon we were all seated. The two policemen refused my offer of beverages. We sat in silence for a moment, a silence that made me feel nervous. I pulled at my fingers beneath the tabletop, urging myself to relax. I had nothing to hide. I had done nothing wrong.

"Why don't we start by hearing your theory," Detective Lapley said. "What do you think happened to Brianna?"

"I have no idea," I replied honestly. "If I thought I knew where she was, I would have told you the last time you were here."

"You must have a theory, though," Officer Peters put in. "After we left, you must have considered what had happened."

"Of course I considered it. I thought about nothing else for hours," I said. "But I didn't come up with anything groundbreaking. She didn't say anything about where she was going next, and I had no reason to think she was going to do anything but follow her normal routine. I can only assume that she either left town of her own accord without bothering to let anyone know, or that someone got her to pull over and took her or something."

"Then where is her car?" Officer Peters asked. "If someone took her, wouldn't her car still be where she left it?"

"I have no idea," I said honestly. "Like I already said, I don't have any explanation for her disappearance."

"If I were in your position, I might have tried a little harder to work out why she didn't turn up to see Mr. Davidson, her next appointment that day," Detective Lapley said.

"Maybe *he* did something to her," I said.

"Mr. Davidson informed us that she didn't arrive for the appointment she had with him, and a phone call to the office asking about her whereabouts confirms this," Officer Peters said.

"Oh, and of course this Mr. Davidson couldn't be lying, yet I could be? I hope you're harassing him like you're harassing me," I said.

"I would hardly call this harassment, James. And Mr. Davidson has CCTV footage that corroborates his story," Detective Lapley said. "So, I will ask you again. What happened to Brianna?"

"I don't know why you're even bothering to search for her, Detective. I mean it's obvious she ran off with one of her guys," Janet said as she came into the kitchen.

"Janet, this is a private conversation," I said.

"No, she can stay," Detective Lapley said, eyeing Janet suspiciously. "Take a seat."

Janet did as she was told, giving me a smug smile.

I resisted the urge to roll my eyes.

"What do you know about these guys she was seeing?"

Detective Lapley asked Janet. "Do you have their names? Addresses? Anything like that?"

"No, I don't know them personally. But you just know she had multiple guys on the go, don't you?" she said. "She's the slutty type; got it written all over her."

"Janet," I exclaimed, "that's enough. You have met Brianna once for all of about thirty seconds, and you're talking as though you know her."

"That was all the time it took to get a handle on her," Janet replied.

"Just because she put you in your place when you tried to interfere with her job doesn't mean that she's a slut or a bad person," I said.

I saw Detective Lapley and Officer Peters exchange a glance as I said that, and I cringed inwardly. Had I said the wrong thing? It sure seemed like it. The two policemen were staring at Janet now, their expressions hungry like sharks who had smelled blood. At least she no longer looked quite so smug.

"In what way did you try to interfere with her job?" Officer Peters asked Janet.

"Oh, take no notice of James. He loves to be melodramatic. Brianna came for one of her scheduled visits, and James wasn't feeling too good. I merely asked her if she would prefer to come back at a different time when he was more lucid."

"That ... that's not true," I said. "You tried to make her leave. She had to threaten to get you arrested."

"Ohh, James," Janet said, looking at me with pity in her eyes. "I don't know why you keep having that same hallucination, but do you realize that's the second time today that you have said someone in your life has tried to have me arrested. It was Dr. Sellers earlier, and now Brianna."

"But it's true," I said, suddenly confident that it was. I was trusting my gut instinct, and it told me if she had tried to stop Brianna from doing her job, she might well have done the same to Dr. Sellers. I looked at the policemen. "Call Dr. Sellers and ask him. He'll tell you it's true."

"What happens between you and your therapist is of no interest to me because it's not relevant to this case," Detective Lapley said. He shifted his attention back to Janet. "What does interest me, however, is this dynamic between you and Brianna. It's clear you don't much like her. Is that because, as your brother put it, she put you in your place?"

"I didn't say I dislike her. I dislike her morals. I am a God-fearing woman, Detective, and I find women who disgrace themselves in the eyes of the Lord to be trouble. However, the blame doesn't lie solely with them. It lies equally with the Devil, who tempts them away from the ways of the Lord."

"And it's your job to rid the world of people like that?" Detective Lapley pushed on.

For a brief second, Janet appeared nervous. She looked down into her lap, and when she looked back up, she was biting the skin on her bottom lip. She smiled. "If you are asking me if I did something to Brianna, the answer is no, Detective. If you are asking in the more general sense, I believe it's all our responsibilities to rid the world of a lack of moral fiber, not through violence, and certainly not through murder, but through education. I believe we need to bring these errant young women back into the arms of the Lord."

The look I had seen earlier passed between Detective

Lapley and Officer Peters again, only this time, rather than a look of suspicion, their look said one thing: nut case.

While it was nice that the heat was off me for a bit, it wasn't ideal that it fell on Janet. I didn't care how much Janet claimed to be in my corner, if it came down to a choice of me or her, she would pick herself every time. With that in mind, I knew I had to speak up, and in a way that wouldn't have Janet hating on me as soon as the policemen left me alone with her once more.

"We all have our beliefs, don't we?" I said. "But Janet can't have been helping Brianna find her moral compass or whatever. She only came back into town yesterday."

"Is this true?" Officer Peters asked Janet.

Janet nodded.

"And is there someone who can corroborate that besides your brother?" Detective Lapley asked.

"Before I even came to the house, I filled a prescription at the pharmacy. The one on Oak. I'm sure there will be a record of that," she said.

Just like that, another piece clicked into place. Another time for me to trust my gut instinct. Dr. Sellers had told me Janet had been sacked from her play ages ago. Surely this proved it? Otherwise, she would have said that her fellow actors knew of her planned trip, because she wouldn't have missed the opportunity to brag about her lead role.

"Thank you for confirming that, Ms. Owens," Detective Lapley said. "We will look into it as soon as we can and eliminate you from the investigation."

"Yes, you do that," she said.

Detective Lapley turned back to me. "Again, don't leave town. We may want to speak with you again in the near future," he said, and then he stood up.

Officer Peters stood up alongside him.

I followed them out into the hallway and to the front door. We said some awkward goodbyes; then I watched until they were both in the car and the car had driven away. I closed the door behind them and made sure that the lock had engaged. Then I turned around and leaned back against the door. I felt physically and mentally exhausted, and I couldn't bring myself to face Janet right now.

"Janet? They've gone. I'm going up to bed," I called.

"Okay. Goodnight," Janet shouted back.

"Goodnight," I replied. It appeared Janet didn't want to talk about it any more than I did.

I made my way to the stairs. When I reached the top, I walked to the bathroom, where I brushed my teeth and used the toilet. I took a glass of water to my bedroom. I changed into my pajama top and took my pills from my jeans pocket. I swallowed the ones I needed with the water; then I put the rest in my pajama pocket before finally slipping into bed. It didn't take long to drift off to sleep.

I woke with a start, my nerves jangling and the hairs on the back of my neck standing up. I heard a pounding sound that made me think of someone punching a wall, but it seemed to be coming from the wall opposite me, and there was no one there. The banging gave off a dull echo, and the more I heard it, the more it seemed to be coming from inside the wall.

The sound intensified as I lay frozen in fear. It sounded like hundreds of fists knocking inside my wall. I tried to move, but the paralysis gripped me completely, and I did the only thing I could do—I screamed for Janet. Once I had opened that floodgate, I couldn't stop screaming, and I kept repeating her name over and over until I heard my bedroom door crash open.

"My goodness, James, whatever is wrong?" Janet demanded.

I stopped screaming, and that was when I realized the banging had stopped. I swallowed hard and sat up, pulling the duvet up around my shoulders. "There was banging. It sounded like it was coming from inside the walls."

"It'll be the pipes settling," Janet said. "You know what these old houses are like."

"It wasn't the pipes. Do you think I haven't heard the pipes creaking before? This sounded like people inside the wall banging their fists on it." Even as I said it, I knew it sounded crazy, but was it any crazier than finding the ghost of a corpse in bed with me?

"You're hallucinating again," Janet said, her voice tight, her forehead lined with wrinkles from her deep frown. "If it was as bad as you said it was, how come I didn't hear it?"

"Maybe you were too far away," I said.

"I heard you calling for me," she pointed out.

"Then I don't know," I admitted. "But that doesn't mean the sounds weren't real." I knew what I had heard, and I was trusting my gut instinct once more.

"Oh, James, not this again," Janet said with a sigh. She held her hand out. "Let me count your pills."

"No," I said.

"No?" she repeated, an eyebrow raised.

"Dr. Sellers said it's important for me to take personal responsibility for my pills, and I know I have taken them," I told her.

"You took the ones right before bed? Because you didn't

come back to the kitchen for a drink to take them with after the police left," Janet said.

"I took them, honestly," I reassured her. I nodded toward the half-empty glass of water on the nightstand beside me. "I used that."

"As long as you're sure," Janet said.

I nodded. I was sure.

"The sooner my pastor blesses this place, the better."

34

I managed to drift back into a restless sleep after the banging incident, but still, when I woke up the next morning, I felt like I hadn't slept for months. My eyes were sore, and my head ached. By lunchtime, I was ready to give in and go back to bed, but I knew that Janet's pastor was due any time, so I couldn't.

I really hoped that she could help somehow. I would have given anything to have the house be calm and peaceful and allow me a good night's sleep without fear.

Almost as though my thinking about her had summoned her, the doorbell rang. I started to stand up, but then I heard Janet's feet on the stairs, and I sat back down. I figured it would be less awkward if someone who knew the pastor greeted her.

The door to the living room opened, and Janet walked in, followed by the pastor. I wasn't sure exactly what I was expecting, but it certainly wasn't her. She was young—definitely no older than thirty—and she was wearing a pair of jeans and a yellow blouse. I supposed I was expecting her to wear some kind of robe that would make me think of a priest, but I guessed in hindsight that she would only wear that during her sermons.

I stood up and offered her my hand. She shook it and smiled warmly.

"This is my brother, James," Janet said. "James, this is Pastor McKinnsey."

"Oh, Anne is fine," she said, still smiling. "No need for all of that formality, is there?"

"Thank you for coming," Janet said. "If there was ever a person who needed Jesus, it's my brother."

This was the second time Janet had said something like that about me. I had let it go before because I had been exhausted, but this time, I needed to know what exactly she meant. I opened my mouth to demand an explanation, but before I could ask her, Anne spoke up, and I felt like it would have been rude to interrupt.

"Now, Janet, you know we don't make needing Jesus seem like an insult. Everyone needs Jesus in their lives, but I won't push him onto people before they are ready to embrace him. If that is all you have brought me here for, then ..." Anne started.

"No, no, of course not. I'm sorry. Please don't go," Janet said quickly, not looking Anne in the eye. "The house really does need blessing. Right, James?"

I was so surprised to see Janet bowing down to someone that I almost didn't respond. She was like a little girl, eager to please and upset when she missed the mark.

It would have been fun watching Janet squirm, but I didn't want the pastor to leave either. I really did want her to do what she could to make the house peaceful again. "Yes, we need help with whatever is in this house. Please sit down."

Anne smiled and sat down, and I felt a rush of relief that she wasn't about to leave. Janet and I sat down, too.

Anne smiled at each of us. Her gaze lingered on me. "Tell me about what's been going on."

I thought for a second about where to start, but before I could even gather my thoughts, Janet jumped in.

"Oh, it's been awful, hasn't it, James?" she said. "Just the other night—"

"Janet, would you be so kind as to go and grab me a glass of water? Let the faucet run so it's nice and cold. James can explain what's been going on," Anne said.

I had to bite my lip to keep from smiling as Janet meekly nodded and got to her feet. I liked Anne more and more by the second. She didn't stand for any of Janet's bullshit, and it was clear she wasn't the sort of woman to let herself be manipulated by Janet either.

While Janet was gone, I quickly explained to Anne everything that had been happening, ending with the fact that I believed the corpse had been a hallucination until Janet had confirmed that she, too, had seen it. Anne raised an eyebrow at this, although she made no comment, and I realized there was a fair chance Janet had told her I was mentally ill, and I needed to have this blessing just to prove that nothing was really there. I found that I didn't much care what Janet had or hadn't said at this point. I just wanted the noises and the visions to stop.

By the time Janet returned with the water, Anne had gotten the full story from me.

Anne accepted the glass from Janet, and, after a few sips,

she put the glass down on the coffee table. "So, James tells me you saw the ghost of your mother, too. I do believe that must have slipped your mind when you told me what was going on."

Again, I bit down on my lip to stop myself from smiling. I had been right. Janet had, of course, left out that part. I loved the fact that Anne wasn't letting it go, and by asking her in front of me, Janet could hardly tell Anne I was delusional.

"Oh. Did I not mention that?" Janet stuttered. "Umm, yeah, it must have slipped my mind."

Anne nodded as though she believed her, but I didn't think she did for a second.

"So, what I propose to do is a full cleanse and blessing." Anne leaned down and began to rifle through a bag she had placed beside her feet when she sat down. She pulled out a small bowl filled with greenery and a bottle of what looked like water. "I will burn sage and scatter holy water. We'll start at the top of the house and work down over every single nook and cranny. All of it must be covered, every dark space, every drawer, every cupboard."

I nodded in understanding, and Anne smiled. "Right. Let's begin, shall we?" she said.

A couple of hours had passed since Anne began blessing the house. She was extremely thorough. We had been in every room upstairs, every drawer and closet had been opened, and no corner was left unblessed. She even did the staircase. She had done the living room and the kitchen downstairs.

Now, as we headed for the library, Janet sighed loudly.

"If you want to go and sit down, feel free," I said, emboldened by Anne's presence. "There's really no need for you to follow us through the full house."

"No, don't be silly," Janet said. "I want to be here for you. I just don't think it's necessary to do the rooms you barely even go in, that's all."

"I can assure you, it is necessary," Anne put in. "Why else would I be doing it?"

That shut Janet up for the moment, and together we trooped into the library.

Anne moved around, wafting the sage smoke into the air, and flicking holy water around into all of the corners.

"Dear God," she said, repeating once more the prayer she had said in each room of the house as she had moved around, "I pray over this home and everyone in it. Lord, I pray that you will keep this home safe both spiritually and physically. I pray for the safety of the house against physical damage, and the members of this house against injury and sickness. Amen."

I had expected something a little more dramatic, maybe more similar to an exorcism, but as we made our way through the house, I felt lighter with each room blessing, like all the residual negative energy was being cleansed. Whether that was the case or whether it was a placebo effect, I didn't know or care. I was just pleased to feel it.

Suddenly, though, that changed in this room. I felt surrounded by darkness. I blinked hard, trying to blink it away, but the feeling wasn't shifting. The more I fought the dark, the more it engulfed me until I felt like I was drowning.

Janet was sitting in a chair beside the window, and Anne was still moving around blessing the room. Neither of them seemed to notice anything strange was going on with me.

I felt pulled toward one of the bookshelves. I didn't know why I was being directed there, but I found my feet moving almost of their own accord, and I didn't fight the feeling; I allowed myself to be led, trusting my gut instinct once more. I felt as though the darkness was coming from behind this particular bookshelf, and when I reached it, I stood for a moment, studying it.

I felt a sharp pain in my head, and as it receded, it left behind a fraction of a memory. At least it felt like a memory, and I was once more taking Dr. Sellers's advice and trusting my gut. In the flash of memory, the bookshelf in front of me was gone, and in its place was a dark opening. I started tapping around the bookshelf, listening to hear if it sounded hollow behind it.

"James, what are you doing?" Janet asked, a sharp edge to her voice.

"It's a dark place," I heard myself say as I tap, tap, tapped my fingers around. "It needs to be open, too."

I felt eyes on me, and I glanced over my shoulder. Janet was up on her feet and heading toward me. Anne was watching me, a look of concern on her face.

"Stop that, James," Janet said. "You look crazy."

I shook my head, more to tell her that I wasn't going to stop what I was doing than to tell her I wasn't crazy. I heard footsteps behind me as Anne began to walk toward me, too. I wasn't sure if she planned on trying to restrain me or Janet, but I tapped quicker, knowing instinctively that I was right and also knowing that if I couldn't prove it in the next few seconds, no one would ever believe me.

"James, you need to take your meds," Janet said.

I touched the wall below the fourth shelf, and it felt different from the rest of the wall, hard and shiny like plastic.

I pressed on it, and with a *psst* noise of escaping air, the bookshelf began to move backward. It went about a foot backward, then it slowly slid to the left until it was completely embedded inside the wall, leaving behind the gaping patch of darkness I had felt in my soul.

35

I stared into the black space until my eyes adjusted. I could make out bare brick walls, cobwebs, and not much else.

"It's like something from a movie," Anne said. "A secret passageway. Did you two not know this was here?"

"I ... I don't know," I admitted. "I've repressed a lot of my childhood memories, but it came to me, like in a flash of memory, that there was something behind here."

"Well done," Janet said. "It's good that your memory is coming back. Now, how about you remember how we close this thing back up?"

"Why would we want to do that?" I asked, genuinely surprised. "Everywhere needs blessing, remember? Every dark corner, every drawer, every cupboard."

"But that's not really part of the house, is it?" Janet said. "And, besides, look how dark it is. One of us could break a leg wandering around in there."

I didn't know what to make of this. On the one hand, Janet was right. It was dark, truly dark, and one of us could easily fall and get hurt. But on the other hand, I got the distinct impression there was more to it than that. Janet seemed nervous, like she was waiting for something to jump out of the darkness and attack us.

I turned to face the gaping black maw, at least wanting a slight warning if anything appeared.

"So?" Janet pressed on. "How do we close this thing?" She stepped toward the remaining bookshelves and began running her hands over them, looking for some kind of closing mechanism, I assumed.

"Wait," Anne said, holding her hand up for silence and stillness.

Janet kept tapping away.

"Janet, stop."

Reluctantly, Janet stepped back from the bookshelf, and without the sound of her hands running over the shelves, I heard a noise coming from the darkness. It was faint, but there was no doubting it was real. Still, I felt better when Anne confirmed it.

"It sounds like a cat or something has gotten trapped in here." Anne took a step closer, then another one, and finally she disappeared into the shroud of darkness.

I heard a rough rubbing noise, Anne's hands over the brick walls, I suspected, and then I heard an electrical humming sound, and the darkness was gone, the tunnel lit now by bright neon lights.

"James doesn't have a cat," Janet said. She glanced at me. "Right?"

"Right," I confirmed.

"Oh, well, that's okay, then. If it's not James's cat, we'll just leave it to die," Anne said.

"Okay," Janet said. "Come on out of there so I can try to get it closed up again."

Even I had recognized Anne's sarcasm, and I stared at Janet, shocked she had missed it.

"What?" Janet said. "Oh, the cat thing. Yeah, I didn't think you meant it, obviously. But if it got in there itself, it can get out of there itself, right?"

"Regardless, this is part of the house, and it needs blessing just as much as the active rooms," Anne said.

"I don't know," Janet said. "I'm just getting a bad vibe from in there."

"Surely all the more reason to bless it," Anne pointed out.

"I ..." Janet started.

I had heard enough. I felt like I had finally found my voice. I didn't know if this newfound inner confidence came from having Anne here, someone impartial who seemed to think Janet was the problem and not me, or whether Dr. Sellers's techniques were working. Maybe it was both.

"Janet, you were the one who suggested having the house blessed. You were the one who asked your pastor to come here and carry out the blessing because you trusted her. Now she's telling you what needs to happen, you need to trust her on that, too. Stay here if you want to, but wherever that passage leads to, it's getting blessed."

36

I was shocked to discover that the passageway behind the library wall was just the start of it. As we walked along, Anne blessing the space at regular intervals, it soon became clear that this wasn't simply a passage that connected one room to another. It spanned the full house, and it was so much more than a thoroughfare, although we did pass lots of places with handprints, which, after pressing the first one, we discovered were alternate ways out of the passageway.

As if that wasn't disturbing enough, all the way along were peepholes and two-way mirrors that allowed anyone in there to see into every room in the house. It was clear that someone could have inhabited these passageways and caused the so-called hauntings. A person who knew their way around the maze could cause banging sounds in any room they chose. They could play recordings of creepy laughter and shouting. And they could come and go in various rooms and move things around.

But who the hell could have done such a thing? Sure,

Janet had been there last night when the banging started, but before that, it had happened when I was alone in the house. Or at least when I had thought I was alone. Perhaps I'd had an intruder all along. Maybe a squatter who wanted me out so they could emerge from the shadows and take over the house.

But none of that explained the ghost of my mother. I had seen her as plain as day lying in bed with me. Even Janet had seen her.

"Why didn't you guys tell me about the basement?" Anne said.

"Because we don't have a basement," I responded.

"It sure seems like you do," Anne said, nodding to a flight of wooden stairs leading downward.

I peered down and saw more of the same bare brick walls. I shook my head. I had no idea we had a basement, and I think Anne believed me. She had no reason to think I might try to hide part of the house from her, especially when I had insisted on entering the passageway in the first place.

"Maybe it's not part of our property," Janet said.

I turned to look at her, unable to keep the expression of disbelief off my face. "We don't have any neighbors for miles around, Janet. Who on earth do you think it belongs to, if not us?"

"I don't know," Janet said, her cheeks flushing slightly. "Don't you think it's weird that we have a basement neither of us remember?"

"No weirder than us having a network of secret passageways we don't remember," I said with a shrug.

"Good point," Janet agreed. She turned to Anne, who had already taken the top two stairs. "You're not seriously suggesting we go down there, are you?"

"I'm not suggesting you have to. If you two aren't comfortable, then go back on up to the library and wait there for me. But I'm going down there. For the last time, this blessing won't work unless every part of the house is blessed."

Janet sighed and shuffled from foot to foot, looking like she was about to argue. She mustn't have been able to think of a good enough case to convince Anne not to go down there because, eventually, she simply nodded.

As I followed Anne down the stairs, I thought about how Janet had agreed with me when I said that we didn't remember the passageways. But that wasn't entirely true. My flash of memory had showed me the entrance to these passageways, which means that at one point, I *did* know of their existence. Which must also mean that Janet knew about them. There was nothing in this house that she didn't know about, and she was certainly much more privy to information than I was. If she wanted this area to stay a secret, that explained why she had been so determined to stop me from investigating the bookshelves. But why did she want that? What the hell had happened down here? It must have been something bad. That was why she didn't want to face it again, and that was why I couldn't remember it at all.

We reached the bottom of the stairs, and the passageway curved around to the left. We followed it, only to be confronted by a dead end a few steps away.

"See?" Janet said. "I told you there was no basement down here. This was probably just a larder or something at one point."

Anne wafted the sage smoke around and repeated her prayer.

I looked around. It seemed like Janet was right, but it was

still a good thing we had come down here. Even this small space was part of the house and needed blessing.

We waited until Anne finished and nodded to us; then we headed back the way we had come, first Janet, then Anne, and then me. As we walked, I was sure I heard something that sounded like a muffled scream coming from behind me. I glanced back, but of course, there was nothing and no one there. There was no way I had heard anything. It was my imagination.

Then I felt a pain in my head again like I had in the library, only this time it was a thousand times worse, and I lifted my hands, pressing them to my temples. I tumbled forward onto my knees on the concrete, but even the painful landing couldn't pull me back to the moment. Nor could Anne's voice, although I was vaguely aware of her asking if I was alright.

I am small again, seven or eight years old. My father has a tight grip on the top of my arm. He is hurting me, but if I dare to tell him this or fight to get away, he will only grip me harder. I have learned this the hard way. I let him pull me down the wooden stairs and into the bricked-up passageway.

The whole time he is dragging me, he is yelling at me about having an overactive imagination and how I should live in reality. I am so petrified that I can't even remember what I am supposed to have done or said that's set him off like this.

He runs me toward the brick wall, and I am sure he's going to slam me into it. I brace myself, waiting for the pain, but instead he pulls up just short of collision. He lifts his left hand and presses on the third brick in. My jaw falls, and I forget my fear as the section of wall in front of me slides away to the right.

My fear comes back twofold when my father grabs me again and pulls me through the opening where the wall was. A long passageway snakes away in front of me, doors on either side.

My father pulls me forward, and that's when I see that the doors aren't doors as such. They are bars, the rooms behind them cells. Suddenly, I'm more afraid of what might happen if I get locked in one of those cells than I am of what my father might do to me if I resist him. I can imagine him throwing me into a cell and then forgetting about me and leaving me to die of hunger or thirst down here, cold and alone.

I pull back, digging my heels into the ground as much as I can, but there's nothing to get any leverage on. The floor is too smooth, and my feet keep being dragged along anyway. My father yells at me to stop stalling, and I beg him to take me back up to the house. I tell him I'm sorry over and over, although I have no idea what I'm sorry for.

My pleas fall on deaf ears, and my father grabs a metal key ring from a hook on the wall and unlocks the nearest cell. He lifts me off the ground by my arm and throws me into the cell. It's an almost gentle throw, designed to get me far enough away that he can slam the cell door closed rather than hurt me.

I huddle on the ground where I landed, my knees drawn up to my chest. As the cell door slams and my father locks it, I feel hot liquid spurting over my thighs, and an acrid smell fills the air.

"JAMES, CAN YOU HEAR ME?" a voice called.

I was snapped back to the present.

The voice belonged to Anne, who was peering at me, a

look of concern etched onto her face. "James? Are you alright?"

"Of course he's not alright," Janet snapped. "He hasn't been taking his medication again. I fear I'm going to have to have him readmitted."

"I have been taking my meds, and you'll do no such thing," I said to Janet. I smiled at Anne. "I'm fine, thank you. A memory from my childhood came back to me."

"You mean you had a hallucination," Janet said.

"Maybe, but I really don't think so. We'll soon find out." I pushed myself up onto my slightly shaky legs and moved toward the end of the little passageway.

I stood and looked at the wall in front of me. I counted in three bricks from the left, but I wasn't entirely sure which row the correct brick was on. I tried to work out roughly how tall my father had been and where his hand would have come to, but then I saw it. One of the bricks was different than the others. It seemed to have a yellow tinge. I reached out and pressed it, and then I stood back as a groaning noise rumbled through the wall, and it began to move.

"Wow," Anne said. "You weren't kidding about a memory coming back, were you?"

I felt afraid to go any farther, like I would end up locked away in a cell again. I told myself I was being ridiculous. Of course I wasn't going to end up in a cell. I was a grown man, and besides, who was going to do it? Janet? The pastor? No, I was being paranoid, and I knew it.

"Guys, I don't like this," Janet said.

"Go on back up to the house, then. James and I have got this," Anne said and smiled at me. "Right?"

Her smile melted away some of my fear, and I felt myself nodding.

"It's okay. I'll come along," Janet said. "But every movie about this kind of thing has led me to believe that if you find a sealed chamber, you leave it that way."

"Well, then, it's a good thing this isn't a movie, isn't it?" I said.

"Just don't blame me if it all goes wrong and you end up regretting coming down here. That's all I'm saying," Janet said.

I rolled my eyes, but I was no longer concentrating on Janet. I was listening to the sound coming from farther down the passageway. It was louder now that the wall had slid away.

I turned to Anne. "Can you hear that?" I asked.

She nodded, and we both stepped into the passageway, followed by a reluctant Janet.

As we drew level with the first cell, my jaw dropped open. There, in the middle of the otherwise empty cell, was a skeleton.

It was the one I had seen before.

And it was still dressed in my mom's favorite dress.

I looked at Janet, who stood casually picking at her nail. I had to be hallucinating. She would have reacted far more than she was if what I was seeing was real. I looked back into the cell, but nothing had changed. The skeleton was still there. I didn't know what to do to make the vision go away, but I tried looking away again, and this time, I happened to catch sight of Anne. Her mouth was hanging open, and she was making the sign of the cross.

"You see that, too?" I asked, my voice barely above a whisper.

Anne nodded, and then she began to say a prayer.

It was a prayer for my mom's soul.

37

"Amen," Anne said as she finished the prayer.

I echoed her, and then we stood in silence.

Finally, I couldn't bear to stand looking at Mom any longer, and I turned to Anne. "I'll understand if you want to call this off now."

"We've spent a full day on this." Anne shook her head. "We've come so far, and if we don't finish now, I will have to start over again to complete the blessing. We can address this ... finding later, but just now I'm not receiving any negative energies from her, may the Lord bless her soul."

Now Anne mentioned it, I realized I didn't, either. The bad vibes I had gotten the last time I saw that skeleton had to be because of the extreme shock of finding her in my bed. She was my mom. She was the one person who truly had my back, and I wasn't about to be afraid of her now.

Anne started off again, and we paused outside the next pair of cells while she prayed and splashed holy water into them. Anne blessed the next two pairs of cells without incident. We were about halfway down the long passageway with three more pairs of cells to go when I heard the cat sound again. Only this time, it didn't sound like a cat. It sounded like a person humming.

"Come on, guys, let's go back," Janet said. "Surely discovering Mom's remains like that is enough of a horror show for one day."

I didn't even bother to answer her. I had made my thoughts on the situation quite clear, as had Anne, and if Janet wanted to go back, she could, but I wasn't about to go with her.

We reached the next pair of cells, Anne in the lead. She stumbled slightly and pressed her hand to her mouth. "Oh, my goodness. James, Janet, get over here," she said, her voice shaking.

I dashed forward, adrenaline stopping me from feeling afraid. I reached Anne's side and saw what had made her gasp.

"Brianna?" I exclaimed, hardly able to believe my eyes.

Brianna was lying on her side on the cell floor, her hands tied behind her back, her ankles bound together, and a gag in her mouth. She made a muffled humming sound, and I realized that the catlike sounds we had heard were Brianna all along. I had no idea how she had gotten here, but I knew I had to get her out.

I grabbed the key ring hanging by the cell door and pushed the key into the lock with a shaking hand. I rushed into the cell and dropped to my knees. I reached out and gently pulled the gag from Brianna's mouth. I reached over and started to untie her hands.

"What happened, Brianna?" I said as I worked on the knot. "Who did this to you?"

She tried to speak, but her voice came out as a croak, and I couldn't make out what she was saying.

"It's okay," I said. "You're safe now. We'll get you upstairs and take care of you; then we'll call the police and work everything out."

Brianna kept making the croaking sounds, and something in them sounded urgent enough that, for a second, I stopped pulling at the knot and leaned back to look down at her. Her eyes were wide open, terrified, and she nodded, croaking again.

"Janet," Brianna finally managed to say.

38

When I turned around, I saw what had terrified Brianna so much. Janet had a hold of Anne. One hand covered her mouth, preventing her from crying out. The other hand held a knife, the point digging into Anne's throat hard enough to leave a dimple but not quite hard enough to break the skin.

"Good God, Janet," I shouted. "What the hell are you doing?"

I was vaguely aware of taking the Lord's name in vain in front of Anne, and I almost laughed at the absurdity of the fact that I wanted to apologize to her in the middle of all of this. Instead, I kept my focus on Janet. "Let her go," I said, keeping my voice as steady as I could.

All I could think was that there had to be some mistake. There was no way my sister had imprisoned Brianna and was now taking her pastor a hostage. But I knew this was no hallucination; I knew that much by the reactions of Anne and Brianna.

Janet still hadn't spoken, nor had she eased her grip on Anne.

I didn't know what to say to convince her to release her, but I knew I had to try. I shuffled around on the ground so that I faced Janet. It also put me in a good position to keep working on untying Brianna without having to take my eyes off Janet.

"Janet, please let her go," I said. "Whatever has happened here, we can work something out. You haven't really hurt anyone, and we can help you. But if you kill someone, it's too late for that."

"I should have killed that fucking little slut before now," Janet hissed, her eyes flashing with anger.

"Except you thought you'd do it the coward's way, didn't you?" Brianna said. She still sounded croaky, but there was a new strength in her voice. "Drug me, tie me up, and let me die without getting blood on your hands."

"You think I'm afraid of getting my hands dirty?" Janet snarled. "That's so far from the truth, you have no idea. I just didn't want to sully myself by touching you."

I could feel things starting to get out of hand, and I knew I had to reel them back in or Anne would get hurt. Other than the overwhelming fear that Anne was about to have her throat cut, at this point, I would have quite happily told Janet that she was evidently a full-on psycho.

The knot on Brianna's wrists finally came loose, and I moved onto the binds around her ankles. Brianna clenched and unclenched her fists, bringing the blood flowing back into her fingers.

"Why are you doing this, Janet? What did Brianna ever do to you?" I asked.

"What did Brianna ever do to me?" Janet snorted. "Well,

let's see. She manipulated you into thinking she liked you so that she could take control of your money and your life. That money is mine. I'm the one who was good to our father. I was his special little girl, and dammit, I earned that fucking money."

"You can have the money. Take it. Take every fucking penny because I'd rather be dead-ass broke than allow myself to be corrupted like this," I retorted.

"Oh, and now you're taking the high road," Janet said with a manic laugh. "Oh, that's good, James. That's very fucking good."

Money be damned, I just wanted everyone to get out of this alive. I decided to go back and start over. "Okay, so you wanted to punish me for having our father's money, so you took Brianna to spite me? How did you think that was going to work when you didn't tell me what you had done?"

"I didn't take her to spite you," Janet said. "Don't you get it, James? It's me and you against the world. We don't need anyone else because we've always got each other. And that whore was getting in the way. So I simply removed her from the situation."

Janet looked away from me and focused on Brianna, who was now sitting up and rubbing her ankles where I had managed to loosen the rope.

"You had to fuck him, didn't you?" Janet screeched. "You couldn't just do your damned job and move on with your life. You had to manipulate him, make him think you were special. You had to try to take what was mine. Well, you know what? You can have him because I don't want him anymore now that he has succumbed to your ways. I'm out of here."

Janet removed her hand from Anne's mouth, and, for the first time, Anne spoke.

"Janet, listen," she said. "We can—"

"Oh, fuck off," Janet interrupted. "The Lord doesn't approve of slutty women who fuck like animals outside of a marriage, and neither should you. But you're just like them, aren't you? You do whatever brings you pleasure with no thought for anyone else. You make me sick."

On that final word, Janet suddenly dug the knife into Anne's throat and dragged it across. A slit like a second mouth opened up across Anne's throat, and her hands came up to press against the awful wound. Her mouth hung open; her eyes were wide. Blood spurted between her fingertips as her knees buckled, and she fell to the ground.

Janet didn't hang around to see how this would end. She turned and ran.

"Get her, James," Brianna croaked out. "I'll help Anne; you need to stop her from locking us down here."

I didn't want to leave Brianna or Anne in that state, but I knew Brianna was right. I had to get Janet. If she got away, she might never pay for what she had done. I leaped to my feet and ran to the cell door. I spotted Janet just as she turned at the end of the passageway. I sprinted after her and followed her up another set of wooden stairs.

Janet yanked open a door at the top of the stairs, and I felt cold air rush in. I had no idea where this door came out, but I ran up the stairs and threw myself through it. I found myself in the back garden. I wondered briefly how I had never questioned a door here, but as I ran and glanced back, I saw that the door was on the back of the toolshed; I wouldn't have seen it from the house.

I had to give Janet her due. She was a hell of a lot fitter

than me, and she was widening the gap between us. I couldn't let her get away. I forced myself to see Brianna lying on the ground, helpless and terrified. I forced myself to see the shock in Anne's eyes as blood gushed from her throat. Those images, those terrible things Janet had done, gave me a spurt of adrenaline, and I managed a fresh burst of speed.

I followed Janet across the grounds and saw that her car was parked just out of sight of the house. I knew that if she was able to reach her car, this was over, she would somehow manage to get out of this, and I forced myself on even faster. I darted through the open gate without a second thought, and the wailing sound of the alarm from my ankle monitor cut through the stillness of the night, taking us both by surprise.

I was lucky. I had momentarily forgotten about my curfew when I sprang through the gate, but I knew what the sound was, so I recovered my wits quicker than Janet and closed the gap between us. I reached out to grab Janet, but she slashed toward me with the bloody knife, the blade barely missing my knuckles, and I pulled back.

"What the hell is wrong with you?" I demanded.

Janet and I stood facing off against each other for a moment, the blade flashing silver in the moonlight and clouds of our breath pluming out white against the night.

"What's wrong with me? What the hell is wrong with *you*?" Janet said, shaking her head. "I did everything for you, James. It was meant to be us until the end. Don't you get that? I took Brianna away because she was trying to manipulate you. I took the pastor out because she knew too much. I know you'd never cope if I was in prison, so I made sure our only witness was gone."

"You're crazy," I said, the realization hitting me that it was indeed Janet who was crazy and not me. At least not anymore.

"I must be for thinking you could be anything but selfish. The things I did so you would have me at the house and see that things were better when we were together. I created a full-on haunting, and I made it go away when you called me. I thought you'd see then that you needed me and only me. But no. Dr. Sellers tried to get into your head then, didn't he, making me an outcast in my own damned family."

"So the banging sounds, the whispering, the laughter, the things moving around on their own. That was all you?" I questioned.

Janet nodded.

"How?"

Janet gave me a smug look. "Haunted house effects I picked up from a specialty shop."

"And my missing pills?" I asked, although the answer was obvious.

"Guilty," Janet said with a manic laugh. "But, James, try to understand, I didn't do it to keep you ill. I did it so you would blame Brianna and see what a bitch she was. But even when presented with a clear-cut case of her being bad news, you couldn't see it. Her claws were in you too deep."

I shook my head in total disbelief. "I just ... I ... When I asked you for help, you always made me feel like I was a burden on you. Now you're saying you went to such lengths to get me to need you."

"I didn't mean to make you feel like you were a burden. I was short with you, I know I was, and I'm sorry. I was hurt that I had to go so far to convince you to reach out to me," she said.

"But you could have reached out to me. You could have

called, visited; hell, you could have moved in if you wanted to," I said.

"You say that now," Janet said sadly. "And maybe you even believe it. Yes, I think you *do* believe it. But then Brianna or the next one after her would have come along, and at some point, you'd have asked me to leave so you could be with your lover." She said the word *lover* like it was the vilest concept she could think of.

I opened my mouth to tell her that wasn't true, but before I could, she went on.

"Don't try to tell me it wouldn't have happened, because it would have. Look how close we were as kids," Janet said.

I frowned, trying my best to remember a time when Janet and I had been close as kids. It had always been her and our father, and me and our mom. She had joined forces with the one person who made my life hell, and had done whatever it took to impress him, even if that meant harming me, and now she wanted to say we had been close.

"But as kids ... you were always with Dad, not me—"

"No!" Janet's face was full of anger. "He made me be with him! I didn't want that, but I couldn't say no. I did it for you; he threatened to beat you more if I didn't."

My head was reeling at what she was saying. Did she mean that Dad was abusing her too, but sexually? I wanted to be sick. That had to be what that picture I'd drawn meant; I'd seen something back then.

"Then you met that Terri girl, and it was like, 'Janet who?'" she spat.

"Oh, Janet," I said, as everything started to make horrible sense.

"Don't try to tell me you weren't at least a little bit relieved that she was no longer controlling you," Janet said.

"No," I said, refusing to let myself believe this could be true. "No. No. Please tell me you didn't."

"Oh, I did. I killed Terri. And I made damned sure no one would ever have suspected me," she said.

It was only in that moment of profound understanding, when my whole world stood still, that I realized my ankle monitor was no longer making a noise, but I could still hear an alarm-like sound. I focused on that as it got louder rather than allowing myself to focus on what Janet had just told me. I recalled the last time I'd seen Terri. I remembered Janet walking behind me, taunting me, telling me my girlfriend wasn't good enough for me, that she was a dirty little whore, shouting all kinds of awful things. I had yelled at her, telling her to shut up and go away. She'd laughed at me, but she went away. Or I'd thought she had. She had killed Terri. A surge of anger flooded me.

"You killed Terri and ruined my fucking life!" I screamed at Janet as I lunged for the knife.

I missed the knife, my fingers closing on empty air as Janet moved back quickly, laughing, taunting me even now.

"Oh, don't be such a drama queen, James," she said, her voice high-pitched and almost tuneful.

"You murdered my girlfriend and let me take the blame," I said. "Tell me: How am I being a drama queen?"

"Yes, that part was unfortunate," Janet admitted. "But it's all over now. We can get on with our lives. Just us."

"There is no fucking 'us.' Stop saying there is. I want nothing to do with you, you absolute fucking maniac!" I shouted.

I had to shout to be heard over the sound that I now realized was a siren. A police car was approaching, the blue light cutting through the air.

"You don't mean that," Janet said, tears running down her cheeks. "Take that back."

"I mean it," I said. "I—"

With the knife held high in the air, she flew at me, bringing the knife down toward my face.

I grabbed her wrist, holding the knife away from me as best I could. Her strength surprised me, and I could feel my arm muscles tiring, the knife moving closer to my face.

"Police!" a male voice yelled. "Drop the weapon."

Janet pushed against me a moment longer, and then she opened her hand and let the knife drop.

"There's someone in there who needs urgent medical attention," I managed to say to the nearest police officer as I fell to the ground and watched as the police surrounded Janet and handcuffed her.

EPILOGUE

SIX MONTHS LATER

So much had happened since that fateful day of the house blessing that it felt like a lifetime ago. At the same time, it felt like everything that had happened with Janet had happened just yesterday. I kept going over that night in my head. I still couldn't quite believe how far into the realm of crazy Janet had ventured. And she had the nerve to say that I was the crazy one.

Anne needed a ton of stitches and a blood transfusion after Janet's knife attack, but Brianna's first aid had saved her, as did the fact that Janet's blade didn't slice a main artery.

Janet was arrested that night, and Detective Lapley had called around to the house a couple of days later to inform me that Janet had admitted to not only everything that had happened with Brianna and Anne, but also to the murder of Terri. Her trial was coming up in the next few weeks, but I thought it was fairly obvious that she would be found guilty. It was looking more and more likely that she would spend her incarceration in a secure mental hospital rather than a prison, as her short stint in prison seemed to have made her even more violent, which brought about more charges.

I wanted to say I was pleased Janet was getting the help she needed, but all I felt was relief that she was no longer my problem. Anne told me every day that I should find it in my heart to forgive Janet, as she has. And maybe one day I would, but I didn't think that day was coming anytime soon. Without Janet hindering my progress and undermining my treatment, Dr. Sellers had worked wonders with me. He had made me see that me and my mom, the so-called crazy people in our family, were never the problem. The problems stemmed from Janet and my father. There were still childhood memories I might never get back, but I had made my peace with that, and with Dr. Sellers's help, I was learning to move on from the past and look to the future.

Speaking of the future, Nick and I had made plans to get together more often. It was good having a friend I could talk to about everything, someone who understood what I'd been through. And he was working on his next book, which I was anxious to hear all about since it would be loosely based on my life. We would be meeting up to discuss details once I was finally off probation.

Finding Mom's remains amid everything that had happened felt so surreal, but I had wanted to find a way to honor her, so Anne and I had given her a proper burial in holy ground. I was relieved that she was finally at peace after Dad beating her and leaving her for dead down in those cells.

Although I still got anxious at the idea of being in large groups of people, I was working on it, and Anne had convinced me to attend church and run an art group for some of the younger members of her congregation. When someone who almost died tells you that life is too short not to do something, how can you argue? I found that the teaching was immensely rewarding, and I was so glad I let her talk me into it.

And today was a very special day. I was officially no longer on probation. I would have my ankle monitor removed, and my mandated therapy sessions would end, although I had already arranged with Dr. Sellers to stay on a little longer as a private patient.

I smiled as I heard the knock on my front door and went to open it. It was a bittersweet moment seeing Brianna standing there. Sweet because she looked good enough to eat in her pink blouse and black skirt, bitter because this would be the last time that she appeared on my doorstep like this.

We had remained friendly. As much as I felt the same attraction to Brianna as I always had, I didn't want to push things, not after what had happened to her as a result of being with me. She still seemed to be attracted to me—she flirted with me occasionally, but she always pulled away before things went too far.

"Are you going to invite me in, or are you just going to stand there staring at me?" Brianna asked.

I laughed and stood back to let her in. "Sorry, I was a million miles away," I said, following her to the kitchen, where we took our usual seats at the table.

"Already imagining your freedom, I would guess," Brianna said with a smile.

"Something like that," I lied.

She pushed a piece of paper over the table toward me and handed me a pen. "That's a standard release form like we talked about at our last meeting. It's to say you are no longer on probation and that you understand that your status is the same as that of any other citizen now."

I signed my name with a flourish, returned her pen, and pushed the form back toward her.

"Someone will be around later this afternoon to remove the ankle monitor," she said.

"Great." I smiled.

"Now, there's just one more thing." She suddenly looked kind of awkward, biting her bottom lip and glancing down into her lap. "Now that I'm officially not your probation officer, I wondered if maybe you'd like to have dinner with me tonight?"

I felt my face break out into a grin so wide it hurt my mouth.

"I'd love to," I said, feeling as though my world was finally headed in a sunny direction.

THANK YOU FOR READING

Did you enjoy reading *The Patient*? Please consider leaving a review on Amazon. Your review will help other readers to discover the novel.

ABOUT THE AUTHOR

Cole Baxter loves writing psychological suspense thrillers. It's all about that last reveal that he loves shocking readers with.

He grew up in New York, where there was crime all around. He decided to turn that into something positive with his fiction.

His stories will have you reading through the night—they are very addictive!

ALSO BY COLE BAXTER

Inkubator Books Titles

The Perfect Suitor

The Betrayal

I Won't Let You Go

The Night Nurse

The Doppelganger

The Couple Next Door

I Will Find You

The Cole Baxter Box Set

Other Titles

Prime Suspect

What She Witnessed

Deadly Truth

Finding The Other Woman

Trust A Stranger

Follow You

Did He Do It

What Happened Last Night

Perfect Obsession

Going Insane

She's Missing

The Perfect Nanny

What She Forgot

Stolen Son

Before She's Gone

Made in the USA
Monee, IL
15 January 2024